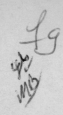

Laura wanted no misunderstanding.

"It will be a marriage of convenience and in name only," she said bitingly. "Once Fairfield is mine, our arrangement is at an end. You will be paid handsomely for the time we must remain together. Clandestine marriages within the prison here are not uncommon."

With each sentence Matthew's expression darkened. "Aye, I know of these marriages," he snarled. "Is it your inheritance you fear for, Mistress Stanton, or in six months' time do I become a proud father?"

Pauline Bentley

Marriage Rites

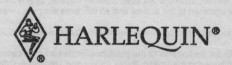

HARLEQUIN®

TORONTO • NEW YORK • LONDON
AMSTERDAM • PARIS • SYDNEY • HAMBURG
STOCKHOLM • ATHENS • TOKYO • MILAN • MADRID
PRAGUE • WARSAW • BUDAPEST • AUCKLAND

ISBN 0-373-30355-6

MARRIAGE RITES

First North American Publication 2000

PAULINE BENTLEY

has long been captivated by history. Born in Essex, she trained as a legal secretary, but always came away from visiting castles or manor houses with the desire to write about them. She now lives in Sussex, is married with two children, has a growing menagerie of dogs and finds inspiration walking over the South Downs.

Chapter One

"I've gone along with some hare-brained schemes of yours, Mistress Laura, but in all your seventeen years this one beats them all." Jedediah Hames shook his grey-wigged head, his weather-hewn features drawn with concern. "If your grandfather learns of it…"

"Grandfather has driven me to this desperate measure." Laura Stanton shivered as she stepped from the carriage into the shadow of the prison gatehouse. The air was foul from the stench of the nearby Fleet Ditch, which was no better than an open midden. Taking the old retainer's hand, she forced a trembling smile. "What choice have I, Jedediah?"

"With respect, Mistress Laura, a beautiful, intelligent woman like yourself has every choice." He looked up at the dark frontage of the Fleet prison and sighed. "I need my head cracking to let you talk me into this devil's pit."

Beneath her black velvet mask Laura's blue eyes were bright with resolution. She took no offence at Jedediah's familiar manner. He had been head groom on her grandfather's estate for more than thirty years.

Ever since he had first taught her to ride and she had begun to spend every spare moment of her time with the horses, a bond of affection had been strong between them. It was to save Fairfield that she was here on this bleak winter's morning in 1694. Her plan must work.

She pulled the hood of her plain woollen cloak over her face, hiding her auburn ringlets. She had no wish to be recognised by any servant delivering their master's food scraps for the debtors in the prison. Without even such pitiful charity many of the inmates in the poorest quarter of the gaol would starve.

Laura's spine stiffened and her chin was high as she stepped towards the prison. "There is no other solution I find acceptable, Jedediah."

Her step was firm as she approached the gatehouse. There she paused, the stench making her gag. Pressing the nosegay of flowers to her face, she fretted with impatience as she waited for Jedediah to pay the warder the garnish needed to gain admittance. With each second her courage wavered. She stamped down her doubts. She was desperate. And desperation called for desperate action.

She suppressed a shudder as the gaoler led them into a courtyard where thirty prisoners glanced hostilely in their direction. Men, unshaven and unkempt, lounged against the walls, or squatted on the ground arguing over a game of dice. Laura quickly averted her gaze from a couple pressed against the wall in the last throes of lovemaking and oblivious to the jeers and encouragement of several spectators. A woman with a baby suckling at her breast and a young child clinging to her skirts thrust out a thin, grimy hand towards Laura.

"Have pity on me, mistress. Five pounds would settle me debts. Just the coal merchant, and back rent for me old lodgings. I was robbed of all me savings.'' The woman pushed the undernourished child forward and Laura caught the smell of stale beer and vomit on the woman's ragged skirt. She also saw the woman's calculating stare upon her clothing as the creature assessed how much money Laura could be tricked into giving. "Just five pounds, gracious lady. You've a kind face. You'd not condemn me poor mites to life in this living hell.''

Laura looked into the woman's hard, prematurely aged face and saw eyes bloodshot and puffy from years of debauchery and hard drinking. Her compassion was overridden. In the last year she had worked with the poor in her local parish in Essex. Gradually she had become hardened to this type of woman, who would put her craving for drink before care of her family. She hated to see the children suffer, but knew it was hopeless to pay the woman's debts. She'd be back in here within a month, all her income spent on drink.

But even Laura's work with the poor and their suffering had not prepared her for the degradation and misery she witnessed in the next minutes. The debtors were the most abused of all prisoners. Without money you could not survive, even in prison. Everything had its price—proper food, bedding, bribes for the guards—else they could be regularly beaten without cause. As she was escorted across the open yard Laura kept her gaze fixed on the down-trodden heels of the gaoler's boots ahead of her.

The single cell she entered was occupied by five men. At her entrance they shuffled upright, their eyes bright with speculation as she studied each of them in turn. Laura's heart plummeted. Jedediah was right. She had been mad to come here. None of the men fitted her requirements. Despite her disappointment she was determined to put her first impressions of the men aside and study each in detail. The previous day Jedediah had selected the men and her servant had assured her that all of them were gentlemen by birth. Each man had been shaved and had taken some pains with his attire. Only two had the bearing of their station, but when she looked into their eyes the bright glitter which met her candid stare betrayed them as wastrels, lechers or pompous ne'er-do-wells. Not one of them had a look she could trust.

She shook her head at Jedediah, who sighed in relief.

"Praise the Lord, you've seen sense at last." Jedediah wiped his wrinkled, sweating face with a large red kerchief.

"It's the men who are unsuitable," Laura said defiantly as she walked out of the cell. "We will try Newgate next. With so many debtors in the London prisons there must be one suitable for my purpose."

On returning to the courtyard, Laura heard a youth screaming in agony. To her horror she saw a young lad being whipped by a brutal-looking warder. As the blows grew in ferocity the youth fell to the ground, curling into a ball to protect his head from the kicks and lashing he was receiving. A crowd cleared around the gaoler, some jeering, seeking any diversion in their dreary lives.

Laura sucked in her breath, disgusted at the brutality. She was about to protest when a dark-haired prisoner with the speed of an attacking wolf sprang out of the crowd.

"Bastard!" he growled, his teeth white against his brown beard. "You killed a lad with that whip last week. What had young Sam done, apart from refusing to be your catamite?"

Grabbing the gaoler's collar to haul him away from the youth, the prisoner then smashed his fist into the man's jaw. The thick-set bully was knocked off his feet and lay sprawled in the puddled courtyard.

"You've had it coming a long time, Hoskins," the man who had attacked the gaoler raged. "It's always the young and weak you pick on, and never anyone who can fight back."

He got no further. Three gaolers brandishing cudgels ran to their colleague's aid. A cheer rang through the crowd as the prisoner fought them. Outnumbered, he faced them with angry defiance. He balanced on the balls of his feet and agilely ducked their first blows. Then, with the swiftness of a seasoned warrior, he swung round and two men staggered back, one clutching his stomach, the other his eye.

The breadth of the prisoner's shoulders strained against the russet broadcloth of his jacket as he hit out at the third gaoler. When he whirled to attack another his open jacket gaped, and his close-fitting, black knee-breeches revealed a flat stomach and slender hips. Despite his lithe build every blow was delivered with accurate force, and Laura knew he was immensely strong.

In the first moments of the fight, when the prisoner held his own, Laura felt her pulse quicken, willing him not to be overpowered. It was an impossible hope. The gaolers' faces were evil with menace as they closed in on him. They were armed and the prisoner was not. The heaviest gaoler, with an eye-patch and a scar down his right cheek, laughed cruelly as he thudded his cudgel into the prisoner's ribs, and another struck him upon those broad shoulders.

Laura cried out and started to move forward. She was only a few feet from the prisoner when the man with the eye-patch shouted, "It's the solitary hold again for you, Thorne. This time I'll break you, you bastard."

Thorne staggered from the impact of several more blows, but continued to fight until he was eventually overpowered. When he was held by the three gaolers Laura saw that Hoskins was again on his feet, and that his cudgel was raised above the prisoner's head.

"Stop! Stop that at once!" Laura ran forward, her face flushed with fury at such unnecessary brutality.

Hoskins hesitated, his pock-pitted face twisting with spite. His mouth drew back in a grimace, showing several blackened stumps which were all that remained of his teeth. Turning from her, he brought the cudgel down on to the prisoner's shoulders.

Laura screamed. The blow had been all the more vicious because of her interference. It had brought the prisoner to his knees. Her hand flew to her mouth and her eyes were bright with tears of remorse. For a moment the man's head was bowed, his shoulder-length brown hair falling forward over his face. She saw his hands bunch into fists, the blood-smeared knuckles whitening as he combated the pain. Then his head lifted.

His skin retained a golden tint from a life in the outdoors. That its colour had not completely faded to the sickly prison pallor told her he had not been incarcerated for many weeks. For a moment eyes the colour of polished bronze burned into her and she inwardly flinched. All his contempt for her wealth and station was defined in that hard, condemning stare. When he straightened, she was surprised that he was little above medium height. The way he carried himself had given her the impression of a much taller man. At only two inches over five feet herself, she was still forced to tilt back her head to hold that blazing stare.

Even when the prisoner was roughly jerked backwards he did not lower his eyes. Laura stood her ground as his insolent stare skimmed over her figure before returning to hold her gaze. His lips twisted into a half-smile and she felt her breath catch in her throat. Whoever this man was, he certainly considered no one to be his better. And, if she was not mistaken, there was now a glint of mockery in that knowing obsidian glare.

Her hand dropped from her mouth and she unconsciously squared her shoulders. To her further chagrin he inclined his head in a brief but derogatory bow. Again the cudgel descended, and when Laura saw blood on the side of his head she had to bite her lip to stop herself crying out in protest. It would only lead to further ill-treatment.

As she watched the prisoner being led away between the four gaolers her cheeks burned with shame. The man had suffered because of her intervention, though she had meant only to halt the gaoler's cruelty.

The warder stood at her side. "I regret you had to witness that," he said gruffly. "Matt Thorne was born mean. He's a regular trouble-maker."

"He was concerned for the youth." Laura saw the boy's beaten body being carried away.

"Thorne were looking for a fight, that were all." The warder snorted. "He has a grudge against the world. Not that he'll be seeing much of it. Like as not he'll rot here for years with his debts unpaid."

There was something about the warder's tone which made Laura stare sharply at him. She suspected he was deliberately blackening Matt Thorne's character.

"Are his debts so considerable?" she asked.

The warder did not answer, nor did he hold her stare.

Anger at the man's rudeness mingled with curiosity about Matt Thorne. From his manner he certainly had no love for the gentry, but there was something about the way he carried himself which told her he was no ordinary commoner. She saw Matt Thorne being taken to a door on the far side of the courtyard. Even restrained by the guards he held himself proudly. She had not been able to see his face clearly beneath the beard and his long hair, but there had been no meanness in his bronze stare.

"Mr Thorne may serve my needs," she addressed the warder.

"That won't be possible."

"Is he, then, not in here for debt, but for a more serious crime?"

The warder clamped his mouth shut.

Irritated, Laura turned to Jedediah, her voice dropping to a whisper. "Matt Thorne may well suit my purpose. I would see him cleaned up and presentable first. Pay whatever this louse wants in bribes to make it possible. If Matt Thorne is the calibre of man I believe him to be, I'll settle his debts. Make the arrangements, Jedediah. I'll return tomorrow to visit Thorne. In the meantime I do not expect him to be ill-treated, or the warder might find the extortionate bribes he demands are not paid. I'll await you in the coach.''

Before many minutes had passed the carriage creaked as Jedediah stepped inside and sat opposite Laura. His expression was grim and his voice heavy. ''Forget this madness, Mistress Laura. Matt Thorne will be trouble.''

''What were his debts?''

''A thousand pounds.''

Laura paled. She was shocked that his debts were so high. Had she misjudged the man's character? He had not struck her as a wastrel or a gambler. She closed her eyes, acknowledging defeat. Before her mind rose the image of Matt Thorne. It was so clear, especially the intensity of his bronze gaze. There had been anger within its depths, not slyness or gullibility. Instead of appalling her, the size of his debts only made her more curious about him.

''What's Thorne's background?''

Jedediah spread his hands in a negative gesture. ''Not much is known of him. He was part-owner and captain of the brigantine *Sea Maiden*. He's spent most of the last five or so years at sea. Hadn't docked long when he were recognised and arrested.''

''This may not, then, be a recent debt,'' Laura probed. ''Who does he owe this money to?''

''On that the warder wouldn't be drawn. He hinted it was to a prominent courtier and a statesman who did not want his financial affairs public knowledge. Five extra pieces of gold loosened the warder's tongue enough for him to imply that the man was a partner in Thorne's ship and cargo. He said Thorne were lucky the man did not press charges of fraud or piracy, by all accounts. The warder only agreed to you visiting Thorne because he said Thorne was an arrogant bastard who needed to be put in his place. He doesn't believe you intend to go through with your plan.''

Despite her earlier reservations, Laura was intrigued. She was rarely wrong in judging a person's character. There was something underhand in the way Thorne's partner wanted his name kept secret. She knew enough about statesmen from her grandfather's associates to know that not all were honest men. She would get Jedediah to check further on the sea-captain. There had to be some records stating who Thorne's creditor was. If they had been deliberately suppressed, then there was something very sinister happening here. Matthew Thorne would not be the first innocent man to be incarcerated and forgotten in prison. Though he had shown contempt for her station, her intuition told her that if he accepted her terms she could trust him to fulfil them.

It was late afternoon the next day when Laura returned to the Fleet prison. Charcoal storm clouds hung menacingly overhead, making the building look more forbidding than ever. All morning Laura had wrestled with her conscience and had almost allowed Jedediah to dissuade her from this folly.

The groom had spent last evening in the dockside taverns and found two seamen who had served under Captain Thorne. Both spoke highly of him, which was rare. Few sailors had much respect for their captains, who were often cruel in maintaining discipline among their crew. Only an exceptional man could earn such loyalty. Of the business partner and debt Jedediah had learned nothing. Apparently the *Sea Maiden* had been sold, and had since sailed for the Mediterranean.

With Jedediah muttering and shaking his grey-wigged head in disapproval, Laura entered the prison. She was not taken to the cell she had visited yesterday, but was led down into the fetid bowels of the prison, where no daylight penetrated. There was a smugness to the warder's expression which made Laura uneasy. Cockroaches ran out of the light spread by the gaoler's lantern. Forced to lift her skirt high above the wet, slimy floor, puddled with stale urine, Laura suppressed a shudder of disgust at the filth and squalor. A surly turnkey stepped back as he opened a heavy, iron-studded door. Inside the cell it was black as soot, and reeked of mildewed straw and rats' droppings. Taking the lantern from the turnkey, she stepped forward.

The edges of the light touched upon the prisoner. He sat on the floor, his arms manacled to the wall. From out of his bearded face his dark eyes flashed with contempt. There was dried blood on the side of his head where his wound had not been treated. The russet jacket was gone and a grimy blood-striped shirt was in tatters about his body. Through the rips she saw the bloodied lash-strokes where he had recently been whipped.

She spun round to confront the gaoler, her voice filled with fury. "Why was this man beaten? I gave instructions he was not to be harmed and that he was to be made presentable for my visit."

"He was beaten for insolence," the warder grunted. "Said he'd no intention of being paraded before some high-stomached doxy like a prize bull on a stud farm.''

Laura bowed her partially masked face to hide her smile. Though she deplored his sentiments, she admired the prisoner's spirit. ''Since the prisoner has an aversion to being paraded like an animal, I'm sure he would prefer this conversation to be conducted while he is not fettered like one.''

''He's dangerous,'' the warder answered sullenly.

Holding the lantern high, Laura moved further into the cell. The appalling musty stench buffeted her, but she was careful not to show her repugnance. She surveyed the prisoner, who had not troubled to stand. He sat with one leg drawn up, and a manacled arm rested negligently on his knee.

''Sir, are you a danger to an unprotected woman, even a high-stomached one? I think not, or you would not have sprung to the defence of that young boy yesterday.'' Laura sweetened her voice, adopting her most docile drawing-room manner. ''I ask your pardon for presuming that you would wish to discuss a business matter with me without first consulting you. Since I am here, perhaps I may call upon your indulgence to grant me a few minutes of your time? It will be to your advantage, Captain Thorne.''

For a long moment silence stretched between them. Without taking his gaze from Laura's forthright stare, the prisoner raised his arm for the warder to remove the manacles.

To Laura's relief the warder nodded to the turnkey, who unlocked the fetters, the chains falling away with an ominous clang.

''It's Mr Thorne now, not Captain,'' Matthew Thorne informed her as he rose to his feet. He executed the same mocking bow he had performed yesterday.

Seeing him wince as he straightened, she asked, "Have your wounds been tended, Mr Thorne? I fear that my intervention yesterday only served to harshen your punishment."

"They would have beaten me anyway," he dismissed her concern. "You have me at a disadvantage, ma'am. My abode is not fitting for a lady to call. And while you know my name, I do not know yours."

Laura waited until the warder and turnkey left them before she said softly, "Your insolence neither impresses me nor will it deflect me from my purpose, Mr Thorne. Until you have heard my proposition there is no reason for you to know my name."

"Then we cannot do business, ma'am." His glare was scathing as it swept over her. "I've no cause to have faith in the gentry. Only those intent upon underhand trickery would remain anonymous. If you don't trust me with your name there's nothing to discuss."

Laura felt her blood run hot at his insolence. She could feel her anger beginning to get the better of her and immediately checked it. She remembered that it was supposedly a man of power and influence who had instigated Thorne's arrest, and he had ensured that his name was kept secret. "The matter is delicate," she answered coolly. "I cannot afford to lay myself open to blackmail."

"Then you do not trust me, and I can be of no use to you."

Laura clenched her fist at his stubbornness. It was rare for her to lose her temper, but this man was infuriating. Wasn't she offering him his freedom? She managed to keep her voice calm as she reasoned. "I do not know you, so how can I trust you?"

"You sought me out, ma'am, not I you."

Her eyes flashed at his continued insolence. The interview was not going as she had expected. She inhaled deeply while she held his stare. Reluctantly, she was impressed by his uncompromising manner, and she was strangely drawn to confide in him. Still she hesitated. He intrigued her. He was bearded and as unkempt as the pirate the warder had proclaimed him. The whip-cuts on his body bore witness to his unruly character. But there was something in his eyes—behind the wariness with which he regarded those of wealth and position—which confirmed her first impression that he was a man of honour. If he had been wrongly imprisoned, or used as a scapegoat to conceal some financial scandal, her sense of injustice was outraged. She found herself wanting to help him. However incautious or dangerous it might later prove, she would follower her instincts and trust him.

"I am Laura Stanton of Fairfield Manor in Essex," she said firmly.

"And how may a hapless and imprisoned debtor be of service to you, Mistress Laura Stanton of Fairfield Manor in Essex?"

Was the knave laughing at her? Laura's cheeks stung with heat and her eyes narrowed.

Jedediah came to her side and whispered, "Come away, Mistress Laura. The man's an arrogant clod; he's unsuitable. Forget this madness."

The proud resilience which had upheld Laura this far crumpled. Her shoulders sagged as she sighed. When her stare returned to Matt Thorne, her disappointment was barely hidden. "I'm sorry I've wasted your time."

Without her realising it, he had moved closer. There was no longer antagonism in his regard. She could smell the intensely male scent of him, feel the power and the strength of the man. As she continued to hold his stare, she was startled to find that his eyes were no longer mocking. They regarded her with a serious gravity and, at the same time, seemed to promise a wealth of experience and bold invitation more profound than she could conceive.

"It took courage to come here." His voice had lost its harshness and taken on a more cultured tone. "What desperation has driven you to such ends?"

The intensity of his stare melted her antagonism. His tone was that of natural leadership and she was drawn to respond. "I am offering you the chance to repay your debts in return for—"

Under that dark, frowning scrutiny Laura broke off, unable to go on. If he had mocked her, or interrupted, she would have left the cell, her plan abandoned. He merely waited patiently for her to continue.

Her stare fixed on a patch of green slime on the walls. The situation was embarrassing, but instinct told her she could find no better man for the role required. Loath to commit herself fully until she knew more of him, she drew a deep breath. Usually she was in control of her emotions, but there was something about Matt Thorne which put her out of countenance.

"Before I explain my proposition, I need to know some facts about you," she continued, her voice strained as she mastered her discomfiture. "You haven't the rough speech of the common Londoner, nor any country inflexion that I can detect. Where do you come from?''

''I was born in London.''

''How old are you?''

''Twenty-seven.''

''Have you a family, Mr Thorne?''

''What bearing has that on your proposition?'' He was instantly on his guard, his eyes hooded as he studied her.

''Close family could make things awkward.'' She paused and asked coolly, ''Are you married?''

When he did not answer, she found herself holding her breath. He turned away and ran a hand through his long dark hair. As the flesh caught the lantern light she was pleased to see that his fingers were long and slender. Her grandfather often said that you could tell a person's breeding as much by their hands as their features. Whether that was true or not, Matt Thorne had hands which could pass for an artist's or a nobleman's.

''I'm not married,'' he said flatly.

''But you have been?'' Intuition prompted her to persist.

He swung round, his eyes glittering with a menacing light. ''My wife died.''

That glare stopped Laura pursuing the subject. Perhaps he still loved his wife, but that was of no consequence to her.

''So what is this mysterious proposition you would offer me?'' He turned the conversation with the skill of a man use to being in authority.

''Not so fast, sir. I need to know more of the nature of your debt.''

''That's my affair.''

"Since the amount is so vast, and to free you from the prison I must first settle it..." She deliberately paused and regarded him sternly.

He held her steady gaze but refused to answer.

"Pride could be your downfall," she said, her patience strained.

"There's much at stake. I believe you are an honest man, but the warder said you were fortunate not to be charged with fraud. Your debt is immense."

"So it was made to appear."

He was being deliberately evasive.

Jedediah cleared his throat. "Come away, mistress. You daren't trust him. If the warder is right, the man's a blackguard."

Matt sprang forward and grabbed Jedediah by his jacket-front. "I was the one who was cheated out of my ship. There was no debt that I knew of."

"Everyone you speak to here is innocent by their reckoning," Jedediah said, unintimidated by the prisoner's threatening hold.

Laura put a hand on the sea captain's arm. "Release my servant, sir. We are not here to condemn you. If I thought you guilty of fraud, you would be the last man I would approach on this matter."

Jedediah was released, and scowled as he adjusted his clothing. "He's mean all right. He won't serve at all. Come away, Mistress Laura."

Laura studied the prisoner. He now leaned against the wall, his arms folded across his chest. The only sign of his anger was in the cording of the tendons in his neck. "No details of your creditor are on record. I suspect he has bribed the authorities to keep it from being known. That makes me suspicious, Mr Thorne. Not of you, but of the man who had you arrested. You clearly know something he did not want revealed.''

''Since I have no idea who my new business partner was, what can I know of the man himself?'' He paced angrily. It was a question he had asked himself a hundred times every day since his arrest. Why had his old partner, Caleb Van Steenis, sold out his share? Who had bought it? And why? Fury ground through him at the injustice of his imprisonment. He struggled to control it. Here was his chance to be released. God knew what plans this woman had for him, but he'd agree to anything to be free of prison. Only then could he begin his investigations to bring to justice the man who had trumped up these false debts and had him arrested.

He drew a steadying breath. ''I was arrested within a few hours of docking in London. I had no knowledge of any debt. All I have been able to discover is that my original partner had sold his share. I have been unable to communicate with either him or my lawyer since my arrest.''

''It seems that you have a powerful enemy, Mr Thorne.'' Laura remarked. ''But since you say you did not steal from your business associate, I believe you.''

''Why should you?'' he fired at her with haughty disdain.

They glared across the cell at each other and suddenly Laura saw the humorous side of their absurd situation. She spread her arms wide in exasperation, and a laugh trilled from her throat.

''The Lord only knows why! Call it female intuition. For if ever a man should be awarded a prize for stubbornness and pigheadedness when offered help, it is you, Mr Thorne.'' The incredulous expression on his guarded face prompted her to add, ''In return for the payment of your debts I would buy a few weeks of your time. All your expenses will be met within that period and a further remuneration paid at the satisfactory conclusion of your service.''

Laura could discern a little of his features beneath the beard. Though his nose was slender and patrician and she had glimpsed even white teeth, the outline of his lips and jaw were hidden. What if he was hideously pock-marked or scarred, which would make him unacceptable for her plans? To succeed he must look every inch a gentleman.

''You have the natural bearing of a gentleman, Mr Thorne, but your speech occasionally betrays you...as do your manners. Are you able to play the role of a gentleman, as will be required of you?''

''To be free of this prison I'd impersonate the devil himself,'' he said gruffly. ''My mother brought me up to consider myself a gentleman, but it takes more than breeding to fill that role truly. Birth has nothing to do with how a man treats another human being. Privilege usually brings with it a callous disregard of others less fortunate than themselves. The gentry think themselves civilised, yet they are often indifferent to the suffering they cause in their selfish need to gratify their own ends.''

Laura was taken aback by his vehemence. ''You have a poor opinion of my class.''

''With just cause.''

''Perhaps you are not the right man for what I intend.''

He shrugged. One sleeve had been torn from his shirt and the lantern light defined the curve of muscles on his upper arm, revealing his strength. There was a fine layer of dark hair along his forearm above the reddened chaffing where the manacles had cut into his flesh. There was something so threateningly and sexually male about that bare arm that Laura hastily averted her gaze. It was drawn to his face to find him studying her in a way which was equally unnerving. Most men, having first been offered their freedom and then believing it about to be snatched from them, would have pleaded for her to reconsider. Not Matt Thorne. The lack of subservience in that forceful gaze convinced her that he would never back down beneath the pompous, bullying arrogance of her cousin Guy Stanton. Despite all the warder had told her, she was certain that his word, once given, would not be broken. And if he was innocent of the crimes for which he was imprisoned, then he deserved the chance to clear his name.

Still her unease persisted. Thorne was a man who stood alone. She suspected that his loyalty must be earned and could not be purchased. There was a smouldering anger within him against her class which needed little kindling to burst into flames. He was a dangerous man. Yet by the same token those very flames, as voracious as a heath-fire, could also beckon like a candle in a window to a lost traveller...and they were compelling. To play with fire was to risk getting scorched, but by harnessing fire man had learnt to survive. Laura meant to survive.

She said thoughtfully, ''Despite your words and the alleged nature of your debt, my instincts tell me I can trust you.''

He raised a dark brow, his lips parting in a disturbingly intimate smile. "Then trust to your instincts."

"I must be assured that you look the part required of you." She refused to rise to his baiting. "Will you permit Jedediah to shave you?"

Beneath dark winged brows the bronze eyes regarded her with searing intensity, golden lights of anger blazing in their depths. Laura's chin came up as she met the challenge in his glare. "I am paying you a great deal of money, Mr Thorne. I need to know that beneath your beard you do not have the face of a cut-throat. In short, you must look the part required of you."

He laughed. "I'm no pretty boy with milksop looks, if that's what you want." He scratched his beard. "But I've no attachment to this and will be glad to be rid of the lice it attracts."

Laura gestured to Jedediah to fetch some water. The head groom had brought soap and razor for this purpose. Alone with the prisoner, Laura clasped her hands together and moved to the far side of the small cell. The close scrutiny to which the prisoner was now subjecting her was making her nervous. While Jedediah was gone neither of them spoke. Defiantly, she forced herself to turn and hold his steady gaze. Though he made no movement towards her, she was uncomfortably aware of the potent strength of his body and the power of his masculinity. His silent watching grated on her nerves, making her feel at a disadvantage.

To her relief Jedediah soon returned, and while he shaved Matthew Thorne Laura rehearsed her proposition if he should prove suitable.

She was so deep in thought at the enormity of what

she planned that she started violently when Jedediah
coughed and stepped back from the prisoner. Matthew
Thorne stood in the light of the lantern, self-
consciously rubbing his bare jaw. Laura was unprepared for the change in him. The lean, hard jawline
was prepossessing, his lips full and sensual. But it was
his thickly lashed eyes which held her transfixed, their
expression challenging her in a way that threatened
to steal her breath.

"In the right clothes you will be perfect." As she
nodded with satisfaction she felt a tinge of colour
wash over her cheeks.

"Perhaps now, Mistress Stanton, you will tell me
what proposition you have in mind?"

"I want you to marry me."

Chapter Two

Laughter reverberated off the dank walls.

Laura, her nerves already rubbed raw from the strain of the meeting, turned on Matthew Thorne in a fury.

"It's no laughing matter which drives me to this desperate plight, sir. The estate is entailed. To secure my inheritance I needs must wed before my grandfather dies, and 'tis unlikely he will last the week." Breathing heavily, Laura advanced on the prisoner. Her cloak parted, revealing the low neckline of her gown, and in her agitation her breasts lifted and fell, revealing to him a tantalising glimpse of their fullness. There was an accompanying hiss of silk as her layers of petticoats rustled with each angry movement.

Nothing of his thoughts was revealed in his expression as he appraised her. "Why are you not already wed? You're an attractive woman. You must have had suitors aplenty."

"None I approved of. I refuse to become any man's chattel and would wed upon my own terms. Terms which will be agreed between us before the ceremony, for I've certainly no intention of relinquishing my fortune to a stranger to squander.''

She regarded him with a hauteur which was regal, and her gaze swept over his ragged appearance. She did not want any misunderstanding. ''It will be a marriage of convenience and in name only,'' she said bitingly. ''Once Fairfield is mine, our arrangement is at an end. You will be paid handsomely for the time we must remain together. Since you are a sea-captain it will explain your absence after we have been wed so short a time. Clandestine marriages within the prison here are not uncommon.''

With each sentence the prisoner's expression darkened. ''Aye, I know of these marriages,'' he snarled. ''Used by profligates to seduce women. Then, once they've bedded them, they discard them, and by the payment you speak of become free men. The women are ruined. Is it your inheritance you fear for, Mistress Stanton, or in six months' time do I become a proud father?''

At Laura's horrified gasp, his stare became icily mocking as he went on, ''Am I supposed to give you my name meekly and enjoy finding myself ridiculed as a fortune-hunter at best, or the village idiot for being duped into acknowledging a bastard as my own?''

''How dare you...?'' Laura began.

Jedediah, who had remained by the door, sprang forward. ''You arrogant swine!''

Laura saw Thorne's eyes flash with fury and his fist bunch, but, undeterred by his hostility, Jedediah ploughed on. ''There ain't no cause for such talk. Mistress Stanton is as pure as the day she was born. Since she was fifteen she's never been short of suitors. She's rejected them all because none of them matched up to the father she idolised.''

Jedediah was red-faced with anger and breathing heavily as he paced for some moments before adding, ''Charles Stanton was no ordinary man. He was a brilliant and courageous soldier. At twenty-seven he became colonel in the King's Own Company of Foot-guards. He resigned his commission and became a Member of Parliament when James II came to the throne. Both Charles Stanton and his father Lionel were advisors to William and Mary and many wa-gered Master Charles would become Secretary of State.''

Matt unclenched his fist, but his expression re-mained unimpressed. Jedediah jabbed a gnarled finger at him. ''You should show Mistress Stanton proper respect. When her father was drowned the King and Queen mourned him. Now her grandfather is dying, and she could lose her home to that scheming cousin who—''

''That's enough, Jedediah,'' Laura cut in sharply. She had only let him go on for so long because she had needed to compose herself after Matt Thorne's ridicule. ''Mr Thorne is not interested. You were right, Jedediah. It was a foolish notion.'' Trembling with anger and disappointment, she turned to leave.

''I did not say I was not interested,'' Matt rapped out. ''I just wanted to make sure I was not being taken for the village idiot.''

Laura paused by the door and looked back at him over her shoulder. There was no mockery in his ex-pression. He stood, shoulders squared and proud, his stance self-assured, a hand resting on his hip for all the world as though he were the benefactor and she the supplicant. That strength of character and assurance ruffled her ire, but the knowledge that her cousin, Guy Stanton, would be no match against such a man made her control her antagonism. When he lifted a dark brow in bold appraisal of her figure she felt her heart pound harder. Instantly she was on her guard. This would be a dangerous man to underestimate.

"Tell me the whole story," he insisted quietly. "Such an arrangement cannot work if you keep secrets from me. Entails, from what little I know of them, are complicated. Do you not fear that as your husband all that you own will become mine? A married woman's property belongs to her husband."

Laura hesitated. The man was clearly well-educated and no one's fool. To tell him all would be to lay her pride bare and expose her innermost fears to a stranger. He resumed his position of leaning against the wall with his arms folded across his chest. His stare never left her face and though his manner appeared relaxed he clearly expected his command to be obeyed.

She had held out against marriage because none of her suitors had stirred her heart, or even won her respect. While they had praised her beauty they had patronised her intellect, their greatest interest her fortune. While friends and cousins of her own age married and became mothers, Laura had begun to enjoy the freedom of her life. Until her grandfather had been taken ill...

Now, with the dread of losing Fairfield throbbing in her mind, she knew that if she did not marry before her grandfather's death she would lose her inheritance. Fear clenched her stomach. All that she loved in this life was bound in Fairfield Manor. She could not bear the thought of losing it. It had been in her family since the time of Queen Elizabeth. Her blood heated with anger at the thought of her wastrel cousin, Guy Stanton, managing it in her stead. For the last thirty years, since the Restoration of Charles II, her grandfather had been restoring the house, which had been damaged by a fire started by the Parliamentary army. He had replaced the livestock slaughtered to feed the Roundhead troops, and today more land than ever was under the plough. Many of the local villagers worked on the estate. If it was allowed to run down they would be laid off, and their families would starve. Guy Stanton would gamble away the profits and soon destroy all that her grandfather had worked for.

Holding Matthew Thorne's stare, Laura silently cursed the circumstances which had brought her to this.

"No unmarried woman can inherit Fairfield, even if they are the direct descendant," she began to explain. "The entail was enforced in 1580 to ensure my great-grandmother married the man chosen by her father, or lose everything. I have no intention of bowing to male tyranny."

"You take a great risk in what you do," he said laconically. "How do you know you can trust me?"

"Instinct," she said with a strained smile. "I believe you are a man of honour. You will not break your word on any bargain we make. Am I right?"

He nodded, his bronze eyes still wary as he studied her. There was a compelling force in his stare and she knew she would have to tell him everything before he agreed to her plan. "I love my home," she said simply. "It's not just losing it which would be painful to bear, but I could never allow my uncle Cecil to inherit. Not out of greed for myself, but because he and my cousin Guy would bleed it dry and bring it to ruin. They want Fairfield for its wealth and have no care for its people."

"Yet this marriage between us is to be one of convenience," he persisted. "If you have no child of your own, surely then, by this entail, on your death the property passes to your uncle's family…or to your husband."

Laura's heart clenched with foreboding. Did he see Fairfield as a means to secure his future? That was not her intention. "The entail was merely to ensure that any female who inherited was married. In normal circumstances my husband would share my control of the estate. Do not think that after we are wed you can steal my inheritance from me. The people of Fairfield are loyal to me. I could raise a small army to protect my interests if I had to. As to the lack of a child…" She swallowed with annoyance that he had spotted the flaws in her plan. "Without a child to inherit, and since I intend that our marriage will later be annulled, then in the present circumstances my cousin Guy would eventually inherit. But not in my lifetime. I can achieve that much at least."

Casting complications aside, she concentrated on the immediate dilemma, not one which would need resolving some years ahead. She went on, "Before my grandfather suffered the seizure, he had petitioned the King to have the entail revoked. His Majesty refused as he did not feel a single woman was capable of the responsibility of running so vast an estate without the support of a husband."

Her gaze slid from his piercing bronze stare, which seemed to be looking into the depths of her soul. Her head came up and she began to pace the tiny cell as she continued to explain. "My grandfather is seventy. Last month, while attending the funeral of Queen Mary, he collapsed from a seizure. During the years of the Protectorate he was forced into exile. He served Queen Mary and William of Orange at The Hague and has done so ever since. The Queen's sudden death from smallpox deeply upset him—"

She broke off, finding it difficult to talk of such matters to a stranger, and for several moments her eyes were unfocused with fear for her grandfather's life. Drawing a shaking breath, she forced herself to continue her explanation. "Grandfather's loyalty to the late Queen and King William has been unswerving. His voice was one of the loudest when James II was deposed for his Catholic sympathies and his eldest Protestant daughter approached to take the throne. Only when his health began to fail last year was he allowed to retire from his post at Court. Yet throughout his life his home, Fairfield Manor, has been his greatest pride. As it is mine."

A passionate light gleamed in her blue eyes as she faced the prisoner, willing him to understand the plight which drove her. "During the conflict with parliament in the 1640s he struggled to make it prosper," she went on proudly. "His involvement with the failed attempt of Charles II to regain his throne in 1651 drove him into exile. For a time his youngest brother Cecil, a supporter of Cromwell, claimed Fairfield as his home."

She pressed a hand to her temple to control her anger at those events. "Cecil plundered its wealth and neglected the land and people. At the Restoration, Fairfield was returned to my grandfather, and since then there has been no love lost between the two brothers. Cecil wants Fairfield's restored riches for his son.''

Laura paused in her pacing to stare across at Matthew Thorne. He was frowning, but made no attempt to interrupt. He would clearly make no decision until he knew the whole story. Reluctantly she admired his astuteness, though it galled her that she must speak of painful and private emotions which she had confided to no one before.

"Lionel Stanton, my grandfather, had three sons to succeed him," she went on heavily. "He believed his own direct line was assured. Fate decreed otherwise. His eldest son Samuel died in a hunting accident in 1690 and last year in 1693…'' Her voice broke and she needed several moments to control the grief which threatened to overwhelm her. "Last summer my father, Charles, and his younger brother Robert were drowned when their yacht capsized in the Thames estuary.'' She resumed her restless pacing. "I am the only grandchild. But only by marrying will I prevent my uncle and cousin claiming my inheritance.''

As she continued to pace the floor Laura slipped her hand inside her cloak and touched the legal contract which had been specially drawn up. The lawyer had sworn it would be binding. It would give her control of her life. She quashed a momentary unease that Matt Thorne was not a man to let anyone control his destiny.

"I'd not seen myself as a knight-errant rescuing beautiful maidens in distress,'' Matt said softly.

"Even to be free of this place and my debts, I do not relish being beholden to a woman. Marriage is a serious step."

"A marriage of convenience," Laura amended. "After my inheritance is secure you are free to take up your own life again. The entail does not stipulate that I must remain married. My grandfather is not expected to last the week. In the circumstances, we will not be expected to socialise so I anticipate no difficulties. If you agree to my proposal, you will be required to sign a document outlining our agreement. It states that the marriage will be in name only and will be annulled at the first appropriate time. As I said, the fact that you are a sea-captain will explain your absence to any curious enough to enquire. After a year or so I will simply announce that you have perished at sea, since my annulment would cause a scandal I would rather avoid. You will, of course, be rewarded by a sum to provide security for your own future as well as your present debts being settled."

As she spoke he rubbed his clean-shaven jaw, and a lock of hair fell over his brow, softening the severity of his expression.

"How came you by one thousand pounds to settle my debt? No woman of your age is in control of such wealth."

"That is my affair," Laura blurted out, resenting being put to the question over so sensitive an issue.

"I thought we were to be honest with each other, Mistress Laura Stanton of Fairfield. I've no intention of agreeing to this sham marriage only to discover that once the ceremony has been performed I remain incarcerated for my unpaid debt."

Laura flushed at the insult, but could understand

his suspicion. It heightened her respect for him. Matt Thorne did not leap at opportunities without weighing the consequences. He would need cunning as well as strength if her uncle and cousin proved difficult over her inheritance.

She swallowed against a lump of guilt which had risen to her throat. "Although my allowance from my grandfather is extremely generous I could not at short notice raise such a vast sum. I have pledged my grandmother's jewels against a loan to pay your debts and set you up in the manner suitable for my husband. Once we are married my dowry will secure their return, and provide adequate funds for us to live on and provide you with the necessary accoutrements needed for your lifestyle as a gentleman."

Her voice lost its reassurance. It had been a desperate gamble to pledge the jewels. Those emeralds had remained intact throughout the terrible years of her grandmother's exile during the Commonwealth. They had been a wedding-gift to her great-grandmother in the reign of James I, and her grandmother had refused to sell them no matter how impecunious the family had been. Laura had wrangled with her conscience for days. Only by convincing herself that they would be rescued from the moneylender immediately her dowry was paid to her husband had she offered them for security. She had been anxious ever since. If Matt proved dishonest and fled with her dowry, she would lose not only her home but her grandmother's jewels, the sentimental value of which was irreplaceable. She was not very proud of her action, but how else could she save Fairfield? Her grandfather was too ill to confide in.

Matt was watching her like a hawk hovering over

a rabbit. "Your uncle and cousin do not sound the type of men to give in so easily," he said after consideration. "They are bound to cause trouble."

"I expect they will. That is why I was impressed at the way you defended the youth in the yard yesterday. The speed of my marriage will arouse their suspicion. Therefore it must be obvious to everyone that ours was a love match. During the time we are together you must play the enamoured lover."

"You've chosen the wrong man if you want a fawning lapdog," he snapped.

"I said enamoured," she retaliated, "not moonstruck with calf-love. I don't expect you to serenade me with love-songs, or swear undying devotion with every breath."

"I'm relieved to hear it," he replied drily. "Your terms are generous, but even so a man does not lightly give up his freedom. Before I agree, would you remove your mask? If I'm to play the besotted husband, I'd be reassured that I'm not to be bound to a plain or hideously scarred woman."

He was paying her back for making him shave before she accepted him. She was surprised that such audacity amused rather than angered her. There was a smile upon her lips as she pushed back the hood of her cloak, revealing the cascade of thick, shining auburn ringlets. Slowly she put her hand to the mask which covered the upper part of her face, and lifted it away.

She felt a glow of satisfaction as his eyes widened with admiration. Then, as quickly, their expression was hooded. Used to extravagant compliments, she was piqued when he said nothing.

"Will you be capable of performing the role required of you, Mr Thorne? Or do I fill you with repugnance?''

''A man would have to be blind not to be moved by your beauty.''

He had moved out of the light of the lantern and his voice conveyed nothing more than pleasantry, as though he were remarking upon fine weather. Used as she was to flattery from her suitors, his offhand manner rankled. She conquered her antagonism. His indifference would make their roles easier. She certainly did not want a husband who was hot with desire for her and would later demand his marriage rights. There was one matter she still had to resolve before completing the arrangements.

''Will you now tell me about the nature of your debts?'' She had to ensure that the man would not be tempted by her fortune and seek to rob her of her inheritance.

He did not immediately answer, clearly disliking having to explain. There was tension in every line of his figure when at last he spoke. ''My business associate, who had a quarter-share in my vessel, sold his share without informing me during my last voyage. Then apparently my signature was forged on loan papers drawn up by my anonymous new partner, supposedly lending me finance to pay for extensive repairs to *Sea Maiden* and to purchase cargo for my last voyage. There was no loan. My new partner's lawyer arrived on board the *Sea Maiden* an hour after I docked. I denied the debt, which was the preposterous figure of several thousand pounds. I was immediately arrested. My ship was sold to cover this fictitious debt, and still they say I owed another thousand pounds.'' He hit out at the wall with his fist in impotent anger. "I'll sign any document you want to get out of here. I want no claim on your estate. All I want is to bring to justice the man who put me in here. Three months I've been forced to suffer in this hell-pit."

Laura's skin prickled at the lethal edge to his voice. This was not a man to make your enemy. "That's monstrous. Your partner must of course be brought to justice."

"When I am free from this prison he will be." The handsome contours of his rugged face could have been hacked from a glacier. "I've yet to discover his name. Any questions I've asked have been met with a beating. I've not even been permitted to contact my lawyer since my arrest. Someone has gone to a great deal of trouble to keep me in prison. And I intend to find out why." His tone was that of a judge delivering a death sentence. "All I know is that he is a man of wealth and influence. Like all his kind, he thought that made him immune from justice."

Laura shivered at the suppressed fury in his voice. Had she made an error in judgement in trusting him? There was an untamed and dangerous element about him which made her uneasy. But then was not his rage justified? Laura felt her own sense of justice outraged that Matthew Thorne, for no apparent reason, had lost his ship and his freedom. And, worse, that the corrupt gaolers had been bribed to ensure that the outside world was kept ignorant of his plight.

"Why should a man act like that against you?" she asked, needing to know that the prisoner was not keeping anything from her.

Hatred contorted his features and she saw his throat work as he battled to control his anger. "When do the gentry ever need a reason? What they want they take. Enough bribes can pervert justice. For most of my imprisonment I've been kept in the solitary hold. Yesterday was my first day out of it in weeks.''

"If you hate the gentry so much, then I fear you are unsuitable for our arrangement. You will have to live among them for a few weeks.'' There was a quality about the prisoner she knew she could never control. Although she was appalled at the injustice perpetrated against him, she could not risk losing Fairfield by choosing the wrong person.

"This matter will not affect our agreement.'' He closed the gap between them and she found herself staring into a penetrating bronze gaze. The anger had gone from his eyes but the light in their depths was indefinable, something between a challenge and coercion. "I will not fail you. You're not my enemy. You've nothing to fear from me.''

The husky cadence in his voice increased the frantic pounding of her heart. When he reached out to lift the hood of her cloak to cover her hair, she braced herself not to pull away from his touch. He chuckled softly.

"I'm no Sir Galahad, Laura, but when I give my word I keep it.''

Matt stared deep into Laura's brilliant blue eyes, trying to fathom her thoughts. He could not believe his luck that this ravishing creature would pay his debts. Once free, he would discover the identity of the man who had perverted justice to steal his ship and have him imprisoned.

The heady scent of Laura's skin and jasmine perfume wafted around him, bringing a breath of seductive softness to the bleakness of his cell. Behind the defiance of her tilted chin he had glimpsed the vulnerability which had driven her to such desperate measures. A latent chivalry stirred, which he quickly stifled. Her beauty was but a shell, hiding the canker bred by affluence beneath. He distrusted all those of her station. Wasn't she prepared to deceive her grandfather, whom she professed to love, in order to cheat the entail governing her inheritance? She had frivolously bartered the family jewels to gratify her selfish aims. She had no concept of family loyalty and was typical of all her kind. How he despised them all.

It was one of her kind who, six years ago, had destroyed everything he loved and cherished in this world. Until now that man had been beyond his retribution, protected by his wealth and position. No longer. As Laura Stanton's husband he would be on equal terms with his adversary.

He viewed the woman in a kinder light. His gaze took in her small figure. Her cloak had parted, displaying a lilac gown of the finest linen which was draped back over her hips to display an underskirt of cream brocade embroidered with violets. The tightly laced bodice nipped in her waist and enticingly pushed up her full breasts. In the soft amber glow of the lantern her skin glowed pale golden, warm and seductive as silk. He felt his body responding. He had been a prisoner for three months and in that time had fastidiously shunned the dubious charms of the prostitutes plying their trade in the prison.

The building ache of his need brought a mirthless smile to his full lips. Beauty alone could never override his contempt for her high birth. She was using him for her own ends. As he meant to use her to gain his freedom and honour a vow he had made on a double grave six years ago.

Laura stood rigid, feeling the touch of his breath warm against her bare throat. She felt stifled by his nearness, a slow blush spreading through her body at the boldness of his appraisal. She pulled the edges of her cloak together and was alarmed to hear a tremor in her voice as she said, "Jedediah will have your debts settled by noon tomorrow. He will also bring suitable attire for the wedding ceremony, which will take place in the Fleet chapel. We will spend an hour in a private inn parlour discussing the story we must tell about our courtship and your background before I present you to my grandfather. Good day, Mr Thorne."

Matt did not move as Laura Stanton swept out of the cell, taking the lantern with her. It was a dream— a hallucination—it had to be. But he could still smell her perfume, sweetening the fetid stench of the air.

There was a jangling of keys and a gaoler shuffled in.

"Ain't you a lucky bastard?" he said, chuckling as he put down a tray containing the first hot food Matt had received since his imprisonment.

The impact of Matt's fist smashing into the gaoler's face sent him staggering back against the wall. Surprisingly, he did not call out for assistance. Instead his mouth split into a toothless grin.

"That caught you on the raw, did it? By-blows ain't got no cause to get uppity when their mothers ain't no better than they should be."

Matt glared at him, suspecting ridicule if not another whipping.

"No offence intended, Thorne," he surprised Matt

by saying. "Don't ruin yer chances of getting out of 'ere just 'cos of a slip of me tongue."

Matt relaxed. The man was not one of the prison's bullies, and it was years since he had picked a fight after taking offence at that most common of insults. But Laura Stanton had got beneath his guard. She was of a class he despised, a class which had condemned him to a shameful birth and his mother to poverty and degradation.

He crushed a rush of bitter memories. He had been given no food since yesterday as part of his punishment for attacking the gaolers. A mouth-watering spicy sauce tantalised his nostrils as he lifted the cover from the food. There was a whole chicken, a partridge pie in a delicious golden pastry, and a large slice of apple and cinnamon tart, together with a flagon of Burgundy wine. The warder took another packet out of his pocket and sniggered as he tossed it to Matt. Unwrapping the linen around it, Matt saw a small pipe, a tobacco pouch and a tablet of soap. The soap Matt threw aside, but he sniffed the tobacco pouch with appreciation.

"After you've eaten you're being moved to another cell." The gaoler grunted. "One with a fire, light and bedding. Instructions were fer yer to take a bath. This ain't no bloody Hampton Court Palace. You'll get a bowl of water if yer lucky, no matter what's bin paid."

"Water will be fine," Matt responded.

Left alone to eat his meal, Matt's thoughts returned to the change in his fortunes and especially Laura Stanton. The image of her loveliness, her figure, petite but with unawakened sensuality, refused to be banished. Distrust had made him goad her. He had known women enough in the last six years to recognise innocence. Her beauty had startled him. She was the siren of every man's dreams. There was an unconscious invitation in her movements and the boldness of her stare. A boldness he did not mistake as brazenness. Laura Stanton would be a woman capable of great passion when the right man nurtured it. That latent sensuality was a lure, tempting men to seek to become her master, her tutor in the delights of love—

Matt cut off the treacherous route of his thoughts. That man would not be himself, even though she would call him husband. The meal half eaten, he snatched up the flagon and, angered by his thoughts, paced his cell. What madness was possessing him? He would love only one woman, and she was dead these past six years. He dishonoured Susannah's memory by entering into this sham of marriage. He tipped the flagon to his lips and drank deeply. He would not do it.

He paced until the gaoler returned, his appetite gone as the grief and loss which had been with him all those years gave him no peace. To make it worse he could hear Susannah's voice, telling him to use this opportunity to avenge the death of their daughter. In prison he could do nothing.

He was still wrestling with his conscience as he was escorted to the far side of the prison where, on payment of garnish, the better quarters could be found. The cell was smoky from the damp wood burning in the tiny grate, but at least the smoke would keep the fleas and cockroaches away. There was even a thin, stained, straw-filled mattress on the wooden bed, and two worn blankets. Luxury indeed after the nights he had spent with teeth gritted, his body curled up into a ball to combat the freezing winter air. Placing the half-empty flagon of wine on the floor, he tossed the contents of Laura's bundle on to the mattress. With a contented sigh he stretched out on to the bed and rubbed a hand across his clean-shaven jaw. His thoughts remained upon Susannah and his daughter, and his peace of mind shattered. He closed his eyes, but he could no longer summon the images of his dead wife and child, though their souls cried out for judgement upon their murderer.

Swinging his legs to the floor, he dropped his head into his hands. Laura Stanton, with her absurd proposal, had given him the means to escape prison and avenge the deaths of his loved ones. This marriage of convenience would not be a betrayal of his love for Susannah. It was simply a means to an end. His conscience cleared, he felt better. He could smell the stench of his unwashed body and the blood from his beating and flinched from it. There was a hard lump digging into his thigh and he pulled out the tablet of soap. With a grin, he sniffed it. Sandalwood. A manly, pleasant scent, unlike many of the sickly perfumes favoured by the gentry. To wash the prison stench and lice from his body and hair would make him feel more like a man and less like an animal.

Absently, he scratched at a flea-bite. If Laura Stanton thought he'd adopt posturing, foppish ways she'd be disappointed. The years at sea had roughened his once impeccable manners, but they were not forgotten. Hadn't his mother painstakingly drilled them into him, even if he had led a life little better than that of a guttersnipe?

The memory of his mother thinned his lips into a bitter line. Her life had been ruined because of the callous lechery of a so-called gentleman. Penelope Thorne had been no woman of easy virtue. She had been the only child of a parson, who was himself the youngest of five sons. Without an inheritance, Simon Thorne had entered the church. Although a Puritan with Royalist sympathies, during the Protectorate he had been given a living in an affluent parish of Bath. For a time they had prospered. Then had come the Restoration, when Puritan incumbents had been cast from their livings and the Royalist preachers reinstated.

Matt stretched out on the bed, his hands behind his head as his thoughts lingered on the past. To support his family Simon Thorne had preached in the marketplace, relying on the charity of the citizens. One afternoon he had been caught in a thunderstorm, and huddled in a church porch for shelter. Two drunken cavaliers had come upon him and, despising his Puritan garb, had beaten him senseless. He had never recovered consciousness. Penelope and her mother had been forced to take in sewing for the gentry, which was how she met her lover. He had sworn to love and honour her. When he told Penelope that his father had refused to give his blessing to their marriage they had eloped and been married in a small country church. Three months later Penelope had been abandoned and had discovered herself pregnant.

The old anger which had burned in Matt for years returned and, too restless to be still, he paced the cell, his eyes grim with the need for vengeance upon the man who had ruined his mother's life. Betrayed by her lover, Penelope Thorne had been too ashamed to return to her mother and had fled to the anonymity of London. There she had struggled to bring up her son by working for a seamstress. The hours were long and the pay poor, forcing them to live in the poorest quarter of the City. Matt had spent his childhood days in the streets. Penelope had instilled in him that by birth he was a gentleman. But she would not reveal the name of his father. With no money for his education, she had taught him to read and write as her father had taught her. Matt had struggled with his studies, seeing them as a means to make life easier for his mother when he reached manhood.

There had been other lessons to learn about survival. These he had mastered among the street urchins where only the wiliest and strongest reached manhood. His expression became bleak as he recalled the poverty of his childhood. At twelve, scorning the life of crime taken up by so many of his companions, he had taken work as a scribe to a city alderman and hated every second of it. At fourteen he had saved a little money to support his mother for some months ahead and had run away to sea to make his fortune.

In the following years fate had smiled on him. He had enjoyed his life at sea and he had prospered. His quick wits and obvious education had won him the attention of a grizzled captain, who had recently lost a son of his own. By the end of the first voyage he had started to teach Matt how to navigate by the stars and read maps. Three years later Matt was his second-in-command.

"You were a good man, Captain Boscombe," Matt said affectionately. He lifted his goblet in reverential salute. "I hope your retirement in the Americas was long and contented."

As he drained the goblet Matt's memory travelled on a year, to his first meeting with Susannah. She had been an orphan, and worked as a milkmaid to a kindly farmer and his wife who doted on her. At sixteen she had been as innocent as the sunrise.

Matt inhaled sharply as the familiar pain again wrenched his chest. He drained the wine flagon and flung it aside. His mood now dark and menacing, he snatched up the pipe and lit it. As the blue smoke curled around his head he stared into space, the black pit of his memories hardening his features to a demonic countenance sworn upon vengeance. All his hatred for the gentry rose up and threatened to choke him and one name pounded through his brain... Sir James Breten. Sir James Breten, the man he had vowed to bring to justice or die in the attempt.

Even before their deaths Matt had hated the gentry. He had been obsessed with finding out who his father was. He had wanted to make the lecher pay for all the misery his gentle mother had suffered. But he had never learned the man's identity. Penelope Thorne had taken her secret shame to the grave when she had died of the lung fever.

There was only one way to get revenge upon the gentry and that was to become accepted in their circle. He'd spent a month in a drunken stupor after his wife's death, before thoughts of revenge had proved more powerful than his misery. He'd gone back to sea. A year later Captain Boscombe had died, and to Matt's surprise he had left him enough money to become a one-sixth sharer in a ship. For five years, to make his fortune, he had spent most of his time at sea, putting into England's shores for just long enough to reprovision and buy the most profitable cargoes to be sold abroad. Gradually he had bought out the other sharers, until only Caleb Van Steenis remained. Three times he had rounded Cape Horn, taking settlers to the Americas. They'd paid high prices for their passages, and the furniture he bought in England and sold in the Americas had been a lucrative trade. He'd sailed to the East and the Indies, bringing back expensive spices, delicate china and the finest silks, and from Russia exotic furs. He had chosen each cargo with care, aimed at the highest profits, and to achieve this he had frequently sailed in the most dangerous waters. Twice he had fought off pirates and, upon capturing one such ship filled with bounty, he had received a vast reward for the treasure by the authorities.

In those years he had spared himself nothing in his labour, every spare penny of his income ploughed back into his business to ensure higher profits. At last his goal had been within reach. Once Caleb had been bought out, with the profits from his last voyage, it would only take two or three years for Matt to add another ship or two to his fleet. He had given himself ten years to become established as a gentleman seacaptain. Then he would be able to exact his revenge upon James Breten.

Yet all he had striven for had been wiped away in a charge of false debts devised during his last voyage. Someone would pay for that. And pay dearly.

He would start by tracking down Caleb Van Steenis. He had moved from his old address. That was the only information he had been able to gather about his old partner. Caleb would tell him whom he had sold his share to. Then the hunt would begin.

"Curse you, Caleb Van Steenis," he ground out savagely. "What made you break our agreement and sell your share of my ship? You knew I'd buy you out at the end of the last voyage. Fine friend you proved to be.''

Matt had put up a fight to prevent his arrest, but had been outnumbered and beaten into unconsciousness. He had woken up in the Fleet and been shown what was purported to be his signature on the fraudulent loan papers which pledged the *Sea Maiden* and all its cargo as security. The forged signature was good. It must have been copied from one of the genuine legal papers held by Caleb. The corresponding signature of the supposed lender of the money, however, had been carefully withheld from Matt's view. He had lost everything, and in prison was powerless to discover the identity of the man who had brought him down. That fact alone smacked of underhanded deceit. Why had this new partner taken such pains to hide his identity? But to have acted so swiftly and to have so sewn up the course of justice, it was obvious that he held a place of position and possessed wealth. Though why a wealthy stranger should act against himself with any motive other than greed Matt had no idea. He was not aware that he'd made any influential enemies.

His eyes slitted with hatred. At last he was in a position to learn the identity of the gentlemen who had callously used their position to destroy all he held dear. They would pay for their disregard of others, and would learn that Matt Thorne's justice would be swift and exacting.

As Laura entered the high-gabled house in Lincoln's Inn, Jedediah put a hand on her arm. ''You can't mean to go ahead with this madness. A dozen men have offered for your hand this last year. When your grandfather dies you will be a wealthy woman.''

"That wealth is a curse. It's what drives me to this necessity."

Jedediah shook his head. "Too particular you are, that's your problem. And this Matt Thorne… There's more to him than meets the eye. It could mean trouble. No amount of money can buy him. There was an anger burning deep within him; I could sense it. I don't like it, mistress."

"I sensed something too, Jedediah," Laura voiced her unease. "I promise you I will sleep on it before I make a final decision."

"Mistress Laura." Barker, the major-domo, hurried towards her. His smooth face beneath his grey wig was drawn with anxiety. "Thank heavens you've returned, Mistress Laura. The master's been asking for you all day. He's very fretful. The doctor's with him now."

"I'll go to him at once." Laura handed her cloak to Barker and sped up the two flights of stairs to her grandfather's bedchamber. She knocked and entered, her eyes taking a moment to adjust to the gloomy interior. The shutters were closed across the window and only a single candle burned, its feeble light barely penetrating the dark confines of the vast four-poster bed.

"Is that you, Laura?" The voice was a thread of its usual vibrant self.

"Yes, Grandfather." Nodding brief acknowledgement to the doctor, who was replacing a jar of leeches in his bag, she moved to the bedside. When she lifted the candle, the better to see her grandfather, the old man raised his hand to shield his eyes.

"The light hurts."

She replaced the candle on the bedside table and sat on the edge of the mattress. Her eyes brimming with tears, she took his hand. "Are you feeling better?"

"I'm dying, Laura."

For a moment she looked down at the freckled hand between hers. It looked so strong and capable. A hand which had in the course of its life wielded a sword in the bloody conflict between Charles I and Parliament in the forties. A hand which had been taken by no less than four preceding monarchs: Charles II, James II and Queen Mary and her husband, William of Orange. A hand which had set aside the sword to take up the pen of diplomacy and correspond with all the courts in Europe. Just a month ago Lionel Stanton had ridden as hard as any man in the hunt on their estate in Essex. As Laura had kept pace with him she had marvelled that at seventy he had the vigour of a man half his age.

How was it possible for a man to change so drastically in a week? The sudden death of Queen Mary from smallpox had hit him hard. They had come to London to attend her funeral. As the coffin bearing the Queen's wooden funeral effigy passed them by he had clutched at his heart and collapsed outside Westminster Abbey.

"Save your strength," she urged now gently. "You must get well."

Through the gloom the faded blue eyes stared at her. "You know I have only one wish...to live long enough to see you safely wed. Don't fail me, Laura. Don't fail Fairfield. Cecil and Guy will bleed it dry.

Have you chosen a husband from the names I gave you?''

Laura hung her head. Her every instinct was to rail against the ultimatum, but he was so frail that she dared not risk causing another seizure. On the journey home from the Fleet prison she had again been beset with doubts about her plans. When she had entered the house she had decided to abandon the scheme as madness.

"I am considering them."

"You must decide," the husky whisper commanded. "My friend Archbishop Halroyd knows the men on the list. He will marry you this week."

She turned her head away to hide her anger, and it took her several moments to regain her composure.

Her grandfather's breathing came in hoarse gasps as he fought for breath. "I must know Fairfield will be safe in your hands."

The physician reached across from the other side of the bed and put a hand to her grandfather's chest. "You must rest, sir." He frowned at Laura as he straightened. "Mistress Laura, I must ask you to leave the room. The slightest upset could prove too much for your grandfather's heart."

Laura rose slowly to her feet. Duty won over pride. "Do you know what you are asking of me, Grandfather? But I agree."

"Whom have you decided upon?" A fierce light entered his pale eyes.

"I will tell you tomorrow."

Overcome by a sense of foreboding, Laura fled the room, and spent the night pacing her chamber. By morning she knew she could not bear to lose Fairfield. She would wed Matthew Thorne, and would at least have some control over her destiny.

Chapter Three

Laura was grim-faced behind her velvet mask as the coach pressed through the crowded streets on its return to the Fleet prison. Inside her fur muff her hand, which was closed around the silver hand-warmer holding burning charcoal, was white-knuckled with tension. It had snowed overnight and the rooftops were capped with pristine whiteness while the sludge pressed underfoot by the shivering, pinched-faced citizens was an icy hazard to vehicles and pedestrians. Beggars wrapped in rags squatted on street corners, their pleas for alms vying with the raucous cries of the street-sellers. Two carts had overturned, blocking the road ahead, and it was a half-hour before Laura's carriage could pass.

Her nerves were frayed to breaking-point. When she raised the leather blind over the window and saw a sign "Rainbow Tavern and Marrying House" she knew she was in the Fleet district. The area surrounding the prison was notorious for the ease with which a clandestine marriage could be performed. Unmarried women, or widows, seeking a father's name for an unborn child, could do as Laura had done. Many,

for the settlement of a prisoner's debts, would marry
a stranger to give them respectability, and when they
returned to their village never set eyes on the man
again. Many a scoundrel had coerced a gullible heiress into elopement and been married here. Not to
mention the profligates who used the marriage ceremony as a means to seduction and once the maiden-
head was won disclaimed any knowledge of the ceremony. A bribe soon ensured that any record of such
a marriage was either never entered in the records or
could later be erased. The preachers performing the
service were often prisoners themselves and, provided
that the bride and groom both consented to the match
and declared they were not already wed, no other for-
mality was needed.

Her stomach clenched with panic. How could she
go through with this madness? Even as the cold ten-
tacles of fear unfurled through her body she knew she
had no choice. Her head came up. She must do it for
Fairfield. Jedediah had visited a lawyer and settled
Matt Thorne's debts. He had then gone to the prison
to arrange the ceremony in the chapel. Laura needed
the marriage to be put on record temporarily in case
it was checked by her uncle or cousin. Jedediah had
also taken suitable clothes for the groom.

Ten minutes later Laura was at the chapel door, her
determined step concealing her inner quaking. The
bare walls of the chapel were poorly lit and as she
approached the altar she saw two figures move out of
the shadows. For a moment she could not believe that
the taller man was Matt Thorne. Her critical stare
flickered over the knee-length, full-skirted jacket of
grey velvet trimmed with silver braid, which em-
phasised the broadness of his shoulders and slender

waist. The grey hose below his knee-breeches revealed a shapely calf. At his neck and wrist was an expanse of white lace which accentuated the swarthiness of his skin. In his hand he held a wide-brimmed beaver hat, trimmed by a single black ostrich feather. The clothes she had purchased for him fitted to perfection. To complete the image of the gentleman which he must present to her grandfather he wore a silver-embossed baldric across his chest from which hung a sword. A long brown periwig curled magnificently about his shoulders, but it was his face which made her breath catch in her throat. She had not expected the lean, hawk-like features to be so handsome, or that he would hold himself with the natural grace of a born commander.

Her stare ran the full length of him again. In looks and dress her grandfather could not fault him. She prayed his manners and speech would not prove the lie of their masquerade.

A wry smile touched his lips at her critical study. Taking her hand, he bowed and raised it to his lips. "I trust I do not disappoint you?"

Now that he was freed from his cell and no longer in rags, his self-assurance was disconcerting. Even the roughness to his voice was no longer apparent.

"I am not disappointed, Mr Thorne. You look the part required of you." To calm the quickening beat of her heart she kept her voice cool. "I take it Jedediah informed you of the contents of the document he brought with him? Have you understood it and made your mark upon it?"

"I read it and signed it."

She acknowledged the correction with a bow of her head. That he was literate was another surprise.

Clearly she must take care not to underestimate this man.

The chaplain shuffled forward as Laura took her place by Matt's side. The warder appeared from behind a column to stand as witness to the ceremony. Laura felt detached from the proceedings as the chaplain mumbled over the words. She heard Matt respond, and her own voice was clear as she spoke her vows. There was an embarrassed cough as the chaplain fell silent and appeared to be waiting.

"Is there a ring? It is not necessary, but I thought in the circumstances..."

Laura blushed. She had forgotten the ring. Pulling off her gloves, she prised a band of twisted gold set with a sapphire from her right hand. She hesitated before handing it to Matthew Thorne. It had been her mother's betrothal ring. She suppressed her qualms that her actions today desecrated the love of her parents by using the ring, and she dropped it into Matt's palm. A candle reflected in the sapphire winked at her. She could almost feel the presence of her father, laughing over her shoulder at the way she was duping Cecil and Guy Stanton. Then the ring slid, warm and unfamiliarly, upon her wedding finger. When she would have pulled her hand away, she found it held fast. Her gaze lifted to hold the stare of the man she had just married, and with the light of a cresset burning behind his head his face had all the beauty of a dark angel.

"Do I not get a kiss to seal the contract between us?" he whispered against her ear.

"That was not part of our bargain."

Instead of releasing her, he chuckled softly. His face remained close to hers and his gaze fastened upon her lips. Wishing to avoid a scene, she turned her head to offer him her cheek, bracing herself against the touch of his lips on her flesh.

It did not come.

She glanced at him and found his expression closed against her.

"If that's the best you can offer," he said crisply, "I'll not drink at an arid well." Instead he raised her fingers to his mouth, but his lips stopped short of touching her skin before he stepped back from her.

Jedediah was handing a pouch of coins to the chaplain and another to the warder and noticed nothing of the exchange. Why, then, did Laura feel humiliated? She certainly had no desire for this man to kiss her, but during the ceremony she had felt a bond of conspiracy weaving between them. Now that he had moved away from her side the spell was broken. It was misplaced that she should feel disappointed but, uncomfortably, she did.

To cover her unease, she said more sharply than she had intended, "While Jedediah completes his business here we will wait in the carriage."

Laura walked out of the chapel without troubling to see if her new husband followed her. She was halfway across the frozen courtyard when her foot skidded on an icy puddle. A firm hand gripped her elbow, saving her from falling. Then Matt's arm was around her waist as he briskly marched her through the prison gate.

The coachman jumped down from his seat and opened the door of the carriage. With little gentleness or ceremony Laura was bundled inside. Matthew Thorne put his foot on the step and addressed the coachman. "Take us to Mistress Laura's home. The servant will be following later." His figure filled the doorway and the door was banged shut behind him before Laura found her voice to protest. Outraged at his behaviour, she leaned forward to put her head out of the window and order the coachman to stop. A hand on her shoulder pushed her back against the velvet upholstery.

"No, you don't!" his voice grated with barely suppressed anger. "What I've got to say to you is best said in private, before we continue this ruse to deceive your grandfather."

"How dare you speak to me that way? I'd planned we take a private parlour in an inn and discuss the story we will tell about our meeting and courtship."

He silenced her with a cold look. "Your haughty airs cut no ice with me, madam. I agreed to this ruse because I needed my debts cleared. In prison I was powerless to bring to justice the man who perjured himself to put me there. What do you think you were playing at in the chapel just now? Our agreement is off if you can't act out the role required of you."

Her blue eyes flashing with anger, Laura flared back, "Just what do you mean by that?"

"The role of two people supposedly in love. Isn't that the only way you will convince your grandfather why you did not choose one of the men he selected for you?"

Laura bit her lip, hating to admit that he was right. "There was nothing wrong with my conduct. My grandfather is the only one we have to impress."

"You're wrong there." His voice was laced with contempt. "From this moment we act our parts every waking second of the day. You said you married me to stop your cousin inheriting Fairfield Manor. He doesn't sound to me like a man who will meekly allow such a prize to be snatched from him. A hasty marriage is always open to speculation. If this cousin is the type of man I think he is, he won't accept this marriage lightly. If he suspects that we have a signed agreement—that ours is a marriage in name only—he could make your life very difficult. For all I know he could even have the marriage declared illegal, or at least spread vicious scandal about us. I'm sure you'd wish to avoid that. Have you looked into that side of the contract?''

"Marriages of convenience are conducted every day over matters of property," she answered defiantly, though her alarm widened her eyes. "There is nothing in the entail which states that the marriage must be consummated. Though of course it is grounds for having the marriage dissolved.''

"Even so, disinherited kin make dangerous enemies.'' Seeing her pallor, he said more gently. "People will accept a love-match without too much question. After all the pains you've taken to secure your home do you want anyone prying into my past, or risk having your cousin take you to court to contest the validity of our marriage?''

"Of course not, but I acted perfectly correctly. A genteel lady does not flaunt her affections in public.'' She was bristling with anger that he should address her in such a manner.

"You acted like a frizzled-up old spinster who had never been kissed in her life.''

Laura gasped in outrage and responded before she considered her words. "I have most certainly been kissed. Not that it is any of your affair.''

His bronze eyes were flecked with golden lights as

he regarded her, and with a derisive laugh he leaned back in the opposite seat. "Perhaps some milksop has stolen a chaste kiss or two, but I doubt you have ever been kissed as a man in love kisses the woman of his heart."

"And just how is that?" Her sarcasm was out before she had considered the challenge in her words.

Resting his elbows on his knees, his hand falling between his legs, Matt leaned forward and his lips parted in a wicked smile. "Since you are not the woman of my heart, that is one lesson I cannot show you. A woman in love looks at her lover with softness and invitation in her eyes. You had better learn to feign some warmth and passion when we are together."

Piqued by his censure, Laura resolved to teach him a lesson. She tossed back the hood of her cloak. As she stared at him with bold invitation, she ran the tip of her tongue around her upper lip. With a soft sigh she pouted provocatively and looked up at him through her lashes in a way which had made several suitors declare their devotion to her. She held his mocking stare until she saw his eyes darken with desire. Laughing with triumph, she said, "Did I feign passion enough for you then, my husband?"

"It may convince a casual observer." He shrugged. "It had all the calculation of a whore and none of the warmth of a loving wife."

"Oh!" Laura flounced back on the seat, her cheeks stinging with shame.

"With practice you could improve upon it and make it more natural. It would help, of course, if your grandfather had failing eyesight."

"Grandfather has the eyes of a hawk."

He spread his hands in regret, his expression darkly challenging. "Then I fear we are undone. Our ruse will be discovered."

"No, not necessarily."

Laura's mind was racing. She had not come this far to fail now. It was true that her experience of men was limited. She spent hours each week among the tenants of the estate, tending their ills and needs, but the sons of the local gentry held no interest for her. Most were selfish, arrogant and with no conversation other than about themselves and their own importance. On her visits to London she had been interested in the conversations of the elderly statesmen who'd dined with her grandfather and father. The younger fops she'd found self-opinionated and boring. Though her suitors had been many, few she had cared enough to grant an occasional kiss. On every occasion the experience had left her unmoved.

"Then you must show me," she said firmly.

"Passion comes from within." There was a curve to his mouth which alerted Laura that he had deliberately goaded her. "It's not something that can be taught, especially if a woman is naturally frigid. But…"

He paused, studying her intently for a long moment, and as her gaze was held by that worldly taunting stare Laura felt her pulse quicken.

"But you are not frigid, are you, Laura?" His eyes glittered wickedly. "You merely have not discovered what passion is. When you do, you will know it is not something you can light a fuse to without expecting the powder-keg to ignite. Ours is a marriage of convenience. What part has passion in our life?"

She dragged her stare from his. She had never

heard a voice so velvety and seductive. His words said one thing, but his eyes—curse his eyes—they spoke of so much that was forbidden and mysterious. She curbed her wayward thoughts and sharpened her tone. "You are contradicting yourself."

The slow smile which parted his full lips infuriated her. "The terms of the marriage contract were laid out by yourself. Now, if you wish me to be your paramour..."

"I need you to act the part in as far as we must convince my grandfather and my uncle and my cousin. That is all."

"And the servants," he provoked, lifting a dark brow. "They are the greatest gossips of all."

"Of course, the servants." Aware of the blush staining her cheeks, she strove to keep a tremor from her voice. "How, then, are we to succeed?"

To her surprise Laura found herself holding her breath as she awaited his reply. Such was his commanding presence in his new clothes that she forgot that until an hour ago he had been a prisoner. She felt only a link strengthening between them, growing, forging a chain of necessity and something more...something intangible as yet, but which was binding them in a conspiratorial web.

"You arranged our marriage to save Fairfield," he said softly. "That, then, is the great passion of your life. When we stand in judgement before your grandfather and family you must think of me as the saviour of Fairfield. When you look at me—see Fairfield. Do it now."

Laura evoked the image. Her lips softened into a knowing smile, her eyes becoming dreamy as she saw the fourteenth-century timber-beamed house with its battlemented tower and filled-in moat.

Matt felt the blood pound in his head at the transformation in the woman. It was obvious now what was the passion which drove her. Her proud beauty brought the inevitable response from his body and his voice became husky as he continued his instruction. "Keep that image of Fairfield when, as a suitably doting husband, I would brush a stray tendril of hair from your cheek like this."

Her cheek was smooth to touch and he saw her lips part as she drew in her breath. His voice gentling, he went on, "Or in a moment of feigned tenderness I would take your hand like so..."

His fingers curled around hers, squeezing them gently, his thumb running over her flesh as he lifted her hand to within an inch of his lips. As he stared deep into her eyes their ardent blue depths beckoned as enticingly as the exotic waters of the Caribbean. He was cloaked in the sensual fresh perfume of her skin and, keeping his gaze upon her eyes, he turned her hand and pressed a kiss against her palm. When his thumb moved over the pulse at her wrist he felt it throb to a more rapid beat. So the haughty Laura Stanton was not immune to him as she would pretend. He had not seen this marriage as leading to dalliance but she was an exceptional beauty, and that and her proud spirit were an irresistible combination.

The carriage hit a rut in the road and Matt reached out to take her shoulders as they were thrown together. Before she could tense in his hold he coerced, "And if I should touch you, it is not me you feel, but the spirit of Fairfield gathering you into its embrace."

His arms were around her now and his own body

was pulsing with the need for her. Thoughts of Fairfield had roused her hidden sensuality; she was pliant and unresisting as he drew her closer. Her skin held a hauntingly sweet fragrance which tantalised his senses. "Fairfield will never harm you as I will never harm you. You must think of us as one."

His voice was satin-smooth, compelling her to have faith in him. Laura thought the frantic beating of her heart would stifle her. She had summoned all her senses to visualise Fairfield and been guided by the subtle persuasion of his voice to transpose the image of her home and himself. Now she was tinglingly aware of the scent of him, manly and virile, the warmth and strength of his arms around her. He was watching her, constraining her, the spell he was weaving so real and powerful that she felt a quivering of longing break like waves through her body.

"Can you play the role demanded of you, Laura?" he pursued in the same sultry voice. Her hand was trapped between them and pressed against the hard muscle of his chest. The steady pounding of his heart set the rhythm of her own heartbeat, commanding, dominating her sense and will-power.

"Yes." Her answer came on a soft sigh of breath.

"Then we must seal our bargain."

He bent his head and his mouth closed over hers, lightly skimming, tasting, then warm and insistent. His tongue tantalised the softness of her lips until they opened, at first hesitantly accepting, then, as his kiss deepened, she responded with the first heady delights of awakened passion. Her hands moved to bind him closer, sliding beneath the long curls of his periwig to lock behind his neck. He curved her back over his arm and she could feel the heat of his body searing

her from breast to thigh. Her senses were dominated
by the taste and pleasure of his kiss. The voices in
the street outside dimmed and she was powerless to
halt her answering response. Her body seemed to float
on a weightless cloud, her thoughts scattered in a spiralling circle of sensation which made her ache to be
crushed against him. A delicious throb began low in
her stomach and, beneath the seemingly endless onslaught of his kiss, spread out in a golden glow to
encompass her entire body, until a soft purr rose from
her throat.

Her eyes were still heavy-lidded when he drew
back, and she stared mistily up into his deep bronze
gaze. Then she was abruptly released and Laura realised with a start that the carriage had halted before
her grandfather's house. Flustered, she sat up. Matt
was leaning back against the upholstery, his expression amused.

"Now that was an improvement. With a little more
practice you should give a credible performance."

To her horror, Laura realised he was mocking her.
He had tricked her into kissing him. Worse, like a
fool, she had responded. Embarrassment heated her
cheeks, but its flames were dwarfed by the fury which
exploded like a torch to gunpowder.

"I will remember your lesson well," she blazed.
"There will be no need to repeat it. I will keep the
image of Fairfield before me to ensure I do not flinch
away from your loathsome touch."

Matt bowed his head, revealing nothing of his
thoughts, and when the door of the carriage was
opened he stepped into the street. Their bargain had
been struck and it would be honoured. A swift glance
up at the large, tall-gabled house confirmed the wealth

of the woman's family. As the husband of Laura Stanton he would take his rightful place among the people of his own station, denied him since birth by his father's lecherous betrayal. Only when society regarded him as an equal would he be in a position to bring Sir James Breten to justice for the deaths of his wife and child. If the law failed him, then by his marriage he would be of a class able to challenge Breten to a duel. He had used the years since Susannah's death to become an accomplished swordsman and marksman. He meant to use his new position as ruthlessly upon the men who had acted against him as they had abused their position in believing themselves immune from retaliation.

And as to the outcome of his liaison with his new wife... Now there was a tempting challenge to heat a man's blood. With a courtly bow, he held out his hand to assist Laura from the carriage. The moment her foot touched the ground she made to snatch her hand away. Laughing softly, Matt held it fast and drew her close, his voice a sibilant warning in her ear.

"Beware whose eyes are upon us, sweet wife." He pressed a kiss upon her fingers, devilry bright in his dark eyes.

Laura forced a dazzling smile. "The stage is set, my darling. Let us not forget our part, or step above our place."

The set-down was meant to remind him of his lowly status. Instead she saw a dangerous gleam flare behind hastily lowered lashes.

Laura assumed an air of confidence she was far from feeling as Matt followed her into her grandfather's bedchamber. The way Matt had virtually abducted her after the ceremony meant that they had not rehearsed the story of their meeting and courtship. Lionel Stanton was a shrewd politician and would not be easily deceived.

Nervousness prickled her spine. How could she have allowed Matt to get the upper hand? Any hesitancy or slip of the tongue could ruin everything.

"Leave the talking to me," she whispered to Matt. "And back me up in everything I say."

"Then choose your words with care. Unlike the gentry, I find that dissimulation and lies do not come easily to me."

His mouth was close to her ear and as he straightened she caught the contemptuous glitter in his eyes. A quiver of fear iced her flesh and she glanced anxiously at the bed. To her relief the shutters were open wide and her grandfather was propped up on his pillows with his eyes closed. There was more colour in his face than yesterday and his eyes looked less sunken.

"We have an agreement," she whispered fiercely.

"Then do not play me for a fool, Laura." He nodded significantly towards the four-poster where her grandfather was stirring.

Gently she touched the old man's hand to wake him.

"Laura, my dear. Where have you been? I've been worried. Have you made your decision?"

Laura drew a sharp breath. "Not only have I made my decision, but I would present to you Matthew Thorne, my husband. We were married this morning."

Disbelief brought a frown to her grandfather's face. Matt stepped forward and bowed. "I know this must appear as very sudden, sir. I should, of course, have approached you in the correct manner. But Laura was worried about your health. She thought the excitement might cause a relapse.''

"And who the devil are you, sir?" Lionel Stanton snapped. "Laura, if this is some trickery..." His breath came in laboured gasps and he fell back on the pillows.

"It's not trickery, I swear it." Laura hastily assured him, her alarm growing at his high colour and weakness. "Don't over-excite yourself, Grandfather. That's what I wished to avoid. We were married this morning. Aren't you pleased?" she said with all the defiance she could muster.

For a frightening moment his face flushed with scarlet colour and she feared he was about to suffer another seizure.

"And where did the ceremony take place?"

Laura could not hold her grandfather's stare, and looked down at her clasped hands. "We were married in the Fleet, for the sake of expedience.''

"Married in the Fleet!" he expounded with blood-chilling censure. "What means this?"

"You wanted me wed before the week was out," Laura declared. Then, remembering that it was supposed to be a love-match, she took Matt's arm and gazed lovingly up at him. "I could never accept any of the suitors you selected because I had already fallen in love with Matthew.''

"And who is this man?" The old man's stare travelled over Matt. Apparently satisfied at what he saw, some of the antagonism mellowed in his voice. "Why must you always be so contrary, Laura? You were supposed to choose from the list...not present me with a stranger.''

Hating the deception she must weave, Laura took another breath and plunged on. ''I feared you would not approve. I love Matthew. I have done so since last summer when we met in Vauxhall Gardens.'' She removed her hand from Matt's arm and sank to her knees at the bedside. ''Please don't be angry with me. It was because of Matthew that I refused to consider other suitors. He's not a wealthy man, but he is an honourable one.''

From her grandfather's bleak expression she could see that he was not convinced. Despising herself for the lies she must now tell him, she forced out in a voice fraught with anguish, ''When I came to London last week we had not seen each other for months. That was on Matthew's insistence. He said I had to give myself a chance...to find a more worthy husband. I could not forget him.''

Her grandfather snorted in disapproval and glared up at Matt. ''You look presentable enough. Not that appearance means anything. You could be up to your eyes in debt. Worse, you could be a fortune-hunter. Is that why you paid court to my granddaughter in secret?''

Laura looked up at Matt and saw the tension in his face and body. She forced a tremulous smile, encouraging him not to take offence at the insult. When he returned her smile there was a grimness in the depths of his eyes which made her shiver. He despised the lies forced upon him and though she resented his judgement of her she respected that quality in his nature. Didn't she despise herself for stooping to such deception, even to save Fairfield? But there had been no other way. To sell herself in a loveless marriage where she would remain trapped to the end of her days would have meant condemning the rest of her life to a lie and to hypocrisy.

Fortunately, her grandfather was too far away to have discerned the censure in Matt's stare. Outwardly her husband's expression was tender as he superbly played the part she had demanded from him.

Placing a hand on her shoulder, he stood behind her, and she felt the hard muscle of his thigh against her back. Its heat sent a tingling threat through her body. When he lifted his gaze to hold Lionel Stanton's accusing glare, his voice was warm and affectionate, showing none of his antagonism.

"Laura is a beautiful and determined woman. From the moment I met her I was lost beneath her spell. I never dared hope for marriage. But when she came to me so distraught at having to wed or lose Fairfield, I admit to my shame that I could not resist her."

He had erased the rough edges from his voice and spoke in a tone more cultured than many country gentlemen. Matt paused, and, taking Laura's elbow, raised her to her feet. One hand rested possessively upon her waist, the other took her hand and lifted it to his lips. The adoration in his gaze bathed her in its warmth and she felt her skin heat, his touch burning like an ember into her flesh. Matt's smile broadened and Laura suspected that the knave was enjoying himself at her expense. Though, to give him his due, he was faultless in the role of ardent lover. Yet still she felt threatened by his presence in a way she could not understand.

With apparent reluctance he dragged his gaze from her face and again addressed her grandfather. "I still cannot believe my good fortune that Laura forsook all other suitors to marry me. I'll not fail her, sir.''

"Not while I'm alive, you won't," Lionel rasped. "I won't allow Fairfield's riches to be plundered, or Laura made unhappy." The brief flare of battle in his blue eyes dimmed as he again laboured for breath.

"Grandfather, you must not upset yourself so." Laura bent over him, worried by the sheen of perspiration on his brow and the painful way he drew each breath. "We will leave you to rest."

"How can I rest?" he groaned. "I no longer know you, Laura. You've never kept secrets from me. Yet you say you've loved this man for a year. Why did you not mention him? Am I such an ogre you could not tell me?"

The pain in his voice that she had not confided in him tore at her heart. She shook her head. "No, Grandfather." Laura paused, struggling to find the words to continue. "When Father and Uncle Robert drowned, you were so desperate that Uncle Cecil would never gain control of Fairfield that I knew I could not fail you. But when you have lost your heart, duty becomes even more onerous. I wanted to do right by you and Fairfield. When Matt sent me away I hid my misery. I thought I could forget him."

Again unable to hold her grandfather's piercing blue stare, she was forced to continue with her deception. She turned to the man she had married. Matt should have been a player on the stage for the tender way he was regarding her. Only when she moved closer to him did she see that the glitter in his eyes was one of contempt, not admiration.

Her voice choked with self-loathing as she dragged up the courage to go on. "From the moment I first saw Matthew I knew he was the man I would marry. Forgive me for being such a disappointment to you, Grandfather.''

''I had not realised that I had caused you so much pain, my dear.'' Lionel Stanton seemed to sink further into the pillow, his voice frail with emotion. He turned again to Matt. ''Do you love my granddaughter, Thorne?''

There was a heart-freezing pause when Matt did not immediately answer. Laura thankfully had her back to her grandfather as her eyes beseeched Matt not to betray her. A flash of insight warned her that he was not a man to resort to lies to save his hide. Fear clutched at her heart as she visualised Fairfield slipping from her grasp and her plans reduced to dust.

''I'm no fortune-hunter, sir,'' Matt announced finally in a firm voice. ''Who could not spend even an hour in the company of this glorious woman and not fall in love with her? I count myself the most fortunate of men.''

Laura closed her eyes in relief. Perhaps she had not been mistaken in choosing Matt. He was showing qualities she had not dared to hope for.

''Hmmph!'' her grandfather grunted. ''You look an honest enough man, I grant you that. Now, I would know something of your family before I give my blessing on this union.''

''Shouldn't you be resting?'' Laura interrupted, fearful that the interview was about to pitch into disaster. She bent over him, fussing with the lace-edged sheet and pulling it higher over his chest.

He waved her away. ''I'll be resting soon enough in my grave. I want to know the man you took such pains to marry without my permission.''

Laura shot Matt a warning look before stepping back from the bed. Her future was again in his hands.

"My grandfather was a preacher in Bath during the Commonwealth. Later my mother moved to London. That was where I grew up."

"And your father? What is his background?" Lionel persisted.

Laura saw Matt's face harden and his jaw set at a defiant angle. "Thorne is my mother's name, sir."

"Then you are a by-blow," her grandfather rasped. "Did you know of this, Laura? Is that why you kept silent?"

Laura saw Matt's hand clench into a fist at the insult to his birth. It had not occurred to her that Matt could be illegitimate, or that he would openly declare it. Her heart plummeted. Why hadn't Matt told her he was born out of wedlock? Her grandfather would never accept him as her husband. She should have checked. She could again see all her plans crumbling, but grudgingly she had to admit that, among so much deceit, Matt had evaded actually lying to support her claims.

"I married Matt, not his parents," she defended. "I have never known him to be other than honest."

For a long moment she was regarded by Matt's obsidian stare. Though his features were rigid with affront, his head remained high and his back proud and straight. Transferring that uncompromising stare upon her grandfather, he continued in a clipped voice, "My mother believed she had been honourably married. When she was expecting their child the man deserted her. Apparently the marriage was bigamous. Though she was to bear the shame and dishonour with proud dignity until the end of her days, the dishonour was not hers. It belonged rightly to the scoundrel who used his position as a gentleman to abuse the innocent.''

"Grandfather, you can't condemn Matt for the sins of his father,'' she said in desperation.

"Quiet, Laura,'' Lionel ordered. "I think you've done and said quite enough this day.'' His stare remained upon Matt. "Obviously you are that child. Who was your father that I may know the degree of bad blood my daughter has brought into our family?''

"I am proud to be my mother's son and no one else's.''

"So you won't name your father?'' Lionel persisted.

Matt did not answer. His stare locked with the older man's until her grandfather was the first to look away. Laura felt her heart hammering in her breast. Her grandfather pursed his lips as his stare returned to regard her husband's rigid countenance. Finally he nodded. "In the circumstances most men would have lied about their parentage.''

Matt lifted a dark brow in disdain by way of reply.

"And you're proud, too.'' Her grandfather chuckled. "Tell the truth and shame the devil. Laura would have admired that in you. Perhaps you are the right man for my granddaughter. Is your mother still alive?''

"No. So she will not cause you any embarrassment, if that's what you feared.'' His voice was hard.

Lionel shook his head. "You mistake me; I never thought that she would,'' he said, and despite his frailty studied Matt intently.

At that moment the bedchamber door burst open and a tall, barrel-figured man advanced across the room. His long scarlet cloak was flung back over his shoulders, revealing a full-skirted coat of gold brocade. The ends of his immense blond wig billowed out like the snakes on the Medusa's head.

"Uncle Lionel, I came as soon as I heard you were ill," he declared.

"You mean you heard I was at death's door," Lionel sneered. "Like the vulture you are, Guy Stanton, you came seeking your inheritance. Well, I'm pleased to say your journey was in vain. The entail has been honoured. Laura gets Fairfield Manor. May I present her husband, Matthew Thorne?"

The large figure whirled. Eyes black and malevolent as a rodent's glared at them from the sharp, pointed face. "Husband! What husband?"

Laura found herself drawn close against Matt, who was playing his role to perfection. Her cousin's angry, mottled expression was murderous as it swept over the apparently loving couple. His fleshy lips pulled back over discoloured teeth and a shower of spittle sprayed from his mouth as he demanded, "When was the marriage?"

"Today," Lionel informed him, showing more animation than he had in days. "You get nothing, Guy. With her marriage, everything goes to Laura."

Guy puffed out his chest and, glaring his hostility at them all, marched back and forth across the room. "This is a ruse to deny me my birthright. You won't get away with it, Stanton. When I visited Faifield last month Laura had refused to consider any of the suitors you suggested."

"That's because the minx had another in mind." Lionel laughed and pulled himself higher in the bed, showing a surprising return of vigour for a man at death's door. "It's a love-match."

"Love-match be damned!" Guy rounded on Laura, his eyes bright with venom. "There's trickery afoot. Fairfield is mine."

"I take exception to your conduct, sir." Matt stepped in front of Laura to shield her from Guy's rage. "I will not allow my wife to be spoken to in such a manner. Nor will I permit such a scene to take place in her grandfather's sickroom. You will leave at once, or I will be forced to remove you myself."

He stepped forward to give weight to his threat. There was no feigning the admiration in Laura's eyes as she regarded the man she had married. Guy was a head taller than Matt and at least four stone heavier. All his life her cousin had used his size to intimidate and bully. Now that bluster withered beneath Matt's searing glare and Guy took several hurried steps back. Like most bullies when challenged, he revealed his cowardly heart.

"There's foul play here." Guy stabbed his arm towards Matt to emphasise each word. "This is no love-match. The matter won't rest here. Fairfield is mine and no conniving bitch is going to take it from me."

Matt crossed the floor and, grabbing Guy's cravat, pushed him up against the wall. The moment the arrogant bully had stormed into the room he had felt sympathy for Laura's plight. Her cousin was all he despised in the gentry. Debauchery and brutality were stamped on his pompous features.

"I don't take kindly to threats, Stanton," Matt warned. "And I'm not impressed by bullies. If I were you I'd keep your nose out of my wife's affairs and well away from Fairfield. Now get out."

He released him and stepped back. Guy hastily adjusted his crumpled cravat as he backed to the door. On the far side of the opening he blustered, "I won't forget this. You're a marked man, Thorne. Where and when did this marriage take place?"

"That's none of your business," Lionel said sharply. "They are legally wed and have my blessing."

Laura was amazed at her grandfather's vigour. He seemed to be thriving on this confrontation.

Guy jabbed a finger towards Laura, his expression murderous. "I won't be cheated out of what is rightfully mine. The matter does not end here."

Turning on his heel, he stormed from the landing, his cloak billowing out like the wings of an avenging demon behind him as he disappeared from view.

Matt checked his anger. It would be a pleasure to teach Guy Stanton that he could not get his own way by bullying and disregard of others. When he returned to Laura's side his anger mellowed towards her. It was obvious why she was so desperate to stop her home falling into the clutches of her brutish cousin. A man like Guy Stanton would bleed it dry and have no care for the welfare of his workers and tenants. In Laura he had from the first sensed a passion which was not only for the property, but for the people who lived and worked there. He was determined that she would not lose it.

When he placed a proprietial hand on Laura's waist he felt her trembling and hastened to reassure her. "If Guy Stanton is wise he will not cross your threshold again, or seek to meddle in our affairs."

The incident had shaken Laura and the strain of the morning was beginning to tell on her taut nerves. Unconsciously she leaned into Matt's strong embrace, comforted by his support. At the hoarse laughter coming from the bed, she looked at her grandfather. He had struggled to sit up and, regarding Matt with admiration, held out his hand towards him.

"Welcome to the family, Thorne."

Laura was amazed at the transformation in the old man. The gauntness was beginning to disappear from his cheeks and his eyes gleamed with pleasure at the contest of wills he had witnessed. He gave a wheezing laugh.

"I wonder if Laura knew what she'd taken on when she wedded you?" He paused to get his breath, his shoulders still shaking with laughter.

"Thorne, you're the man Fairfield needs. Any good at managing an estate?"

"I can learn, sir. But by profession I am a sea-captain."

Lionel nodded. "Happen you can learn. And you'll know how to handle men." He was grinning as he turned to Laura. "I should have known I could not force you into a marriage you did not want. I've never judged a man by his wealth or his birth, but by his strength of character. Now out of here, the pair of you. All this excitement has tired me. Knowing Fairfield has escaped Guy's avaricious clutches has proved a more potent physic than all the blood-letting and purging that fool physician subjected me to. You must both dine with me this evening in my room."

"Are you sure you are strong enough, Grandfather?" Laura studied him with concern.

"To know that Fairfield is safe and your future secure is a great burden from my mind. I want to know more of this man you married."

Laura foresaw an evening ahead filled with more deception. She hated deceiving her grandfather, but how could she tell him the truth about her marriage?

She had not eaten all day and Matt's behaviour in the carriage had shown her that he could not be easily manipulated. She glanced at him now, and again felt a quiver of danger. Things so far had not gone as she had planned. At any moment she felt a fresh disaster could strike.

Chapter Four

The sickroom was hot and stuffy and her cousin's threats spiralled like a whirlpool in Laura's mind. They had not been spoken idly. Guy was vindictive and a bully. He made a dangerous enemy.

She heard Matt address her grandfather, but his words appeared to come for a great distance. There seemed to be no air in the bedchamber and the panelled walls looked to be closing in upon her. Lifting her hand to her temple, she drew a long breath, but still the plasterwork on the ceiling dipped crazily towards the floor. As her body swayed she was caught in strong arms, and her hazy gaze met the mocking stare of bronze eyes.

"Come, my dear, today's excitement has proved too much for you." He scooped her up into his arms. "I fear you are about to swoon."

There was a delighted chuckle from the bed. "That's it, Thorne. Sweep your wife off her feet. Time the bride and groom had an hour or so alone."

"Put me down. I never swoon," Laura whispered fiercely. With her grandfather watching them with evident pleasure it was impossible to struggle against Matt's hold.

Without paying heed to her, he carried her out of the room and along the corridor. ''Which room is ours, dear wife?''

''Ours? No room is ours,'' she seethed, her fury mounting with each step.

A dark brow lifted. ''Remember your role. Remember the servants. It would not do for cousin Guy to know that the loving bride and groom spent their first married night apart.'' Matt slowed his stride and regarded her. When she stared up at his dark visage, the expression in his bronze eyes was bleak. ''Don't say you never thought about that side of a marriage. This coil is of your making, Laura. Now it seems you have to make the best of it. So which room is ours?''

Laura was appalled at the implication of his words. ''Of course I have given it thought. My rooms are on the next landing. There is a day-bed which can be moved into the ante chamber for you to sleep upon.''

''Damned hare-brained virgin... This marriage will be the scandal of London... Just what have I let myself in for?'' Matt muttered beneath his breath as he strode purposefully towards the stairs.

She was about to protest when Joseph, her grandfather's valet, appeared, carrying an ewer of steaming water. ''May I congratulate you on your marriage, Mistress Laura?'' He smiled at Matt. ''And you also, Mr Thorne. If you have no valet to attend you, I will be honoured to serve you.''

Matt inclined his head in acceptance and strode on. Outside Laura's chamber her maid Sarah was waiting. The middle-aged servant curtsied, her round face breaking into a smile. ''Such a romantic wedding,

Mistress Laura. And you not letting on at all. Will you be wanting anything?'' Her smile became knowing. ''I expect you and your husband wish to be alone.''

Laura tensed in Matt's arms. The entire household knew of the wedding. From this moment every servant's eyes would be upon them. When Matt carried her into her rooms Sarah closed the door behind them.

''You may put me down now,'' Laura said irritably.

One hand slid from beneath her knees, but the other remained firm about her waist, holding her close against him.

She drew back, her eyes flashing. ''Let me go!''

Laura was pulled against Matt's hard body. His expression darkened, but no emotion showed on his rigid face. He did not move, but all Laura's senses warned her that this was when Matt was at his most dangerous.

''What are you planning to do...scream?'' he goaded.

The taunting in his voice and his slow smile told her that he expected her to destroy the fabrication that their marriage was a love-match. Her head came up and her tone was as mocking as his. ''Why should I scream? We agreed upon a marriage in name only. I do not take you for a man who would break his word.''

A muscle pumped along his jaw as he looked pointedly at the day-bed positioned near the fire.

''That must be moved,'' Laura reminded him.

''And won't every servant comment upon the strangeness of its removal?'' Matt glowered at her. ''We are newly wedded. Think of Fairfield.''

"I wouldn't be in this humiliating situation if I weren't thinking of Fairfield," Laura snapped, her embarrassment acute at all he was implying. She had not anticipated this complication. Her grandfather had been so close to death that she had expected to spend every night at his bedside until he died. Yet how could she regret that her predicament was brought about by her grandfather's recovery? For that, at least, she was delighted.

Matt watched the passage of emotions cross Laura's expressive face. The hours since accepting her proposal had been a grim ordeal for him. The memory of her response to his kiss had teased his emotions. The wench was beguiling, and too sensual for his peace of mind. The sunlight filtered through the diamond lattice panes of the window, its rainbow hues turning the rose blush on her creamy complexion to an opal lustre. It touched the curls of her auburn hair, turning it to a flame-coloured silk. Matt was cloaked in the heady scent of her perfume as his gaze deepened in fascinated intensity. Her eyes, so reminiscent of the blue of a Mediterranean sky, were large and slightly slanted, holding all the promise and mystery of a pagan priestess.

Beautiful and strong-willed, the maid was a temptation and a trial. The deceitful side of her nature left him cold, but beneath the hard shell of independence she showed to the world he sensed a vulnerable core.

"It won't be easy for either of us," Matt warned. "But you will be perfectly safe with me and your modesty preserved behind the hangings of your bed. Any unconsummated marriage is grounds for annulment. What if your cousin should learn that we sleep apart—?"

"I understand your meaning," Laura interrupted with a shudder. "But can I trust you?"

"You'll have to trust me as much as I trust myself," he answered with a grin. "But I don't force myself on unwilling women."

Reluctantly accepting his word, she turned her back on him and spoke over her shoulder. "I must change before we dine with my grandfather. It will invite gossip if I summon Sarah; will you assist me with my laces?"

"It will be a pleasure, dear wife," he taunted.

A frigid back remained presented to him as she stared straight ahead.

He closed his mind to the seductive perfume of her skin as he unlaced the back of her gown. It was impossible to avoid contact with the warm, inviting flesh. Whenever his fingers brushed it, he cursed his body's response and the necessity which had driven him to this bizarre marriage.

Crossing her arms over her breasts to hold the loosened gown in place, Laura walked into the dressing-room adjoining her bedchamber. She did not emerge until it was time to join her grandfather for the meal. She had changed into a sapphire silk gown with a low, scooped neckline. On returning to the bedchamber she was surprised to see Matt reclining on the bed, reading the book of John Donne's poetry which had been by the bedside. Meeting the amused sparkle in his eyes, she felt a blush rise to her cheeks as she remembered the erotic love poems.

"At least you found something to keep yourself occupied," she said tartly as she again presented her back to him for her laces to be fastened.

The bed creaked as he swung his legs to the floor

and came to stand behind her. He did not speak, but the warmth of his breath touched her neck in a way that sent a shiver through her body. The deftness with which he dealt with her laces could only have come from experience, and her unease at his nearness increased.

To cover her confusion, she said, "Tomorrow a tailor will call to fit you with several outfits suitable for your position. If you give Jedediah instructions he will obtain anything else you need for your personal use."

When she made to move away from him a hand on her shoulder restrained her. "All my possessions were taken when I was arrested," he said darkly. "I don't want your charity, Laura."

"You will have everything you need as befits your role," she responded softly, aware that his pride rebelled at being beholden to her to such a high degree. "If it is easier for you to accept, then some of the items you may consider as purchased by means of a loan. You may pay me back when you have funds. What is purchased to suit your role as a gentleman is done for my benefit, and I should meet those bills. Do you agree?"

He considered for a moment before answering. "Very well. But fine clothes do not necessarily a gentleman make."

"Is that a warning?" She eyed him stonily. The heat of his hand burned her skin and when he ran a finger along her cheek she flinched back from his touch.

His eyes were unreadable as he considered her gravely. "When we join your grandfather, don't you think he's going to expect you to look like a woman who's just been made love to?''

Laura stiffened. "That's not part of our bargain."

"No. But then you have so much more to lose than I."

"We have just spent an hour alone together; everyone will assume we have—'' She broke off, unable to continue.

"Not if you continue with this frosty maiden's air about you."

"I don't believe you. How could anyone tell that we have not…?"

"I told you before, it's in the way a woman looks at her lover. There is a special softness in her eyes. Your grandfather is no fool."

Matt spoke softly, without mockery. His lean face betrayed nothing of his thoughts. He was simply waiting for her to respond and yet she was stingingly aware of the danger even his immobility presented. His was the stillness of a predator assured of his ascendancy over his prey.

Without her being aware that he had moved, she found herself trapped against the door-frame. His hands rested on the wood each side of her shoulders, caging her and preventing her flight. She glared into eyes which had darkened with an emotion outside of her experience.

"This is just a ruse to you, Laura. A means to an end," his velvet voice mocked. "The stakes are high. Think of Fairfield. Remember the parts you dictated we play."

He caught her hands, drawing her to him. Her eyes widened and her heart thudded wildly, but she refused to show her alarm. The last rays of the sunset played over his skin and danced in the amused depths of his eyes.

"You must at least look as though you have been kissed, wife."

His face was inches from her, filling her vision. The quiet authority in his voice halted her refusal and his nearness had a suffocating effect upon her senses, causing her heart to flutter and her breathing to suspend in anticipation. He bent his head and gently kissed the corner of her mouth. Her lips parted in protest, but only a soft gasp escaped them. His mouth moved to her brow, his kisses tender upon her lids, then her cheeks, before they skimmed across her throat. Their touch evoked sensations more heady than wine. Her heart was pounding with a suffocating beat. Appalled at the way her body was responding, she struggled against his embrace and pushed against his chest in an effort to break free, but his hold tightened, holding her captive as his mouth returned to hers, his tongue gently probing, coercing, until against her will her lips were pliant, parting beneath the dominance of his kiss. Deep within her a flame sparked into life, spreading its heat like the sun's rays through her veins.

As his lips moved over hers his hand slid down her spine to her waist, pressing her against him. Even as her body responded to his mastery, her mind rebelled. As she continued to struggle her soft curves were crushed against the unyielding iron of his body. Her breasts grazed against the silver-embossed baldric and were more tender and vibrant with sensation than she'd believed possible. Her spine burned beneath the span of his hand, and beneath the persistent onslaught of his mouth her body glowed with sensations she had never before experienced. The subtle persuasion of his lips stilled her rebellion. Her senses were absorbed by the taste and mastery of him; reality was abandoned as her mind became dominated by the power of the feelings roused by his kiss.

At a rap of the bedchamber door Laura found herself released, though Matt kept a hand tenderly upon the bare flesh of her shoulder.

"Come in." She was startled that her voice sounded so low and breathless. She held a hand to her swollen, throbbing lips where Matt had kissed her so passionately.

Sarah put her head around the door, her expression alight with pleasure as she saw the flush on her mistress's face.

"Yes, Sarah," Laura said, fussing with her ringlets where several pins had come loose from the ardour of Matt's embrace.

Sarah's smile broadened. "Cook asks if you're ready to dine now."

"Yes, please serve us in my grandfather's room."

Matt's smile was devilish as he held out his arm for Laura to take, and as he escorted her to Lionel Stanton's bedchamber he whispered wickedly, "We've passed the maid's inspection. Now to more discerning eyes."

Ignoring his goading, Laura smiled sweetly as Barker appeared to open the door of her grandfather's chamber. To her delight, Laura found her grandfather seated in a chair by the roaring fire where the table had been laid for their meal.

"It's wonderful to see you looking so much stronger," Laura said, stooping to place a kiss on his leathery cheek.

He grinned. "It's this news of your marriage. It's given me new life." He took her hand and squeezed it. "Just by looking at you I can see that Matthew is the right man for you. Love has put stars in your eyes and a bloom in your cheeks. Aye, it won't be long before I can hold my first great-grandchild. Only then will I rest content. Your future will be secure and Fairfield will continue to prosper."

Laura laughed nervously. "It's too early to consider children."

"Not with two young people so in love as yourselves. There is much to plan for the future. That fool physician is still urging me to rest, but I refused to let him bleed me again. A week ago I never thought I'd see Fairfield again. Now I can't wait to show this husband of yours over the estate. The sooner I can teach him all I know about management the better, for the peace of mind of us all."

Stepping behind Lionel's chair, Laura gripped her hands together. She was elated that he was stronger and showed every sign of recovering from his seizure. But that joy was tinged with alarm. There would be no easy escape from this marriage. She was trapped. With her grandfather alive she could not set it aside in a few months as she had planned.

Lionel Stanton turned to frown up at her. "My dear, you are not wearing your emeralds. I thought on such an occasion they would be fitting. You know your grandmother wore them at our wedding."

Laura paled. "They're…they're with the jeweller. The clasp was loose. I feared I would lose them."

Her grandfather's sharp gaze was unnerving, and when his frown deepened Laura's heart thudded against her breastbone.

"I had the clasp repaired before I gave the necklace to you on your sixteenth birthday last year."

Her quick wits deserted her. So many lies. Would they never end?

Her grandfather was looking at her sternly. "Laura, is aught amiss?"

"No," she said weakly. "It's been a long day." She knelt and threw her arms around his neck. "A momentous day. I never thought to see you out of your sick-bed. I was so terrified of losing you."

He chuckled, his humour restored. Putting her at arm's length, he stared into her tear-bright eyes. "I intend to be around for a good while yet. I wanted to live to see you safely wed." He smiled as he looked from the bride to the groom and gave a nod of approval. "A love-match," he added with a chuckle. "You've chosen a fine man, Laura. Though I doubt you realise that just yet."

"Of course I do," Laura answered, uneasy at the way he was looking at her. "Why else would I have wed Matthew?"

"Aye, why indeed?" He chuckled again. "Give me a great-grandchild, Laura. Then I can die happy, knowing your future and Fairfield are secure."

Laura rose shakily to her feet. Her stricken gaze fell upon Matt. There was tension in his proud figure. He was looking at her steadily, but since he stood within the shadows cast by the candlelight she could not discern the expression in his eyes. She was certain it would not be one of pleasure. They were both trapped in a marriage neither wanted.

The meal strained Laura's nerves to their limits. Her grandfather was remorseless in his questioning of Matt. With each new barrage of questions Laura's appetite waned, and she picked at her food. By declaring his illegitimacy Matt had proved that he would not stoop to lies, and her stomach knotted. She dreaded what new revelation might be disclosed.

"So you were married before," Lionel persisted. "How did your wife die?"

Matt tensed. Beneath his tanned complexion his skin paled. Alerted to danger, Laura picked up her wine goblet and drained it. It was the third she had drunk during the meal, when usually she was abstemious. She laughed brittly to dispel the tension.

"Grandfather, you're putting Matt through an inquisition with all your questions. It's not much of a welcome for him to our family."

"Just want to know him better." Lionel eyed her sternly, then looked across at Matt who was twirling the stem of his goblet, his lashes lowered over his eyes. "Not taking offence, are you, Thorne? Forgive an old man's curiosity, but in the circumstances..."

Matt looked up. A vein pulsated at the side of his temple beneath the dark curls of his periwig. Fortunately, from where her grandfather was sitting he could not see it. Outwardly Matt appeared composed, but Laura, sensitive to the atmosphere in the room, could feel the tension underlying that carefully relaxed pose.

"How can I take offence when you are concerned for Laura's future?" Matt replied suavely. "My wife and daughter died six years ago in an accident while I was away at sea."

Laura's own curiosity was aroused at this insight into Matt's life, but she curbed it. It was best not to pry too deeply, but her instincts told her that Matt had been in love with his first wife.

His lips stretched into a smile and he reached across, covering her hands with his. "I never thought I would marry again."

To all appearances the loving bridegroom, he raised her hand to his lips, his eyes gleaming as he felt her fingers tremble from his touch. As usual he had answered without avoiding the question, but had managed to twist his words to make it sound as if theirs had indeed been a love-match.

"That was before I met Laura," he went on smoothly. "From our first meeting it was obvious that we could offer each other so much. Is that not so, my dear?"

His touch was brief, conveying to the servants waiting on them and to her grandfather that they were a devoted couple. None of them suspected that the long glances and emotional vibrations between them were evidence of anything other than tenderness. It apparently satisfied her grandfather.

"So, Thorne, now you are wed to Laura, what income have you to support her?" Lionel leaned forward, his expression intent.

"I'm a merchant sea-captain. I earned enough in the last five years to purchase a ship and invest in cargo."

Laura saw the muscles tighten along Matt's jaw. Again he had refused to lie, although he was avoiding the whole truth.

"Fairfield needs a man at its helm," Lionel said sharply, "not someone who spends half his life at sea."

"My ship is in the Mediterranean at the moment, and I am here." Matt lifted a dark brow, and when his gaze held Laura's it was dark with suppressed anger which only she could see. He kept his voice smooth and tender as he went on, ''Is that not how it should be between a newly married bride and groom? I will not desert Laura while she has need of me. It is obvious that her cousin means to cause trouble. My presence will stop him.''

Lionel nodded, apparently satisfied. ''Then it is time we discussed the marriage settlement. Laura's dowry is large. That is yours to do with as you will. Fairfield is a wealthy estate. Now she is married, Laura inherits it on my death. However, since I hope you will remain at her side managing it even while I am alive, you will receive the same income from the estate as my granddaughter—five thousand pounds a year. By the entail the estate will pass to your eldest son, or daughter if there is no son. If Laura dies before you, you cannot inherit outright, but would be the guardian of your children's property with provision for you to live there until your death. If there are no children then I fear the estate will pass to my brother's family. I trust the terms are satisfactory to you, Thorne?''

''I did not marry Laura for her money,'' Matt said tersely. ''I will not be supported by my wife. I am a sea-captain. That is how I earn my living.''

Lionel flushed. ''The hell it is. There is Fairfield to think of.''

''Grandfather, you must not overset yourself,'' Laura hastily intervened. ''Matt has the interests of Fairfield at heart, as I have. Surely it is a measure of his integrity and honesty that he prefers to take nothing from the estate unless he has worked for it?''

Beneath the table she rapped Matt's ankle with her foot. The colour in her grandfather's face looked dangerously high and his breathing was becoming laboured.

"Sir, you mistook my words," Matt said smoothly. "Because I want none of Laura's money, it does not mean I intend failing in my duties while I am her husband."

Lionel regarded him gravely. Matt sat straight-backed and rigid in his chair, his face pale beneath his tan. Pride snapped in his bronze eyes as he held the older man's piercing glare.

"Very well, I will speak to my lawyer. Though I hope that you will reconsider. I will give him instructions accordingly, so that when you change your mind…"

He let the matter rest there, and though Matt remained tense he did not argue. The meal finished, Laura wanted to escape further questioning, but the prospect of returning to her bedchamber knowing she must share it with Matt filled her with apprehension. All evening she had tried not to dwell upon the consequences of spending the night in the same room as him. Now they swamped her. How could she escape his attentions without rousing the suspicions of the household? But escape them she would. Traitorously, the memory of his kiss was branded into her mind. With a sinking sensation she recalled how easily she had succumbed to the mastery of his embrace.

She glanced across at her husband, who was again relaxed and talking to Lionel of his voyages. At least that was safe ground. Aware of her stare, Matt turned to smile at her. To her grandfather the action would appear to be one of intimacy, but Laura felt every nerve-end prickle with alarm. Those full lips were tilted in mockery, accurately guessing her thoughts upon being forced to retire in his company.

"You are looking tired, Grandfather," she said. "I think you should rest now."

He laughed. "I can take a hint that you wish to be alone with your husband."

Laura started, and knocked over her wine glass. That was the last thing she wanted. To cover her confusion she dabbed at the spilt wine with her napkin and answered softly, "I was thinking of your health."

"If you say so." Her grandfather laughed again, and to her astonishment winked at Matt. "This is your wedding night. Time enough for us to be better acquainted when we return to Fairfield."

Lionel lifted the handbell to summon his valet and Matt held out his arm for Laura to take as they left the chamber.

Unable to face returning to her rooms, she suggested, "Would you like to see the rest of the house?"

He lifted a dark brow, guessing her true reason for her delaying tactics, and leaned closer as they passed a maid carrying a warming-pan. "I am yours to command, my dear."

"I'd feel easier if I could believe that," she returned.

His step slowed and he turned to regard her. "At last some honesty."

She resented his mockery, and as they entered the main parlour which covered the front of the first floor of the house she rounded on him. "Despite what you think of me, I do not enjoy lying to my grandfather. You saw Guy. Surely you could see the wastrel and bully he is?"

She paced the panelled room. For once the ruby hangings over the window and the high-banked fire brought her no feeling of peace or warmth. Several full-size portraits hung on the walls, and she stopped before the one of her father. He was in his scarlet colonel's uniform and mounted on a black charger. The portrait was a good likeness, and he looked so strong and handsome, so invincible, that her heart ached with grief at her loss. She moved slowly to the next portrait and stared into the face of the auburn-haired figure of her mother. It was the same face which stared back at her from her looking-glass each morning.

"That must be your mother," Matt said. "She is very beautiful."

"I never knew her," Laura answered. "She died when I was born. This is my father." She pointed to the portrait. "And over there are his two brothers, Samuel and Robert. They were all remarkable men and all died tragically young."

Matt was studying the portrait of her father and was smiling as he turned to face her. "You have your mother's looks but it's from him you must have inherited your wilful streak. He has the face of a man who would carve his own destiny."

Matt walked away from the portraits to examine paintings of hunting scenes before he halted before a spinet. "Do you play, Laura?"

"Of course."

"Would you play for me?" he asked, pouring himself a brandy from the silver-chased flagon placed in readiness on a walnut table. The gold and enamel Louis XIV French clock on the marble mantelpiece struck the hour of nine. It was still early. Matt sat on a ruby velvet-upholstered couch and raised his goblet in salute to her. Not once during the evening had she been able to fault his manner or speech. This self-assured, elegantly attired man was a far cry from the ragged, rough-speaking prisoner who had caught her attention yesterday. She should be relieved that he fitted his role so well. Instead he looked too much at his ease for her comfort. She no longer felt in control of the situation and that alarmed her.

She was about to refuse his request when she saw the amused challenge in his stare. An intimate moment between the bride and groom in the parlour would be expected by the servants.

She spread her sapphire skirts as she sat on the stool and began to play. The music flowing from her fingers eased some of the tension in her body. Matt was sitting opposite her, sipping his brandy, his expression relaxed but unreadable. To delay the moment when they must retire she played several pieces, and finally her fingers came to a halt.

"Well-played, my dear. But no love-songs? Surely a groom would expect to hear tender words upon his wife's sweet lips on such a night as this?"

"I do not sing. My singing teacher despaired of me. He said I had a voice like grinding millstones."

"That I do not believe," he said, standing up and coming to her side.

Laura rose quickly to avoid close contact with him. "Believe what you will." Her melodic voice was spiced with honey as she reminded him of words he had flung at her in the prison. "I'll not serenade you with love-songs."

He grinned and silently offered her his arm to escort her to their bedchamber. Instantly Laura froze, her throat working as she struggled to overcome her fear.

"We have a role to play, wife," he reminded her softly. His gaze was not mocking, but there was speculation within its dark depths that filled her with dread as to what thoughts were going through his mind.

She swallowed against the dryness in her throat and placed her hand lightly upon the hard muscle of his forearm. His hand covered hers and his breath ruffled the curls by her ears as he whispered, "I gave you my word, Laura. Don't you trust me?"

She wanted to believe him, but she knew the devastating effect that his masculinity could have upon her. The thought of being alone with him in the intimacy of her bedchamber...and all that that intimacy implied...left her with a feeling of wading in water out of her depth.

When they entered the bedchamber it was worse than she had imagined. The coverlet was laid back and the bed strewn with dried rose-petals. Sarah and the other housemaids must have scoured the flower-stalls for what few blooms were available. They had garlanded them together with sweet-smelling herbs and greenery to turn the bed into a bridal bower.

The gesture was so well-meant, but so sadly misplaced that it destroyed the last of Laura's composure. "What have I done? What have I done?" she groaned, and hugged her arms tight about her body.

Matt looked at her in astonishment. He had hardened himself to her beauty, believing her heartless and faithless to her family in her greed to possess Fairfield. Guy Stanton's virulent outburst had shattered one of those illusions. And seeing her shoulders shaking with silent sobs told him that she was not entirely uncaring of others' feelings.

"Go to bed, Laura."

She whirled to face him, her eyes wide with fear. "Don't come near me."

He snatched up two pillows from the bed and tossed them on to the day-bed. "For God's sake, woman, what do you take me for? I've no intention of forcing my attentions on you."

"You haven't?" she said in a shaky whisper.

"Not unless you're offering yourself," he mocked. "I don't force myself upon quaking virgins. Even if all the world believes we're married."

She looked at the day-bed, which was too short for him to be able to rest comfortably, and felt another stab of guilt. "The day-bed is rather small."

"My dear—" his voice was heavy with sarcasm "—for the last three months I've been half frozen, my bed mildewed straw on the prison floor." His dark brows were drawn together in an accusing frown, his formidable expression reminding her that there were many sides of his character which she knew nothing about. Dangerous sides which she would be wise not to provoke. There was a predatory calmness which made him remote and unapproachable. He gave her an impatient and exasperated glare. "Do you think this is any easier for me than it is for you?"

"Oh!"

"Is that all you can say?" His lips twisted into a sardonic line. "Or had you simply not thought of my feelings at all? All your life you've thought of no one but yourself—you're gentry, aren't you?"

Turning his back on her, he picked up Donne's book of poems from the bedside table. With a derisive laugh he tossed it on to the bed, and took up a volume of Milton's *Paradise Lost*. Without looking at Laura, he stretched out on the day-bed and began to read.

From the way he held his body rigid, revealing the powerful undercurrent of tension in him, she could feel his hatred and contempt. How dared he condemn her so? What did he know of her life?

The angry tirade which almost burst from her was stifled. To give in to any emotion now could make that tension volatile, and she dared not risk goading Matt too far. She was too much at his mercy, and the rogue knew it.

Chapter Five

Furious at Matt's attitude, Laura strode into the adjoining dressing-room and kicked off her shoes. With shaking hands she pulled the pins from her hair and shook it loose. For fifteen minutes she twisted and turned to untie the laces at the back of her gown. It proved impossible. She refused to ask for Matt's help. Neither could she summon Sarah and thereby betray that the bride and groom had quarrelled on their wedding night. Wriggling out of her petticoats, she began cursing in a low voice as she again struggled with her laces. With each failure her frustration mounted. Finally defeated, and acknowledging that she must sleep in her gown and the restricting corset beneath, she flounced down on to a stool, unaware that by her terse, angry movements she was banging her toilette pots on the table.

As she wrenched a brush through her unruly auburn curls the enormity of what she had committed herself to by this marriage hit her. Throwing down the silver-backed hairbrush with a clatter, she propped her elbows on the toilette table and sank her head into her hands.

"God, you must be ripe for Bedlam, Laura Stanton," she groaned in frustration. "It's your own ass-witted fault you're in this mess."

"I couldn't agree more." Matt's amused tone came from behind her.

Laura swivelled around to glare at him and sucked in her breath when she saw him leaning against the doorpost. He had removed his long periwig and stood in his shirt and close-fitting breeches which encased his thighs like a second skin. With his bronzed skin darkened by the candlelight and his own long, dark hair waving to his shoulders, he looked devastatingly handsome and as untamed as a buccaneer. The smile on his lips and the dancing light in his eyes made her feel as if she was being drawn towards some inevitable fate over which she had no control.

It was an alarming feeling. To fight it, she forced herself to hold his taunting stare, refusing to let him see her unease. If he suspected any sign of weakness on her part, she knew she would lose control over the situation between them.

As she studied him in silence he thrust his shoulder from the door-frame and moved two paces into the dressing-room. His expression remained amused as his gaze took in her dishevelled hair and the sapphire gown clinging to the outline of her legs. The way he was looking at her stifled the breath in Laura's lungs. There was a subtle change in his expression, softening the harsh planes of his cheeks, but she could not read his thoughts. What she felt was a force as strong as a lodestone, drawing her to him. He was willing her to come to him. She was astonished at how much will-power she needed to exert not to give in to that potent lure. Her whole body tensed as she refused to submit to it.

"It's obvious you cannot sleep in your gown." His voice was smooth and deep, but she sensed he was combatting some inner struggle of his own. "Just think of the speculation it will cause for your maid to find you thus garbed in the morning."

"You're enjoying my humiliation, aren't you?" she retorted, inwardly wincing as she heard the shakiness in her voice.

"If you feel humiliation, it is by your own doing," he said softly. "If you want the world to believe that we are lovers, we must learn to cope with that role within the terms of our agreement."

"I thought it would be so easy." Her gaze dropped from his. "It's a nightmare. I can't blame you for hating me for dragging you into all this. We're trapped in an impossible situation."

"How can I hate you? Were it not for you I'd still be in prison." He moved closer. The armour which plated his emotions briefly slipped and she saw beneath that guard the pain of a loss he would never put into words.

She stood up, unwilling to remain at the disadvantage of being seated. They stood very close, aware of each other and of the enormity of the events which now bound them together. The intensity of his gaze darkened as he studied her auburn hair, hanging in disarray about her shoulders and falling in shiny curls to her waist. She saw him look briefly at the full curves of her breasts and the outline of her hips and thighs beneath the clinging silk of her gown. His throat worked as he swallowed.

"Turn round, Laura. I will deal with your laces."

Neither spoke as he loosened the laces of her gown and those of her stiffened corset. "I'll remain here while you undress in the bedchamber. Call me when you're in bed." His voice was like crushed gravel, and as she moved past him he scooped up her neatly folded petticoats and held them out to her. At her puzzled expression he added, "Scatter these around the room as though I had disrobed you, together with your gown and hose."

At seeing the pink flush rise up her neck to her cheeks he grinned wickedly, unable to resist taunting, "Yes, my dear Laura. If we were indeed lovers, and I were truly your loving husband, I would have peeled each garment very slowly from your lovely body and clothed you with my kisses." His hand touched the soft skin of her shoulder and traced a line to the swell of her breast before he snatched it back with a caustic laugh. "Go quickly to your virginal bed, dear wife. And tempt me no more."

With an indignant gasp Laura ran from the dressing-room. At each item of clothing she scattered on the floor she looked over her shoulder, her heart hammering wildly lest she find that Matt had broken his word and pursued her. Throwing aside her corset, she was about to climb beneath the covers when his voice carried to her.

"Don't forget to also remove your shift."

"I most certainly will not," Laura answered coldly.

"Ah, well, I suppose a well brought up, prudish young gentlewoman would keep herself covered like a nun. Let's hope that is how your maid will expect to find you."

Laura hesitated. Was he deliberately provoking her, or would Sarah expect to find her lying naked in her bed? How was she supposed to know? She already felt far too vulnerable with Matt in the same room without discarding what little protection her shift awarded her. She leapt into bed and pulled the covers to her chin.

"You may come in now," she called, wishing she did not sound so nervous.

Not daring to close her eyes, she watched Matt stroll back into the room and adjust the pillows and cover on the day-bed. As he pulled his shirt from his waistband he turned to her with a chuckle. "If you don't blow out that candle by the bedside, you may see more of your husband than you bargained for."

He pulled his shirt over his head and heard her outraged gasp as she blew out the candle and the room darkened.

Laura lay immobile as marble, the pounding of her heartbeat thudding in her ears at the sound of Matt's movements as he settled on to the day-bed. The fire had been banked high and its flames cast long shadows on the walls and ceiling. Through a narrow gap in the bed-hangings, left open to allow some of the fire's heat to warm the bed, Laura cautiously peeped at the day-bed. Matt's naked back was turned to her. The shadowed firelight revealed the dark stripes on his skin from his whipping. Unaccountably she felt the need to reach out and touch him, to ask if his wounds needed tending. Just in time she stopped herself. The only way to maintain peace of mind between them was to keep her distance.

She turned away, and in the next hour must have turned and tossed in her bed a hundred times. Every sinew of her was aware of Matt's masculine presence. Each time she closed her eyes his image was before them, and with it the taste and memory of his kiss. And what had he meant by saying that if he had truly been her loving husband he would have slowly stripped every garment from her body and clothed her in kisses? The thought brought a blush to her entire body and with a groan she rolled on to her stomach.

"Can't you sleep, Laura?" His voice was husky with amusement.

"Damn you, no!"

"Is it me you fear? You have no need. But unless you stop fidgeting my baser instincts may overcome my honourable intentions. Every movement you make is like an invitation. I'm not made of stone, Laura."

"Conceited jackanapes!" Laura froze in her movements though every limb was restless and sleep was far away. She glared up at the folds of the canopy over the four-poster, watching the firelight make dancing patterns on the pearl-coloured brocade. She resented the way Matt intruded upon her thoughts and made her body so aware of him. She had not realised that being forced into this intimate proximity with a man could make her feel so wretched. Why couldn't she get the memory of his kiss out of her mind? He was just a common prisoner. She had paid for his services. That was all. He was just another servant.

A chuckle from the far side of the room set her flesh tinging with fearful anticipation.

"Devil take you!" she snapped. "How can I sleep if you keep chortling like a lunatic?"

He moved swiftly, throwing back the cover and swinging his legs to he ground. Laura gasped and sat up with a start, clutching the sheet high to her chin. He stood in his breeches, his hands on his slender hips as he scowled across the room at her. The dying firelight turned his torso amber and she saw the broad expanse of his chest with its dusting of dark hair.

"Don't look at me as though I am the devil himself." He picked up his shirt and half turned, clearly revealing the score of criss-cross lacerations across his back for the first time. Some were weeping and obviously must have been causing him considerable pain.

"Shouldn't your back be treated?" Her concern overrode her fear.

"And how would you explain the whip-marks to a servant?" His tone was scathing, but she suspected that he had resorted to anger to cover his surprise at her change of attitude.

"I will tend to your back. I've a greater knowledge of such matters than any servant. I always tend the sick at Fairfield." She reached for her nightrobe, which had fallen from the end of the bed on to the floor during her restlessness. Slipping her arms into its scarlet satin sleeves, she pulled it around her as she slid from the bed and tied the sash about her waist before facing him. "There is no need for you to suffer unnecessarily. Please, if your wounds are painful, I could ease the discomfort. My box of unguents is in the dressing-room."

"As you wish," he answered, sitting on the daybed.

Laura opened a carved wooden coffer and searched through it for the balm and herbs she needed. She lit a fresh candle and placed it on a table behind his back. As its light fell across his flesh she caught her breath. Several of the lash-strokes were weeping and inflamed. Without hot water there was little she could do to cleanse the wounds, but there was a special balm which would draw out the poisons and soothe the pain. With a light touch she smeared it on to his flesh. Even so she felt him flinch, and he turned away to stare fixedly into the flames of the fire.

"It's my fault you were beaten," she said softly. "All I wanted to do was stop them, but I only made things worse."

Again he looked over his shoulder, and Laura felt herself flush under the intensity of his gaze. "I was due fifty lashes for hitting the gaoler. The warder was too eager to take your bribe to have me badly beaten. Besides, he was convinced you'd never go through with your bargain and I'd get the other lashes anyway. So my debt to you is greater than you think."

A tress of her hair fell forward over his shoulder and he wound it around his fingers, his voice gruff with suppressed emotion. "You have glorious hair and the softest touch."

Laura kept her head bowed so that he could not see her expression. "These cuts should be bandaged," she said firmly, but her words were defensive. Again the virile masculinity of him held her in its thrall.

Matt sat rock-still while she continued her work. Every brush of her fingers against his skin was becoming a torture as they moved like a caress over his fevered flesh. From the moment Laura had removed her mask in the prison he had been fascinated by her. He had deliberately fuelled his contempt for the gentry to keep his desire for her at bay. The fresh scent of her body and hair and the sensuous movement of her hands over his back was destroying his honourable intentions.

With his jaw clenched, he bore that sensual torture

until all the cuts were tended and bandaged. The throbbing pain of them had eased, but a deeper ache now consumed him. He controlled it and swung round to thank her. At the same time she side-stepped, and suddenly she was standing between his open legs. The warmth of her thigh against his sparked a fire in his loins. He saw the flicker of awareness which darkened her eyes to indigo, and when she made to move away he captured her waist, pulling her against his chest as he rose to his feet. The heat of her radiated through the flimsy material of her robe, increasing his aching torment. Her lips parted and her eyes widened with wary alarm.

"Laura." Her name was torn from him.

As she stood poised like a deer scenting danger and ready to run, he felt her trembling. The challenge in her eyes made him crave to turn that coldness into the passion that he knew simmered beneath the surface. The magnitude of the desire which flowed through him was like a dam bursting.

He should never have allowed her to tend his wounds. His need to possess her was so fierce that his blood ran furnace-hot through his veins. His senses were enmeshed around her slender, inviting figure like a hunter's net. The candlelight turned her hair to burnished copper and reflections of its light spangled the blue depths of her eyes. The feel of her slender waist in his hands and the delicious promise of the luscious curves just within his reach drove him to the brink of the precipice. He was teetering on the edge of the black pit, battling to exercise restraint.

Sanity returned. Honour triumphed over desire. Abruptly he put her from him and stood up. "Thank you for tending my wounds, Laura."

He pulled on his shirt as she backed away from him. She was breathing heavily and trembling—whether from fear or passion he dared not analyse. He had made a bargain and had never yet broken his word to anyone.

"I'm going for a walk," he said sharply.

"Won't the servants think it odd?"

"Very likely, but I doubt you would appreciate the consequences if I do not," he all but groaned, and then added, "You're a very desirable woman, Laura. And I've just spent a very long time in prison and forgone the usual female companionship a man requires."

"You'll not shame me by seeking a doxy this night?" she said, aghast.

When Matt released her Laura was jerked out of the spell which had spun itself around her senses as she'd tended his wounds. She had never expected that to touch a man's flesh could move her so strangely. When he had pulled her against him she had felt as though her body was melting.

She backed further away as he pulled on his hose. His figure was silhouetted against the dying firelight and she could see nothing of his features as he shoved his feet into his shoes and reached for his jacket. The fiercely exhaled breath cut the air like a whiplash.

"I just need some fresh air. I'll go into the garden and return before the servants are astir. You need not fear. No one will hear me. I spent my childhood with the guttersnipes of London and learnt at an early age to walk with the stealth of the invisible."

"Do as you wish," she said, stung by the change in his mood. Turning her back to him, she pulled off her robe and climbed into bed. "But if you think you can…"

She stopped, aware from the stillness in the room that she was alone. She had not heard the door open or shut, or a single footstep. Scowling at the closed door, she tried to fathom something of the character of the man she had married. It was impossible. Matt's moods were forever changing. With a sigh she willed herself to sleep, resolving to banish Matthew Thorne from her mind. Another impossible task. She heard the parlour clock strike another two hours before she finally drifted into sleep.

Her next conscious awareness was of the mattress moving under a second weight. Before she could open her eyes a hand was placed over her mouth.

"Don't cry out," Matt warned. "The servants are up. Won't your maid be expecting to find us abed together when she comes to tend your needs?"

In the early morning light Laura glared at his face so close to her own. Along one side of her body she could feel the heat of his bare torso as he leaned over her. As she heard the latch of the door being lifted Matt twisted and, sliding his arms around her, dragged her so that she was lying across the upper half of his body. Her gasp of protest was silenced by his mouth hard on hers, his fingers lacing into her hair to prevent her evading his lips.

An inarticulate sound from Laura was muffled as he took her face in his hands and his mouth moved possessively over hers. Laura knew she had only to cry out for the house to be raised against him, but by the same token such a course was impossible. The truth of her marriage would come out.

Keeping her mouth clamped shut, she endured the

assault of his lips. But an insidious flame was melting
the ice of her control. With infinite gentleness his lips
played over hers and she was barely aware that Sarah
had entered the room. Beneath that intoxicating onslaught her lips parted, and her fingers spread across
the bandage on his chest to discover the exciting
touch of his skin, and felt the rapid beat of his pulse
as her hand moved to the hollow of his throat. Her
fingers curled into the silky softness of his hair, her
senses beginning to swirl as his kiss deepened in intensity.

At Sarah's giggle and mumbled apology Laura
found herself released. She was appalled at the way
she had again responded to his kiss, and her cheeks
were on fire when she rolled away from Matt. He kept
one arm firmly around her waist and there was a speculative look in his eyes which made her blush grow
hotter. Confound the knave, she fumed inwardly. He
was making a fool of her and enjoying himself at her
expense.

The maid put down the morning tray of tea and
began to gather up Laura's scattered clothing. When
Laura saw Sarah pick up Matt's breeches, the colour
fled from her cheeks. She glared at him. The knave
was grinning, and he lifted his head to whisper in her
ear.

"You wanted me to play the part of the loving
bridegroom, did you not?"

"That will be all, Sarah," Laura dismissed her
maid.

As the maid left the room Laura snatched up her
robe and bolted for the window-seat. The pillows and
covers had been removed from the day-bed and there

was no sign for the servants to tell that they had spent the night apart.

Away from Matt she found it easy to whip her outrage. "You have overstepped the bounds of our contract."

"Wouldn't your maid have expected to find you in my arms this morning?"

"You are just using that as an excuse."

"Am I?"

Laura's palm itched to slap the insolence from his grinning face. "I will not be subjected to such base behaviour each morning."

"What are you afraid of, Laura? Enjoying it?"

"I'd as soon embrace a viper."

He chuckled. "The lady doth protest too much, methinks."

"Conceited jackanapes! Think what you like. It will do you no good." She twitched the folds of her robe together as she moved to her dressing-room. "Just remember that you're paid to act as you are told."

"I'm not your servant." He sat up in the bed, his eyes glittering with a dangerous light. "So far I've gone along with this nonsensical scheme because I'm indebted to you." He swung his bare legs from the bed, the sheet acting as a skimpy loincloth across his waist as he continued to glare at her. "Push me too far and I might take all I consider to be my husband's right. You are a beautiful woman and you are not immune to my kisses. Stop playing games, Laura, and grow up. This marriage was your idea. Don't forget that now I'm your husband the law is on my side. It is the husband who is the master. And I'll be subservient to no woman. Now pass me my breeches, dear wife.''

''I'll burn in hell first.''

When he flung back the covers to fetch them himself, Laura fled into the ante-room and slammed the door behind her. Her cheeks burned from the sight of his muscled golden body revealed so unashamedly. The sound of his laughter followed her.

''I had only meant to spare your blushes. You are your own worst enemy, Laura Thorne.''

''It's Stanton,'' she flared from behind the safety of the closed door.

''No, my dear.'' His low chuckle was close to the wood separating them. ''By your own choosing it is Laura Thorne. And until our arrangement is rescinded it will remain so. I bid you good morning, Mrs Thorne. You may order a bedchamber prepared for me if you wish. I'm not the one who stands to lose Fairfield because I'm a prude.''

She wrenched open the dividing door, her eyes blazing at his audacity. ''Don't you dare threaten me. I know what you are about. You can cool your lechery, for I will not share your bed.''

Maddeningly, he quirked a dark brow at her tirade. ''Threats, were they, Laura? Have you looked out of the window? That's Sarah, isn't it? She's talking to the coal-carrier. Is he your regular merchant? He could be anyone hired by Guy Stanton to trick a maid into an indiscreet remark about her mistress's hasty marriage.''

Laura went to the window and looked out. Sarah was chatting to the coal merchant, but hovering close by was a road-sweeper who was taking a long time to sweep that section of the road. From where he was standing he could hear every word her maid was saying. Whether the road-sweeper was a spy or not, it brought home to her that from now on, for every second of the day, she must be on constant guard.

Matt's breath fanned her neck as he stood behind her. She jumped violently. She had not heard his movements.

"If you want to safeguard Fairfield, Laura, you are going to have to learn to trust me."

Laura did not answer as she stared down at the street. Her profile was as white as porcelain and there was an unnatural glitter in her eyes as though she was striving to fight back tears. Matt crushed a moment of guilt. He had not meant to upset her. Only God knew why, but this woman could rouse the worst demons in his nature. Her arrogance and the cool way she ordered him about drove sanity from his reasoning. There were times when he hated her and all she stood for. Then he would glimpse a chink behind that icy exterior and his chivalry would be roused. Misplaced chivalry. When did the gentry ever need help from such as him?

But Laura did need his help—more than she suspected.

Matt dragged a hand through his hair. There was no place in his life for a woman, especially this one. And there was certainly no place for him in her future. Last night had buffeted his emotions until they were raw. Having glimpsed the sensuality to be awakened within her, he was consumed with the need to make love to her. He wanted her with a force which defied reason—and he needed her to be subservient to his will, wanting him as an equal. Only then would the debt be truly accounted for between them.

* * *

Delighted as Laura was at her grandfather's gradual recovery, it pitched her into an untenable situation. With each passing day it was becoming more obvious that she could never refute the marriage as she had planned. Too many people now knew of Matt and had met him. How could he just disappear out of her life without a scandal ensuing?

To her relief her grandfather had paid her marriage portion to Matt, and that same afternoon they had visited the money-lender to reclaim the emerald necklace and earrings. Matt had insisted that they visit a goldsmith and place the dowry money in Laura's name for security. That he had shown no desire to wrest any part of that money from her had confirmed her faith in him. She even felt guilty that she had suspected him of dishonesty. At least now she had sufficient funds to finance her plans for the future without having to go to her grandfather for money and so raise awkward questions.

In the week following her marriage Laura's life fell into a regular if uneasy pattern. In the mornings Matt spent an hour with the tailor, and the first of his completed outfits arrived. Then they travelled out of the city to Bethnal village. At discovering that Matt could barely sit on a horse, Laura had insisted that he learn to ride like a gentleman.

"What need has a sea-captain to ride?" Matt had tried to dissuade her. "I've managed thus far to get by without risking my life on those great snorting brutes."

"You don't like horses?" Laura had said in amazement. From the age of seven she had been riding in the hunt. "But all gentlemen ride."

"My mother's meagre income did not stretch to

such luxuries as a pony of my own.'' He had scowled. ''When you're a child playing in London's streets, the first lesson you learn is to keep well away from any stamping hooves. God gave me two strong legs and I've never been afraid to use them.''

''As my husband you will be expected to ride,'' she had insisted. ''We will start today.''

Matt had learned quickly and, apart from the slight stiffness of his gait from his aching muscles unused to the saddle, he had become a competent rider.

On the way back to the city one day, Laura asked the coachman to stop at the horse market and there she selected a black gelding for Matt to ride.

''What do I need a horse for?'' Matt dismissed her generosity as the gelding was tethered to the back of the carriage and they returned to Lincoln's Inn. ''You've already spent a fortune on clothes for me. I don't want to be deeper in your debt.''

She was discovering that he could be very stubborn about such matters. ''The gelding is a good investment. You must look the part in every way, no matter how short the duration of our arrangement. You will also need an allowance. How much does a gentleman require for his personal needs? I have no idea about such matters.''

''I don't want your money, Laura.''

''And you don't want me as a wife either,'' she said tartly. ''You have kept your part of the bargain and I will keep mine. I would expect only the best in everything for my husband.''

His fist clenched and he banged it against the side of the carriage with a violence that made her jump. His body was tense and his face was taut with controlled anger. ''I won't be a kept man, Laura. Spare me some pride. Our agreement was supposed to be for a few weeks. Each day this tangle you devised knots all the tighter.''

Matt saw clearly the look of hurt and fear for the future in her blue eyes. It made his gut twist as if a knife had been plunged into it. He didn't want to hurt the woman, but the situation was running away with itself. Theirs was meant to be a business contract. He had not been prepared for the way her beauty and fiery spirit had chiselled beneath his guard. He did not want such an attachment. His plans for the future were consumed with the need for revenge. They certainly did not include romantic involvement with a woman of the very class he despised.

He was furious with himself for allowing her to distract his mind from his purpose. Laura had no place in his future. With a jolt he realised that it was a statement he had begun to repeat to himself like a litany.

What ate into his pride was that he could not tolerate a woman supporting him and his voice became sharp as he continued, ''Good God, woman, would you have me branded as a fortune-hunter? Guy Stanton will be investigating more than our marriage. He'll ferret into my background. How are you going to explain that you married a penniless sea-captain? Everything I owned was taken in part-payment of my so-called debt.''

''Everyone believes ours is a love-match. I'm the one whose reputation is at risk, who will be shunned by society when it is discovered I married no gentleman.''

Her eyes were bright with defiance and the proud tilt of her chin tempted Matt to take her in his arms and crush her to him. He wanted to make her acknowledge that he was her equal. He suppressed the urge, but it made him short-tempered.

"Society can be all-forgiving when there is a fortune at stake," he snapped. "Once our marriage is annulled you'll not lack for suitors."

"I don't want suitors. All I want is Fairfield."

"And everything Laura Stanton wants in life she gets... spoilt heiress that she is!" His antagonism burst forth. "This time it's not that simple. I have my own business affairs to settle. Our agreement was for a few weeks. Your time is running out."

"You wouldn't do that to me, Matt." Her eyes were large and pleading.

"Why not? Because I'm a paid lackey and should do as I'm told?"

"That's not how I think of you." Her lips quivered and she reached out to take his arm.

He drew back and held himself stiffly away from her.

"I won't be your puppet, Laura. Surely it's obvious that things cannot go on as they are between us?"

He was deliberately goading her to erect a shield against his own emotions. She must never suspect how much he desired her. A woman like Laura did not make love with a man in her paid employ. She had yet to learn that he could not be bought. She would never know the control he exercised not to take her into his arms and tell her everything would work out. Never must she suspect the temptation he curbed. With any other woman he would have seduced her into acknowledging that her kisses had betrayed her sensuality, that she wanted him as much as he desired her. But relations between himself and Laura were complex enough without passion complicating them further.

Chapter Six

Most afternoons Matt and Laura received well-wishers, who called at the house as news of Laura's marriage spread. Today was overcast and, not expecting visitors, Laura suggested that she instruct Matt in some dance-steps. On the table by the parlour window was a score of invitations for musical soirées, dining with friends, or grand balls for them to attend. So far Laura had declined them all with the excuse that during her grandfather's convalescence they dined with him each evening.

A trio of musicians was engaged to play for them in the parlour and a space had been cleared at one end of the large room. To Laura's surprise Matt was a graceful dancer, and learned the formal and complicated steps quickly. Inevitably they made mistakes, and when Matt found himself facing the wrong way for the second time he shook his head and laughed.

"What sort of dance is this that I may barely touch my partner's hand? Give me a country reel any day." He turned to the musicians. "Enough of this prancing nonsense—strike up a lively country dance."

Laura was swept into the circle of Matt's arm as

the music began, and he led her around the room, spinning her first with his right arm and then with his left. The music played faster and the couple whirled to its wild rhythm. Laura was breathless and laughing as the music finally came to an end and she was forced to hold her side and lean against Matt to catch her breath. His arm remained firm about her waist. He had drawn her into the doorway of an ante-room out of sight of the musicians and she could feel his breath against her hair as he laughed.

"Now wasn't that more fun?"

She looked up at him, smiling as she replied, "I always enjoyed the May Day and harvest revels at Fairfield."

The teasing sparkle in his eyes disarmed her. His hand remained possessive upon her waist, and when he drew her closer it seemed natural for her to lean her forehead against his chest. He rested a finger under her chin and lifted her face to regard him. Her every nerve was tense with expectation, and her lips parted as she suspected that he was going to kiss her. Instead he brushed a stray tendril of coppery hair from her cheek, his bronze eyes studying her with a gravity that scorched her to her soul.

Her mouth suddenly dry, she ran the tip of her tongue across her lower lip. A pulse quickened in the depths of her being, a demand so forceful, so alien that her body trembled. Laura could feel the slow spread of warmth move through her. Her gaze melded with his and unconsciously her fingers slid upwards to his neck, unable to stop the need to draw his head down and feel the heat of his mouth on hers. For a breathless moment she lost touch with reality; there was only the sensual world, which held them entranced, enmeshing them until their lips were poised a finger's width apart.

"Matt." She was unaware that she spoke his name or that her voice was a whispering plea as she was drawn closer against the length of his body.

He heard the tremulous catch in her breathing, saw the invitation in her parted lips, felt the heat of her seductive curves against his chest and thigh, and knew that her submission was within his grasp. His mouth slanted across hers, merciless in his need to subjugate this ravishing woman to his will. Her soft moan of pleasure answered the urgent demand of his mouth and an ache filled his chest as he inhaled the sweet fragrance that was uniquely hers. The neckline of her gown was cut low and he could see the line of her smooth, shapely shoulders and the full curves of her creamy breasts. A madness possessed him to pull the gown from those luscious curves and kiss her until she moaned in ecstasy from the thrill that his mouth evoked. He swallowed against the dryness in his throat, his breathing sharp and harsh. This was not in his plans, or his wildest dreams. Seduction, yes, but not this harrowing longing, this consuming agony of need.

As his kiss deepened, he tasted the heady wine of her passion. It acted like a catalyst. Both of them clung together, reeling from the explosion which had ignited their desire.

Laura was caught in the spell of new-found desire that whirled through her, stirring primitive and unexplained longings she had never dreamed possible. With bated breath she waited, craving more of the magic inducement of his touch. She moved so that his hand, which was slowly caressing her back, came into contact with her breast, and she gasped as his palm closed around it, caressing her through the thin silk of her bodice. When his hand moved to the neckline of her gown and dipped inside to take possession of her breast, her breath came out in a long sigh. The slightly abrasive touch of his callused fingers on its sensitive peak was so poignant that she was suddenly frightened by the sensations which were sparking like firecrackers through her body. Pure and virginal, she was unprepared for the storm of emotions he aroused. She shivered, struggling to control the blissful madness which had overtaken her. Instantly his hand withdrew, and instead of relief her sense of loss was devastating.

"Please," she murmured, capturing his hand to lay it over the frantic pounding of her heartbeat. At that moment everything else was unimportant. "Oh, Matt. What spell is this that you weave upon me?"

"It is no spell, my dear Laura," he said against her ear, before his words were silenced by the passionate kisses which he pressed against her throat.

She was intoxicated by his touch and the knowledge that he desired her. She arched eagerly against him, her body consumed by a liquid fire which blazed with such intensity that a lifetime's family pride and upbringing were banished into obscurity.

"Hurrumph!" A cough came from the parlour. "There you are! Barker said you were in here."

Laura sprang back, her face crimson with embarrassment as she recognised Lady Clifton's booming voice. Matt turned from her with an oath. His eyes were narrowed with thwarted longing and his breathing was jagged. Laura was still light-headed with sensation, and smoothed a trembling hand over her bodice as she encountered the amused stare of the wife of Brigadier, Lord Clifton, who had been her father's commanding officer. She was also an insatiable gossip.

"Lady Clifton." Laura struggled to regain her presence of mind, aware of the merriment in the woman's pale eyes. "How good of you to call."

"I was curious to inspect this new husband of yours." Lady Clifton ran her eye as critically over Matt as though she were buying a prize stallion.

He had recovered his composure and bowed to their visitor.

"He looks well enough," Lady Clifton added. She was a large-boned woman of nearly six feet. Most men found her intimidating. However, Matt merely favoured her with his most disarming smile.

"I am glad you approve," he said amiably. "Laura has spoken of you with affection. Your blessing means a lot to her."

"Does it, indeed?" Lady Clifton laughed heartily. "That's news to me. Heaven knows I've felt duty-bound to give her guidance. I was very fond of her father, as was the Brigadier. This marriage has come as a shock. It's set society back on its heels, especially as she keeps you hidden away. I've sent two invitations to dine and both have been refused."

"That was appalling manners, I know, Lady Clifton," Laura said sweetly, linking her arm through Matt's. "But we've been married so short a time, and Grandfather has been so ill that we are spending our evenings with him."

Lady Clifton's piercing stare regarded them knowingly. "Newly-weds! That's a lame excuse and you know it. But at least I can see that gossip didn't exaggerate when it said yours is a love-match. Despite the odd rumours I've heard circling.''

''What rumours?'' Laura bristled.

Lady Clifton waved her hand in airy dismissal. ''Totally unfounded, I can see now that I've met you both. I suspect your cousin Guy is behind them. But gossip, if left to spread, can cause irreparable harm. Best to nip it in the bud. And what better way for you to prove it a lie than by appearing in public?'' She gathered up her gloves and worked her fingers into them. ''I will permit you a few more days in isolation with each other. But I shall be offended if you do not attend my ball next week. You must not keep your husband hidden away, Laura. He's far too handsome.''

With that Lady Clifton swept from the parlour, and Laura became aware of the musicians' curious glances upon them. She dismissed them. Still shaken by her response to Matt's kiss, she then hurried from the room, remarking over her shoulder, ''I must discuss tomorrow's menu with Cook. You mentioned earlier that you had business matters to attend. I would not have our marriage keep you from them. We do not dine for another three hours, if you wish some time on your own.''

She had taken five steps before her arm was gripped and she was swung round to face her husband, whose face was grim with suppressed anger. ''Don't ever dismiss me like a lackey, Laura.''

''That was not my intent…'' She floundered. She could hardly tell him that she was ashamed at the wanton way she had responded to his kiss. The strain of being constantly with him was destroying her calm. She found his company stimulating, and that was too dangerous for her peace of mind. Everywhere she had to be on guard. It had not escaped her notice that every time they stepped out of the house a figure detached himself from the alleyway opposite and dogged their footsteps. Guy Stanton had obviously set his spies upon them.

A maid was polishing the newel-post at the top of the stairs and, looking pointedly at the servant to warn Matt that they were being watched, Laura stepped back into the parlour and closed the door behind them. Swallowing hard, she tried to put her feelings into words. "I respect you too much to treat you like a lackey, Matt." Unable to hold his gaze, she fidgeted with a ribbon on her bodice. "But surely you must agree that what happened just now, before Lady Clifton arrived, cannot be repeated?"

Matt was unprepared for how hard her rejection hit him. Twice he'd known her on the point of submission in his arms and the need to make her his own still throbbed through him. Having sampled the wild abandon of her response, he knew he would find no peace until he had made love to her.

"I want you, Laura. And I know you want me."

"You know that is not possible." She shook her head. "We are being thrown together in this unnatural marriage, forced to pretend an affection which is a lie."

"That was no pretence when I held you in my arms, Laura."

"It was a mistake."

"It was inevitable."

"Then I shall take care not to make the same error again."

He laughed caustically. "You're so adept at lying

and betrayal, you no longer know when you are deluding yourself.''

''That's unjust. We made a bargain. You've made it clear how onerous this arrangement is and that you want it ended as soon as possible.''

For a moment he paled, his face tense as though she had struck him. Then a guard came down over his eyes and he turned on his heel and left her. She heard him telling Barker that he was going out on business and would not be back to dine that evening. He was deliberately flouting her wishes. Rebellious anger rose in her at the way Matt had behaved.

Later that evening she excused herself from playing chess with her grandfather and retired early to her bedchamber. Too angry to sleep, she heard the nightwatchman calling the hour as he passed the corner of their street. Matt had not returned.

''Two o'clock—dampen your fires and batten your shutters. All's well.''

Matt would not get away with this, she fumed.

''Three o'clock—look to your locks. All's well.''

''Four o'clock. All's well.''

It was no longer anger which kept her wakeful. It was fear. What if Matt did not return?

The speed of her wedding had become the talk of London. That was what Laura had wished to avoid. How could she now refute it? With each new day fresh acquaintances met Matt, and he was not a man many people would easily forget. Until the dancing lesson she had not been able to fault his behaviour during the day. Though there was often a deliberate taunting in his speech, she had found herself enjoying the challenge of their verbal sparring. When Matt was not at her side, it was not just her role of devoted wife which drew her gaze constantly to him. In his new clothes he was a commanding and handsome figure. With secret delight she had noted that she was not the only woman who would follow his progress along a crowded street, or through a press of friends in their parlour.

"Five o'clock," the watchman called from below her window. "Servants up and look to your master's needs. All's well."

Laura picked up a pillow and flung it at the shuttered window. "It's not all well," she groaned. "Curse you, Matthew Thorne!"

Through the gap in the bed-hangings she glared at the empty day-bed. From her own restless sleep since her marriage she knew that Matt was often awake like herself. Often in the night, when she pretended to be asleep, she would see him rise from the day-bed, moving silently as a shadow to squat on the floor by the fire and stare into the flickering flames.

The image returned of how she had seen him in that position at dawn yesterday. The bandage no longer covered his cuts, and as the firelight had played over his torso she had seen that they were healing. Always the sight of them roused a sense of guilt and something more, an indefinable need to reach out and touch him. That, she knew, was too dangerous. Their first night together had proved that.

In their roles as lovers the close proximity to each other inevitably led to contact between their bodies. When walking in the street her breast would brush his arm. Crossing the road led to a protective hand being placed lightly against the middle of her back. When they sat in the swaying carriage, it was impossible to avoid contact of thigh upon thigh. Each touch was like a flame held against kindling. It would spread a delicious heat through her body and snatch the breath from her lungs.

Laura clenched her fist and held it against her breast as she fought to control her wayward emotions. If Lady Clifton had not arrived at that precise moment yesterday, what would have been the outcome? Lost in the spell of Matt's kiss, Laura had been incapable of heeding the caution of her mind. Matt had been right. She had wanted him with a longing which defied sanity.

She had thought herself in control in their relations. How wrong she was! Sarah now attended her when she was dressing or disrobing, and Matt never came to her room until she was already abed. They were forced to continue to share the same room as there were no others available in the London house. Each morning when he slid into her bed, moments before Sarah was about to enter, Laura was careful to keep well away from him.

"Curse you, Matt Thorne," she groaned again, refusing to put a name to the agony of loss she was experiencing. It was madness. She could not succumb to base desire. What was Matt? Nothing but a penniless adventurer with a handsome face and the deceptive charm of Lucifer. He had made it very clear how he despised any of her class.

Hugging her pillow against her breast, she finally drifted to sleep.

Moonlight made a tracery of deep shadows from the overhanging storeys of the houses. A single cresset torch burned outside the house Matt was watching. His narrowed gaze scanned the three storeys of the brick-built building, with its ornamental porch and several imposing steps leading up to its doorway. It was a new house, recently acquired by a man of affluence. His investigations had finally brought him to this street, only to discover that the owner was out of town for several days. He was due to return tonight. Until Matt saw his face he could not be certain that this was the man he was searching for.

It was mild for February, but even had there been a storm tonight, Matt would have maintained his vigilance. He was close to learning from his old partner the identity of the man who had forged the documents for a debt he did not owe, and who had condemned him to end his days in prison. Matt leaned against the shadowed wall and waited, his body still as a predator's.

But his mind was not on the encounter ahead. Laura was increasingly dominating his thoughts. He had been glad of a reason to leave the house tonight. There he felt trapped. A watchman in the next street called the hour of ten. Laura would have retired by now. The image of her lying alone in her bed brought a return of the restlessness which constantly plagued him. Every night it became a contest of his will-power over his desire not to make love to her. In the darkest hours temptation whispered loudest in his mind. Had he not the right to make her his? Their marriage was legal. And her response to his kiss this afternoon had proved her willing. And what of their agreement? his conscience berated. Away from her company he acknowledged the voice of reason. But he had only so much self-control. And Laura could be all provocation. Often he would turn to find her watching him. There would be in her eyes a softness which made him burn to possess her. At such times his wit would be at its most caustic and he would see angry pride flare in her eyes, like a talisman to ward off evil. That pride of hers was his salvation. It gave him the strength to combat his desire.

A curse broke from him at the way fate had made a mockery of their lives. This afternoon Laura had been on the point of surrender, but it had been her body answering the skill of his persuasive passion. It would have made her seduction a hollow victory.

"You're a fool not to take what's offered," he told himself for the hundredth time. He'd had mistresses aplenty in the last five years, all of whom he had bedded and forgotten with consummate ease. None had reached his heart. Susannah had shown him the power and the pain of an exquisite love. Pride refused to allow him to take second-best from Laura Stanton. The sooner he was free to take up his own life the better. Away from the woman, she would no longer be a temptation.

Matt was jerked from his bitter contemplation by the sound of carriage wheels. The vehicle stopped outside the house he was watching. The coachman jumped down from his seat and opened the door. A man stepped out, and as he raised his face to the woman he helped down the cresset light fell across his features. The blond wig disguised the grey hair, but there was no mistaking those deep-set eyes, the broken nose and lizard-thin lips. The torchlight picked out the profusion of expensive lace at the man's thick wrist and the glitter of jewels on a beringed hand.

Caleb Van Steenis had prospered, and with his new prosperity he had shed his Dutch identity, changed his surname to Vance, and married a wealthy widow.

All within the months since he ...
nership in the *Sea Maiden.*

The shaft of light from the opened ...
house made Matt draw his black cloak acros...
and move further into the shadows. He did not ...
until the street was quiet again. Then he crossed t...
street and turned down a side-alley. Here he scaled
the wall, and as he looked towards the back of the
house he saw that only a single light burned in a
downstairs window. Caleb had not changed his habits.
He always sat for a half-hour with a nightcap of
brandy before retiring.

Soundlessly Matt dropped on to the dew-covered
grass and made his way towards the lighted window.
The shutters were open and heavy green curtains were
partially drawn across the panes. Inside Caleb sat by
a fire, his profile to Matt. A glass goblet was cradled
in the merchant's hand as he patted his vast stomach
beneath a scarlet and gold embroidered vest. The self-
satisfaction on the man's face brought a bleakness to
Matt's eyes. Because of Caleb's greed he had been
imprisoned.

Taking out his dagger, Matt slid it along the inside
of the casement sash of the window until he felt the
lock slide open. Holding his breath, he eased up the
sash window and put a leg over the sill, then ducked
inside the room. Caleb was still unaware of his presence.

When his dagger-point was pressed against the
Dutchman's fat neck the older man gasped and his
grey eyes bulged with fear.

"I doubt you ever expected to see me again,
Caleb."

"Thorne! Good God, man, are you a ghost?" His

wide mouth gaped and his fleshy hand gripped the gold cross he wore beneath his silk shirt.

"No ghost, Caleb," Matt said with a laugh.

"You scared me half to death. Thought I was about to be murdered before you spoke."

"I was sorely tempted." Matt was no longer amused. "So you had better give me a damned good reason why you sold out on me."

A line of sweat broke out on Caleb's upper lip. "I swear I had no choice, friend. Good lord, man, your last voyage lasted for eighteen months, and you were overdue by two months. I could not contact you. I'd invested heavily in another cargo which was ship-wrecked. Then there was the fire at the warehouse. I damned near lost everything. There were rumours spreading in the docks that the *Sea Maiden* had been sunk in a tempest. Seamen in a ship bound for Rotterdam from the Indies swore they heard your ship had gone down."

"I've been overdue before," Matt said harshly. "And each time to our benefit, for I had acquired a valuable cargo."

"I had creditors snapping at my heels, and Louise's uncle was threatening to end our betrothal." Caleb was now sweating profusely. "She's the best thing that ever happened to me, Matt. She'd had several suitors before she agreed to become my wife. I was desperate. To clear my debts I had to sell my share in the *Sea Maiden* to raise the money."

"Our partnership gave me first offer on those shares," Matt said darkly. "At the end of my voyage I intended to buy you out."

Caleb's gaze refused to hold his. "I delayed as long as I could, praying you'd return. The rumours that wreckage from the *Sea Maiden* had been seen were growing. I thought I'd lost everything with the ship. I couldn't believe my good fortune when an anonymous investor offered to buy out my share, apparently unaware of the rumours.''

"Didn't you question their motives?'' Matt snapped.

"Question such a heaven-sent gift? No, I didn't. I'm sorry I sold out on you. But this was business.''

Caleb wiped a large hand across his sweating face, again refusing to meet Matt's glittering stare.

Matt's eyes narrowed. "There's more to this, isn't there, Caleb? What are you hiding?''

Caleb swallowed nervously. "Nothing,'' he gasped.

Matt grabbed the man's collar and drew him half out of his chair. "Tell me everything.''

Haltingly, Caleb began. "In recent years I was often visited by a man enquiring after you. He was clearly a servant, but in the employ of someone wealthy; that much was evident by…'' Caleb bit his lip, and carried on. "He came to my warehouse about three times a year. He seemed to know a lot about you, so there seemed little harm in telling him…in conversation, like…that you intended to buy land and build a house in England when you next returned. The man came to see me more often then. Every couple of weeks or so he'd be back, wanting to know if I'd had word from you.''

Matt thrust Caleb away from him. "He paid you for information about me, didn't he?'' he ground out, wounded by the betrayal. "Don't deny it. I can see it in your face.''

"What if he did?'' Caleb defended. "He just

wanted to know when you were due to dock, how long you would be in port before you left on your next voyage... I could see no harm in that. And to be paid well for such innocent information..."

"So why the change of name?" Matt's tone was dangerous. "Did you fear I would seek retribution? Was it you who informed this mysterious party when I last docked?"

"No, Matt! They must have had spies working at the docks. The *Sea Maiden* is not a ship which could slip up the Thames unseen. I didn't change my name because of you, but because of Louise. She's a strict Catholic. She would have nothing to do with anything remotely Calvinistic—even a name. I converted to her faith. What's in a name?" He shrugged. "My father was a drunkard and no one to be proud of."

"Aye, what's in a name?" Matt answered drily.

Caleb looked contrite. "I didn't mean it to sound like that. You always were very touchy about yours— or the lack of it."

Matt paced for several seconds before answering. The mentioning of his bastardy could still flick him on the raw.

Caleb had relaxed and was studying him. He let out a low whistle of approval. "You've certainly done well for yourself since you returned to England. Were the profits that high on the voyage?"

Matt's lips curled back. "They were good. Not that I saw a penny of them. The man you sold out to forged documents in my name. I was supposed to owe him a thousand pounds for cargo I'd purchased. I was in prison less than two hours after I'd docked."

"Matt, I never suspected..." Caleb was genuinely astounded. "Even when I was asked about you, I didn't think they meant to ruin you." He again whistled through his discoloured teeth, his expression defensive. "But if you've made enemies, it was nothing to do with me. I had my own interests to look after."

Matt paced the room. A suspicion was beginning to form as to who was behind his arrest. There was only one man who feared Matt could have information which could endanger his reputation.

"Who was it, Caleb?" Matt persisted. "Who did you sell out to?"

"I dealt through a lawyer. Shortly after the warehouse fire, the servant who visited me to ask about your whereabouts told me his master had an offer to put to me. He took me to the lawyer's offices. I never met the buyer. But wait…yes, I remember now catching a glimpse of a name on the Bill of Sale before it was whipped away by the lawyer after I had signed it. Breten, it was."

Matt's suspicions were confirmed. "Breten!" he bit out, his expression murderous. "He's the man who caused the deaths of my wife and daughter. The man I have vowed to bring to justice."

Caleb gulped a large swig of brandy from his glass. "Then it sounds as though you have made a powerful enemy there, Matt." He stood up and rubbed his fleshy chin. "I'm sorry, Matt," he continued, "but, for what it's worth, you must know that I had no idea Breten was connected with your wife and daughter's deaths. I thought it was an accident."

Matt was fighting to combat his fury as the memories stirred. He continued to pace the room, then halted before the fireplace, his clenched fist beating down upon the mantleshelf. "They were mown down by Breten's coachman for trespassing on his land."

Matt gripped the edge of the mantelpiece and stared down into the flames of the fire. "Though what they were doing on Breten's land in the first place I've no idea. It's as though Breten has a vendetta against me."

"Breten's mother, the Lady Henrietta, was reputedly King Charles's mistress, and lady-in-waiting to Queen Mary," Caleb stressed, his voice gruff with concern. "He's high in favour at Court. Why should he have this vendetta against you?"

"Does a man like that need a reason?" Matt growled. "An imagined slight is enough for some of their kind. All my money and property were stripped from me when I was imprisoned, and the *Sea Maiden* sold to pay part of my debt. Thanks to my marriage, I am now in a position to bring Breten to justice."

Laura stirred, aware of warmth where earlier there had been coldness. She sighed sleepily and snuggled deeper under the covers. Her leg encountered a barrier of firm-muscled thigh which scorched her flesh like a wall of flame. Opening her eyes with a start, she found herself looking into Matt's dark visage, the expression in his bronze eyes enigmatic as she lay with her arm across his naked chest.

With a gasp of shock she rolled away. "Keep your distance," she hissed, frightened as much by the rapid pounding of her heart as by the threat of his nearness.

"It is you who were embracing me, madam," his sardonic tone mocked.

She rolled away from him and pushed open the bed-curtains and was pulling on her robe as Sarah opened the door.

"Is aught wrong, mistress?" the maid asked in surprise.

Matt lay on his stomach. Laura put a finger to her lips to silence Sarah and whispered, "Of course not. Don't wake your master. I rose early to deal with some correspondence. I've neglected it since my marriage."

"Never seen a couple so in love as you and Mr Thorne," Sarah sighed. "It's obvious you were meant for one another."

Laura could see Matt lying with one eye open, and the knave was grinning. Sarah was in the middle of the room when Laura realised that the bed-hangings had parted further than usual. Matt's back, with the red weals from his whipping clear to see, would be noticed by the maid at any moment. While Sarah was occupied, placing the morning tray on the table, Laura dived back into bed and lay against Matt, shielding his scarred back from the maid's gaze.

With a loud sigh Matt turned over, and Laura was clasped in his strong embrace, his lips seeking hers. Forcing a light laugh, she pulled back. "My love, we are not alone."

"Good morning, Sarah," Matt said, his eyes sparkling with devilry. "Go quickly and tend to other duties. Your mistress will not be needing you to help her dress for another hour."

Giggling at the manner of her dismissal, Sarah scurried out. Laura was pulled down beside her husband and her auburn hair fanned across his face. He wound it around his wrist like a rope of silk, holding her captive.

"Release me at once," she ordered sharply.

A dangerous light gleamed in his eyes and,

alarmed, she wriggled to free herself from his hold. His embrace was like steel bands around her slender form and, as her hands pressed against the hard contours of his arms and body, she felt the rigidity of uncompromising muscle.

She tensed, but it was not fear which made her breathing shallow, it was excitement. The sheer power of his masculinity, his handsome face so close to her own, played havoc with her sensibilities. Her body tingled with a delicious awareness, fraught with expectancy. Her heart raced and her mind reeled as she began to lose self-control and surrender to the sensations of her body. Unconsciously, her lips parted. Then his mouth was firm and demanding upon hers, stealing her breath away. The warmth of his breath against her throat was seductive and the slight abrasiveness of his chin in the hollow of her shoulder stimulated her senses. Her head lolled back as he pressed kisses along the slim column of her neck and her blood heated with a turbulent fire.

Reason warned her to push him away and to deny what was stirring to life within her. But her hands no longer obeyed her will. She was ignorant of sexual pleasure, of what was being demanded by the clamouring of her blood. The power of his kisses, the firm moulding of his body against hers dominated her consciousness. The roughness of his embrace had subtly changed, and his hands moved over her skin with a delicacy that set each pore vibrantly alive. As his fingers feathered along her back and hip, stroking and caressing, she cried out in pleasure. Reality was frozen. She moved as languorously as a cat; a passion beyond time or place had taken possession of her.

Despite Matt's resolve never to tempt fate and take

Laura into his arms again, his intentions fled as he felt the heat of her body, pliant against him. His mood had been bitter on his return to the Stanton house. He was strung more tightly than a bow, wanting to strike out at Sir James Breten and all his kind. Her expression was beguiling and dreamy, the face of a woman awakening to her own sexuality. Here was his means to be avenged upon the gentry he so despised. Yet he found he could not use Laura that way. He did not want to hurt her. But for days she had tempted him to the limits of his endurance and the need to show her he was her master, and no mere servant, was too powerful to resist.

When her lips parted to rebuke him, he covered them with his own. The taste of her lips yielding caused his blood to sing in his veins. His open mouth laid siege to hers, his tongue exploring and taking succour from a vividly remembered sweetness. His arms closed around her, moulding her pliant curves like a vine against him. He felt her answering quiver of longing. Gazing into her eyes, he saw her desire, dark behind thick veiling lashes. His restraint broke before the storm of his passion. Murmuring her name, he pressed ardent kisses along her slender neck, his hands practised as they slid the nightgown from her shoulder and he heard the low moan of pleasure rising from her throat.

Laura was floundering in the depths of the exquisite sensations that set her pulses and flesh a-tingling from her toes to her scalp. The heat of his lips seared her flesh. The competent but gentle strength of his hands elicited a thrilling pleasure as they moved down her back then, light and enticing as thistledown, skimmed across her taut ribs, and his thumb grazed the fullness of her breast. A ribbon of fire unfurled through her body and as his hand slid inside her nightrobe, freeing her breast, her skin briefly felt the coolness of the air. Then her nipple was circled by the heat of his lips and an inarticulate moan of rapture trembled in her throat.

The rough but sensual touch of his stubbled cheek as he kissed her breasts heightened her sensitivity and her pleasure. His hands grasped her hips and pressed her more firmly against him. She could feel the hardness of his manhood insistent against her thigh, and her own body pulsed in throbbing response.

The touch of his hand beneath the hem of her nightgown, where it had ridden to her thigh, made her writhe and burn. The slow caress travelled over her silken flesh, moving inexorably higher, tantalising and enticing, until he found the moist warmth between her thighs. The exquisitely stroking fingers caused her to arch against him.

"Tell me you want me, Laura," he murmured against her ear, his hands working their magic.

"Matt, oh, Matt," she responded, lost to the sweet pleasure which besieged her mind and senses.

The sound of a servant dropping a coal bucket on the polished floor outside her door shattered the erotic cocoon Matt had woven about her senses. Good God! What was she doing? What was she permitting him to do to her? Her body went rigid.

"No. Stop. Stop at once!"

"Laura…" His husky voice was against her ear.

"No. I said *no*." She pushed frantically at his chest.

"Laura, you are my wife."

"No. This is not part of our bargain." Her voice was beginning to rise to hysteria.

Matt groaned and rolled aside. He cursed himself for a fool. He had not meant to make love to her. And certainly he had never expected her to respond in the way she had. He had just meant to teach her a lesson.

Furious at the way she had submitted to Matt's caress, Laura scrambled from the bed, pulling her shift over her breasts from where it had been pushed to her waist. She had reached her dressing-chamber door before she heard Sarah singing to herself as she laid out Laura's clothes for the morning. Unable to face her maid, she retreated from the door and turned to face Matt. He was leaning on his elbow, watching her from the bed.

She was trapped, but in her mounting anger was about as defenceless as a cornered tigress.

"I suppose you're enjoying this," she said, careful not to raise her voice and have Sarah overhear. "For appearances' sake I'm forced to suffer you in my bed each morning, but you deliberately take advantage of the situation."

"We are both human, Laura. Why don't you admit it?"

"Don't try and cloak your attempt at seduction with excuses. You are quick to point out our agreement was only for a few weeks. Yet you take advantage of my trust and would use me as a whore. I've seen the way you ingratiate yourself with every acquaintance we meet. I suppose you've realised that this marriage is not going to be so easy to escape." In her growing anger she paced the chamber, beating a clenched fist into an open palm. "I should have listened to Jedediah. My life is a lie and my reputation will be in ruins."

"But Fairfield will be secure."

The words were a challenge, delivered without emotion.

"Go on, mock me." She rounded on him, her blue eyes flashing and her auburn hair shimmering to her hips in a glorious mantle of fire.

"The idea of the marriage was yours," Matt returned with lethal calm. "So things this morning got a little out of hand. But be honest with yourself; you were enjoying them. Have I not otherwise acted as you commanded of me and we agreed upon?"

Had Laura not been so incensed she would have detected the dangerous edge to his quiet voice. "Of course you have. You see a fortune now within your grasp. The contract we signed will mean nothing once Society accepts us as truly wed. Five thousand a year from the marriage settlement is more than you can ever hope to earn as a sea-captain, is it not?"

Matt leapt from the bed and, snatching up the sheet, he wound it around him like a Roman toga. "Do you think I want to be bound to a spoilt brat for the rest of my days?" he stormed. "This marriage was solely to get me out of prison. I've my own life to lead." He paced for several moments, his tense movements showing the fight he was having to control his anger. When he swung round to face her, the glitter in his midnight glare made her take an involuntary step back. "I warn you now, madam, I'm growing tired of playing the pet husband at your beck and call." Matt grabbed her arms and glared at her. "Why not end it now? Go to your grandfather. Tell him everything. Tell him you thought he'd be in his grave by now, and that with the deeds of Fairfield safe in your hands you'd pay me off so I was no further inconvenience to you."

"It would kill my grandfather to learn what I've done." Her eyes blazed with fury and her breathing became erratic as she struggled to control her own spiralling temper and keep her voice low. "And wouldn't dear cousin Guy just love to get hold of such a scandal?"

Breathing heavily, she tossed back her hair, her stance proud and defiant. Her breasts rose and fell in her fury, touching the hard muscle of his chest, but even in her anger her body became aroused at its contact and with the thrill of testing her will against his.

"So what is the alternative?" Matt growled.

He released her so abruptly that she swayed. For several moments they glared at each other. His dark hair had fallen across his brow and the rugged contours of his face were sharpened. Even so, Laura could not shake from her mind that he was the most handsome man she had ever encountered. Perversely, she felt a stab of respect and excitement at their quarrel. Then as suddenly as her temper had erupted it subsided. Its aftermath left her weak and shaken.

"I don't know what's to be done." Anguish washed through her and she turned away to hide her feelings from him. She put a hand to her temple, the endless deception eroding her will-power to remain indifferent towards him. Honesty broke through her guard. "I hate lying to Grandfather. I only did it for Fairfield. Not just because I love my home, but because the people don't deserve to have Guy as their master. Now it's all gone wrong." The strain of the past weeks bowed her head. "I hate myself. I'm so ashamed. I'm so wretched; I wish I were dead."

There was a harsh expulsion of breath from Matt

and he put a hand on her shoulder, drawing her round to face him. His expression was grave.

"You did what you believed you had to. I should not have said what I did. Fate must be laughing at us, but we shall win through. But we must understand each other."

He paused and ran a hand through his thick hair. "I'm certainly not the husband you would want at your side. And I told you in prison that I like my freedom too much to be shackled to one woman to the end of my days. Especially to a woman who has purchased my time as she would a slave. I wanted only one wife, and that was Susannah. She was my helpmeet and my equal. I don't want your money. It's a man's place to provide for the future of his family. I want this over with, Laura, and as soon as possible. It will be easier and less embarrassing for us to part once you're back at Fairfield. My ship was stolen from me when I was arrested. I want the price of it back and the man brought to justice. After that I intend to return to life at sea. I'm sure after a year or two you can seek to have our marriage annulled." He grinned wryly. "It hasn't yet been consummated. Grounds enough."

"That would make us both laughing-stocks."

He lifted an eyebrow and shook his head. "Then the sooner you decide what you want, the easier it will be for us all. Things cannot go on as they are. That is the only certainty we have about our marriage."

Chapter Seven

"Mr and Mrs Matthew Thorne will be pleased to accept..." Laura spoke aloud as she broke off in her writing. How drastically her life had changed in the three weeks since her wedding, she reflected.

Seated at her desk in the parlour, she wrote another acceptance to dine with friends later in the week. Everyone wanted to meet Matt. During the day it was easy to play the role allotted by their contract. Matt was an entertaining and charming companion. When on an occasional afternoon he left her to pursue his own business affairs, she was startled at how much she missed the constant challenge of his mockery. Thrown together as they were during the day, it was becoming increasingly difficult not to respond to his smile when they were alone.

With each night they were forced to share her chamber she became more aware of Matt. Sleep would evade her for hours, then, when she finally closed her eyes, her dreams were of strong arms holding her tight. Passionate kisses parted her lips as they had the other morning. So sharp was the image that she could feel his hands, experienced and masterful, caressing, bringing her body alive until she yearned to press closer to his body. Her arms ached to feel the strength of him as he lay above her, and she murmured his name in blissful surrender…

She would awake with a gasp and sit clutching the sheet to her chin. So vivid were those dreams that it always took several moments for her mind to clear. Briefly she would see Matt, standing over the bed. There was a bold, seductive gleam in his eyes and he would hold out his arms, whispering her name as he drew her close. She would press a trembling hand to her temple and the image would fade. There, stretched on the day-bed, she'd see her husband, his broad back turned to her, the slow rhythm of his breathing telling her that he slept peacefully, his dreams apparently undisturbed. Though she would lie back with a sigh of relief there was always an accompanying feeling of emptiness and loss.

Whenever Matt was absent Laura spent her time with her grandfather. His recovery was rapid and he was already fretting at his convalescence. She would read to him or play at chess or backgammon. The physician forbade him to leave the house for another week, but at the end of that time he had decided that they would return to Fairfield. And there lay another problem. Would Matt accompany her to the estate?

She rubbed the end of her quill against her cheek and sighed.

"You look thoughtful, Laura." She started at the sound of Matt's voice, unaware that he had entered the room.

When she turned to look at him, her heart gave a peculiar leap. He was still wearing his hat and cloak, but he looked so handsome in his new clothes, so assured in manner, that the thought of never seeing him again once she left for Fairfield saddened her.

"Grandfather is insisting on returning to Fairfield at the end of the week." She tried to keep her voice light, but failed lamentably. The attraction she felt towards Matt must be controlled before it got out of hand. There was no future for them together. "We will have to think of a story to explain why you will not be accompanying us," she went on. "You have your own affairs to settle and our arrangement was just for a few weeks. I never guessed it would become so involved."

"My leaving now will raise awkward questions for you." He removed his hat and cloak and laid them across the back of a chair, his stare unreadable as he continued to regard her. "In truth it does me no harm to be known as your husband until I can bring the man who imprisoned me for debt to justice. I will not abandon you while you need the protection of my name."

Laura came out of her chair to go to his side. "You would do so much for me?"

He touched her cheek, but his thoughts remained carefully guarded. "I owe you that at least for settling my debts." There was a tension in his voice she did not understand, and he turned from her abruptly and put on his cloak once more. "If we leave at the end of the week there are matters I would settle. I shall return in time to escort you to Lady Clifton's ball this evening." He paused by the door with his hat in his hand. "Once I again possess my own ship, no one will question my absence on a voyage."

When he left the room, although she knew that she had been granted a reprieve from explaining the disappearance of her husband from her life, Laura felt an icy blast of discomfort. Would the lies and deceit ever end?

With mounting trepidation Laura set out that evening in the carriage to attend Lady Clifton's ball.

She was nervous. So far Matt had passed every inspection with credit. But gossip thrived among the people they would meet tonight. They must be doubly on their guard, and that meant that she and Matt would have to play the ardent lovers to perfection. It was disconcerting how easy she was now finding that role. Constantly she forced herself to remember the circumstances which had brought about their marriage.

As they waited in the doorway of a packed ballroom, lit with a hundred candles, the strain of the evening was already beginning to tell on Laura. She cast an anxious glance at Matt. Dressed in burgundy velvet and a long, curling wig, he cut a handsome and imposing figure. Her heart fluttered with pride. No woman here would question that she had married for love.

Sensing her nervousness, Matt returned her stare, and his full lips lifted in a smile. His gaze was ardent as it caressed her slender figure in her oyster silk gown.

"You look beautiful, my dear," he said, raising her fingers to kiss them.

"Mr and Mrs Matthew Thorne," the major-domo announced in pompous tones.

Immediately a hush fell upon the gathering. The rustle of brightly coloured silk and taffeta skirts was the only sound as the ladies turned to scrutinise the couple whose marriage had made them notorious.

Lady Clifton, in a tall lace head-dress *à la Fontage,* stooped to offer Laura her powdered and patched cheek. Beaming proudly, she held out a plump hand for Matt to raise to his lips.

"Such a charming couple," Lady Clifton declared for all to hear. "Let no one here think romance is dead. They are perfect together. Perfect."

Laura blushed. Lady Clifton meant well, but Laura had longed to slip in among the gathering unnoticed. The Brigadier's wife had not finished yet. Taking Matt's hand, Lady Clifton smiled triumphantly.

"The musicians are about to play. I shall make every woman here pink with jealousy by opening the dance with the most handsome man in the room."

"Hmmph!" Lord Clifton grunted, and bowed to Laura. "Then I shall open the dancing with the most ravishing woman present."

At a nod in the direction of the musicians' gallery from the Brigadier the music struck up a slow and stately pavane, and Laura was marched on to the dance-floor. Lord Clifton was short in stature, and in recent years had acquired a vast girth, but he was surprisingly light on his feet and an accomplished dancer. As Laura performed the sedate movements her glance kept straying to Matt, anxious that he should conduct himself well. She need not have feared. Dressed as elegantly as any courtier present, he carried himself with prepossessing grace which set him apart from the foppish courtiers. He danced superbly, and from the number of times Lady Clifton's booming laugh erupted he was proving a charming companion.

"He's not going to run off without you," the Brigadier said with a laugh. "You can't keep your eyes from that husband of yours. Neither can he drag his gaze from you for more than a moment or two. It's positively indecent. So this tale of a love-match is true?"

Laura smiled. "Why should it not be?"

He looked at her soberly. "I've known you since you were no taller than a greyhound. I've never known you to be secretive, Laura. You've made an enemy of that cousin of yours."

"I shall not miss his false affection," she answered crisply.

"There never was any love lost between your families. A pity. Your father would have…" His heavy-set face clouded with sadness. "No good bringing up what might have been. Charles Stanton is sadly missed."

Laura bowed her head to hide her resurging grief. "Yes, he is."

"Hmmph! Clumsy of me to have mentioned Charles." The Brigadier looked awkward. Men quaked at the thought of earning his displeasure on the parade ground, but in a woman's company he was nervous and uneasy. "Thorne looks a good man. I hope you will be happy, my dear."

The dance had come to an end. She smiled at Matt, who was returning to her side. Before he reached her, he was surrounded by a dozen women, bombarding him with questions. He smiled and appeared at ease, parrying their curiosity with a wit which set them fluttering their fans and laughing. Laura was about to hurry to his rescue when an acquaintance of her grandfather's asked her to dance.

Partner followed partner without her being able to return to Matt. Three times she saw him lead an elderly matron on to the floor, and each time the woman at his side was visibly captivated by his company. It set a glow of pride in Laura's breast to hear him praised. He looked so devastatingly handsome that she found it difficult to keep her eyes off him. A stab uncomfortably close to jealousy pierced her. They had been here an hour, and she had not danced with her husband once. Her smile was strained as she accepted another dance from one of her grandfather's acquaintances, unaware of the longing in her gaze as it rested upon Matt. He was not dancing but standing next to Lady Clifton. Although he appeared attentive to his hostess, his gaze followed her around the room. Every time their stares met he smiled, and a pleasurable warmth expanded through Laura.

"Ah, what it is to be young and in love," her partner, an elderly statesman, said fondly.

His words, which had been repeated so often by other partners that evening, nagged at Laura's conscience. It had become so natural to play the adoring wife that at times she found if difficult to drag her gaze from him whenever he was in the room. That disturbed her. His image was too often invading her thoughts and reaching out from the darkness to mock her dreams. For a man who purported to despise her class, he fitted so well into its society that it was obvious that he was born to it. He was an enigma, and that was dangerous. The mystery surrounding him tantalised her peace of mind, and he filled her thoughts as no man had done before.

The next dance brought them briefly together as their partners completed a set measure. Matt winked at her, and as the dance took him past her he reached for her hand and raised it to his lips. It caused a stir of hushed whispers from the matrons seated behind them. The stir grew to a buzz as the dance ended and, with the briefest of bows to his partner, Matt strode across the floor.

He fixed a midnight stare on the pompous young captain who had been about to escort Laura into the salon where refreshments had been laid out. "I've been parted from my wife for an hour," he interrupted with chill politeness. "It's my privilege alone to lead her in to dine."

He whisked Laura away as the red-faced captain stammered a feeble protest. Laura laughed. "Oh, Matt, that was unpardonably rude."

"I've had enough of inane and polite conversation. I needed to regenerate myself on your barbed wit." His dark eyes were teasing. "Besides, I believe I've mangled enough matrons' toes for one evening."

"They adored dancing with you. Why did you only dance with the older matrons? Didn't any younger woman take your eye?"

"There's only one woman I wished to dance with. She was occupied with a dozen partners. When that chinless officer was about to lead you in to dine I was prepared to challenge the fop to a duel to win your company."

She knew his words were just banter, but her heart thrilled to them all the same. A soft laugh rippled from her throat and her eyes sparkled.

"You are even more beautiful when you laugh," he said softly as he led her to a seat in a secluded arbour in the salon.

She looked up at him through her lashes, and the

tenderness she saw in his eyes made her heart snatch. Deliberately, she hardened herself. "There is no one to overhear you, Matt. Save your compliments."

Frost glittered in his eyes, turning his gaze to a winter bleakness. "As you will, madam." The quiet tone of voice was clipped with reproach which brought a flush of heat to her cheeks. He took two goblets of wine from a passing footman, his expression shuttered as he handed one to Laura.

Laura ignored the overpowering masculinity of her husband's figure as he lowered himself beside her. He raised his goblet in salute to her, his full lips smiling for the benefit of any watching guest. Only she could see the coldness in his stare. It coated her skin with ice. But wasn't that what she wanted? To put distance between them?

Aware that curious glances were upon them, Laura forced a bright smile. The cautious side of her nature scented danger, but the wilful, passionate woman within whispered against all warnings. She opened her fan to shield her lower face and leaned provocatively towards Matt. "You haven't danced with me all evening."

"I am your servant, madam."

"No, Matt, you are your own man," she said, gazing intently into his guarded eyes. "You play your role perfectly—sometimes too perfectly. I don't understand you."

He curled his fingers around her hand and looked at her across the top of her fan. "I'm just a man like any other, but I won't be bought."

"I value that. Though it probably goes against my interests."

"Then there is hope for you yet."

The tenderness in his smile filled her with a glowing aura of warmth. She laughed. "There's a brutal honesty to your mockery. I never know when to take you seriously. You are different from any man I have ever met."

"And how many debtors have you rescued from prison and married before?"

"That wasn't what I meant." She saw the amusement in his eyes and retaliated in exasperation, "Don't humour me as though I am a child!"

His gaze lowered to the emerald necklace she had pledged to pay his debts. The largest emerald surrounded by diamonds twinkled between her creamy breasts. Her breath suspended as desire smouldered in his bronze eyes and they were raised to hold her stare. "You are all woman, Laura. But you play with fire like a child, too innocent to know the danger."

He nodded towards the ballroom, where the violins were playing the opening chords of another dance. He stood and bowed to her. "Our audience awaits us, my dear." His voice again held an undercurrent of tension. "There are another two hours for us to perform for their delectation before we can leave."

Laura placed her hand over his and cast a speculative look at his swarthy features. There was a brooding shadow in his eyes she could not decipher. He was gazing at her, his expression attentive, but it seemed that his thoughts were hounded by a dark spectre.

She must stop dwelling upon the mystery of Matt's past life. She had no claim on him. In a few weeks they would part, never to meet again.

Matt led Laura on to the dance-floor. He had learned news this afternoon which was disturbing. He was bound to honour his agreement with Laura, yet his need to be avenged upon Sir James Breten had become an obsession.

The seductive perfume used by Laura filled his senses as they moved together in the formal dance. Beneath his hand he could feel the rapid beat of her pulse and was aware of the shallowness in her breathing each time the dance took her under his arm and their eyes would meet and smile. Her beauty had always stirred him and the proximity into which they were thrown had become a torture. With each day that his desire was thwarted, its flame burned more fiercely. But Laura Stanton was no light of love he could possess and then discard.

His future was set. Sir James Breten must pay for his crimes. That was what had driven him on through the years since Susannah's death. He had puzzled over why the man had such a vendetta against his family. He was nothing to Sir James Breten. Or was there more behind Susannah's death, which he feared Matt would discover? Was that why he had been persecuted? In prison he could have done nothing. The vast sum of his debt had ensured that he would have remained there until he died. Sir James Breten had thought himself safe. So what had the powerful baron, a member of the Privy Council, to fear being exposed, and how had Susannah been a part of it? That had to be the link, and Matt was determined to discover its roots.

He thrust thoughts of Sir James Breten out of his mind. Unexpectedly he was enjoying this evening, especially having Laura so teasing and seductive in his arms. Yet even as his body responded to the allure of his wife's enticing form, Matt knew that Laura was forever out of his reach.

His pride rebelled. Having purchased his freedom from a debtor's prison, how could Laura ever regard him as her equal? He felt hot and overdressed in his periwig and long embroidered waistcoat and velvet jacket. This life was not freedom; it was another form of captivity. He longed to feel the cool sea-breezes in his own hair. To kick off his fashionable heeled shoes and stride across an open deck in his comfortable old boots. He missed his ship, the *Sea Maiden.* The golden-haired figurehead had been specially carved in Susannah's image. There was no other ship which handled like her. His heart had died with Susannah's and Rachel's deaths. If he had loved anything in the intervening years it was the *Sea Maiden;* James Breten must pay for all he had taken from him.

Again the scent of Laura's skin and the exotic perfume she used enmeshed his senses. Laura was so graceful...so beautiful...so spirited... It was so easy to be captivated by her and believe that he could learn to love again. Love! How could that thought come to him? He loved Susannah. He couldn't fall in love with Laura Stanton. They were too different...used to different worlds with different values. She would not accept the life of sea-captain's wife in a small house at Plymouth or Bristol, and he could not live in the shadow of her wealth. Fairfield had brought them together. But Fairfield would forever keep them apart.

Why, then, was he tormented by the fragrance of her, which clung to him like a mantle? Even the touch of her hand evoked memories of her silken body, warm and supplicant, awaiting initiation in his arms. His eyes were grim beneath lowered lashes. She was looking at him again now, in a way which could make a man forget honour. In her eyes blazed a beguiling fire, challenging him to master her.

Tension coiled through his body as he battled against the temptation to make her truly his. It would not change their backgrounds. She could never fit into his world and he despised hers too much to live within it.

His mind was jolted back to the present as he heard a sharp intake of breath from Laura. Her face was paled but her chin was defiantly high, and beneath the thick fringe of her lashes her eyes glittered. He felt her tremble and her hand clenched tight about his.

"Guy is here," she whispered as they crossed in the dance. "He's with Hal Clifton, Lord Clifton's nephew. He must have heard we were invited."

"He can do nothing among company," Matt reassured her.

"You don't know Guy. And from the look of it he's already in his cups." A soft groan escaped her and her nails inadvertently dug into Matt's palm. "He's brought his rake-hell companions. The three men behind him. They are all dissolute wastrels. They roam the streets in the early hours, drunken and abusive, shouting and disturbing the sleep of respectable citizens. Twice they have tied up the watch. A constable who tried to restrain them was dragged unconscious to London Bridge and thrown into the Thames. Fortunately the icy water revived him and a waterman, hearing his shouts, dragged him from the water before he drowned."

There was a perceptible pause in the conversation of the guests. Laura stiffened, realising that many eyes were on herself and her cousin. Guy was standing in the centre of his companions, glaring across the room at her. Laura returned his stare and, refusing to add fuel to the gossip already surrounding her marriage, she forced a brittle smile and inclined her head in acknowledgement of her cousin's presence.

Typical of Guy, he turned on his heel, rudely ignoring her. He whispered something to his companions, who sniggered maliciously as they departed to the room where the gaming-tables were set up.

Matt tensed with anger and his eyes narrowed to dangerous slits as he stared at her cousin's back. The dance had ended and Matt's arm was possessive about her waist as he stooped to murmur in her ear, "Don't allow your cousin to upset you."

"You don't know how unpleasant he can be," she answered as they moved to stand by an open door leading on to the terrace.

"I know his kind."

The wintry night air was cold after their exertions, but it was the hatred in Matt's eyes which chilled Laura.

"Do you hate all our class so much?" she asked. "Do you hate me for making you a part of this?"

The corners of his mouth twitched and his voice softened as he spoke. "I don't hate you, Laura, just what you represent."

"I cannot change what I am, Matt." Her heart hammered wildly at the gentleness of his tone and an odd tingling sensation swept over her at the thoughtful way he was regarding her.

A frown darkened his brow as Lord Clifton approached them.

"Laura, my dear, I have an old friend to introduce

you to. He knew your father, but he's not very often in London. You'll excuse us, Thorne?''

As Laura was led away she cast a regretful look over her shoulder at Matt. He was watching gravely, and there was something profound in the intensity of his stare which made her heart pound with excitement.

A man of medium height and of some fifty years stood at Lady Clifton's side. He was distinguished-looking in a light brown periwig and gold brocade jacket and breeches. A thin moustache gave the impression of a sneer and there was unmistakable arrogance in his brown eyes. As she approached Laura found herself scrutinised by a stare which bordered upon rudeness. A shudder sped down her spine. She did not like this haughty man.

''Laura allow me to introduce...'' Lord Clifton began.

''I will introduce myself while we dance.'' Without waiting for Laura's acceptance, the stranger took her hand.

Laura complied, so as not to make a scene in front of her host and hostess, but inwardly she was seething at his high-handed manner.

''I greatly admired your father,'' he said smoothly and, as though sensing Laura's antagonism, his manner changed. ''Your pardon, Mrs Thorne. I must have appeared very rude commandeering you that way.'' He smiled. It was the smile of a man used to disarming women with ease. Usually Laura had no time for obvious womanisers, but there was something in his manner which, despite her reserve, began to thaw her coldness towards him.

"Charles Stanton was a brilliant soldier and a great statesman."

"Were you close to my father? I met many of his acquaintances when I stayed in London. I do not believe we have been introduced before."

"My duties at Court and in Parliament give me little time for a social life. You could say that your father and I were rivals. Rivals for power within the Privy Council."

The dance took them apart, and as Laura completed a measure she studied her partner covertly. He had a dignified bearing and she suspected that many women had fallen for his smooth charm.

"Your marriage is the talk of London," he said as they came together. "And rather unusual in the circumstances, was it not?"

"What is so unusual about a love-match?"

"That depends where one met and how quickly the marriage took place."

There was an edge to his voice which alerted every nerve in Laura's body to danger.

"Really, sir, that is none of your affair."

"Is it not?" The words were delivered with such silvery slickness that Laura's alarm grew. "I would like to meet your husband."

"He is over there." Laura had just noticed Matt's return to the ballroom and on his arm was the blonde and vivacious Mary Montgomery, a woman reputed to have bedded over a hundred lovers during her five-year marriage to the ancient Sir Humphrey Montgomery. Matt was laughing at something Mary had said, and from the way the woman was clinging so ardently to his arm it was obvious that she was making a play to win him as her lover.

Jealousy speared Laura. It was so intense that it even overrode her fears at what her partner had implied about her marriage. Suddenly she realised she still did not know the man's name. She was about to ask him when she saw Matt halt in mid-stride. He disengaged his arm from Mary Montgomery's hold and stood rigid.

Mary Montgomery, affronted by Matt's abrupt dismissal, laughed shrilly, and Laura saw the cold calculation in the woman's eyes. Her smile was false as she called out, "Laura, you must not neglect your handsome husband, or you may find you have rivals for his favours."

Laura ignored the challenge in the older woman's voice; she was more concerned at the change in Matt's manner as he walked towards her. The fury in his eyes as they rested on her partner turned Laura's blood cold.

"Matt," she said softly. "This gentleman expressly asked to meet you. May I introduce...?" She faltered at the glittering hatred in Matt's eyes. "I'm afraid I do not know his name."

"We need no introduction," the stranger at her side declared. To her increasing alarm she sensed that the man was enjoying the tension he was creating. "This marriage will not save you, Thorne," he announced.

"We have unsettled business," Matt rapped out.

"Not if you wish to avoid a scandal." The older man's stare slid insultingly over Laura's tense figure.

The stranger turned on his heel to leave. Matt was faster, but he took great care not to touch the man as he side-stepped to prevent his departure.

"This is between us and no one else," Matt whispered fiercely. His face was stiff with suppressed fury.

"The mistake was yours in believing you could seek to destroy all I value and escape retribution."

"Stay out of my life, Thorne, or you'll regret it. I make a dangerous enemy, and even your marriage to Stanton's granddaughter will not save you."

The words were equally low and threatening. The stranger marched off without a backward glance, pausing only briefly on the far side of the room to bid a goodnight to Lord and Lady Clifton before he left.

Laura could feel anger and tension vibrating through Matt. "What outrageous behaviour." She tried to make light of the matter.

Beneath his tan Matt's cheeks had paled. He took her arm and led her away from curious glances.

"What did he say to you?" he demanded.

"Like everyone else he was probing about our marriage. He said he knew my father. Who is he, Matt?"

Matt's lips thinned to a dangerous line, but he did not answer.

"What's wrong? I've never seen you look this way."

He shuddered, then his lips stretched into a parody of a smile. "He is no one you need trouble yourself over. We are old adversaries."

"Over the matter of your debt," she said, with a flash of insight. "Then it is he who should be arrested. He has abused his position of power. The Lord High Sheriff is here. He is a friend of my grandfather's. He will have the rogue arrested even if he is a member of the Privy Council."

"I don't want you interfering, Laura." Matt scowled blackly. "This is my affair and I will deal with Sir James Breten in my own way."

The bleakness of his tone resurrected the barriers

between them. She could feel people's curious gazes upon them and fought to contain her anger that he could shut her out so entirely from his life. Remembering her role, she placed a hand on his chest. "This is not the time to discuss such a matter. We are being watched. That scowl of yours will delight Guy and his cronies. They will think that we are quarrelling."

Matt nodded grimly. "I don't want this to rebound on you."

She sighed at his obstinacy. "You've helped me in my most desperate hour. Grandfather has influence and friends. They will clear your name."

"I will clear my own name and in my own way," he said with a quietness which unnerved her. "I don't need a woman meddling in my affairs."

"I would like to think I could help you as a friend." She mastered her anger, intuition warning her that Matt was in real danger from the stranger she had danced with.

"Don't look at me that way, Laura," he said tautly.

Sensing that he was deliberately turning the conversation, she persisted. "I don't understand."

He smiled mockingly. "You're too accomplished an actress at playing the enamoured lover." He evaded the question in her eyes and his expression softened in a way which made her heart thud erratically. "When you become so defensive of myself I want to…" He stopped and laughed derisively.

"You want to do what?" she could not stop herself asking.

The teasing taunt was enough for Matt to cast aside good intent. It was the excuse he needed to stop her asking awkward questions. All evening he had been unable to keep his eyes from her. He wanted her.

Most of all he wanted to erase the teasing in her eyes that denied she did not want him. A glance over her head at the noisy, chatting guests showed him that for once they were unobserved.

For a second a pulse throbbed along his jaw, then devilment brightened his eyes. With a grin he took her hand. "Come."

He drew her outside on to the terrace and pulled her behind an ornamental shrub which shielded them from prying eyes. The light from the windows lit the terrace and for what seemed an eternity they held each other's stare.

Passion, roused slowly, set the blood in Laura's veins pulsing, and tingling sparks prickled through her body. She could not drag her gaze from his. His expression was taut, dominant, the ardour in his hooded eyes kindling a need to be held in his embrace which had been building all evening. Her heart pounded, and as he took her face into his hands her lips were tremulous with wanting, but she knew she should reject his kiss. The touch of his mouth was gentle, his tongue tracing the outline of her mouth.

"Stop!" she moaned in a last attempt to stem the tide of emotion which threatened to overwhelm her. Speech had parted her lips, giving entrance to his tongue. His supple mouth became hard and passionate, his tongue tasting the freshness of her breath and setting her senses in turmoil. Her hands were on his chest, spreading out to feel the masculine strength that was commanding her surrender.

The fierceness of the longing roused by his kiss destroyed her will to resist. An aching throb pulsated deep within her, expanding into a volcanic heat which spread through trembling limbs. His kiss deepened, the sensuous touch of his tongue igniting emotions which neither could deny. She clung to him as the floodtide of ecstatic sensations spread through her. Their bodies melded together, arms locked tight in a fervent embrace. Laura's body glowed with an exquisite urgency, a hunger awakened that shattered resistance. She instinctively moved her hips against him. The sharp intake of his breath was captured by her lips, soft and pliable beneath the demanding passion of his own.

Laura made no protest when his mouth moved down her throat, his hands taking her breast through the material of her gown. When he touched the hardened nipple with a circling motion of his fingers, her moan broke from deep in her throat. She could not believe the aching desire which pervaded her entire being, making her legs weak and her mind abandon any thought that was not centred on him and the sensual world he was creating.

Lost to the abandonment of his kiss, Laura became light-headed, until at last she was forced to break the contact of their lips and draw a steadying breath. Held fast in his tender embrace, she gradually became aware of voices on the terrace. She pulled back from Matt, so shaken by the emotions still enslaving her that she laid her temple against his chest. The hard pumping of his heart echoed the frantic race of her own.

"We must go back inside," Matt said quietly.

Laura tensed. Was this all a game to him? Was he deliberately toying with her emotions to teach her a lesson in some way?

"What's wrong, Laura?"

"Me. You," she replied bitterly. "Everything. Especially the roles we are forced to play."

"Where was the forcing just now?" he said heatedly.

She felt his anger pierce her breast like a flaming arrow. She did not answer. How could she when his words were so uncomfortably close to the truth? She shook her head. He looked so fierce, so remote from her. How could she tell him that she ached to be back in his arms? The knowledge shocked her. If only he hadn't been so scathing in his hatred of her class, or professed so ardently that he still loved his dead wife. If only she could believe that the tenderness in his eyes was not an act. Or that he felt something other than base desire for her.

"You did not force me, Matthew," she said, so softly that he had to lean closer to hear as he escorted her back to the ballroom. "But it is just an illusion, is it not? It is transient."

"As you will, madam, so will it be."

Gazing at his sardonic profile, she fought back the warning prickle of tears and her throat clenched. Pride became her saviour. She patted a loose auburn ringlet back into place and pinned a bright smile on to the rigid muscles of her face. He must never guess how close she had come to wanting to surrender.

Her footsteps faltered upon entering the ballroom and seeing who lay in wait. There was a malicious smile on her cousin's face as he watched them approach. Behind Guy's bullying figure stood three of his companions; their faces were flushed and malignant and their bodies swayed, betraying their intoxication.

Guy moved to bar their passage. Laura felt Matt

stiffen at her side and her fingers tightened over his arm, warning him to do nothing rash.

"Ah, the devoted couple," Guy sneered, his ferret's gaze missing no detail of Matt's rich attire. "Since your marriage you've acquired quite a wardrobe, Thorne. Not a day passes without the tailor visiting Stanton House, his assistants laden with parcels. Then there was the acquisition of a superb gelding. You don't hesitate to spend your wife's money, do you?"

Matt stepped forward, his face taut and his fists bunched. Laura intervened rapidly. "The gelding was my wedding-present to Matt. If your spies have informed you correctly, you will know that the seamstress has also called daily on my account. Neither Matt nor myself had originally planned to spend so long in London and be invited to attend so many social engagements. Then, of course…" she paused and smiled adoringly up at Matt's dark countenance, her agile mind forming another excuse "…once grandfather is fully recovered, it is likely that we will be travelling to Paris, and on to Vienna and Rome in the spring. We wish to be attired accordingly. But that really is none of your business, Guy."

"Being cheated out of what is rightly mine is very much my business." Guy's grating voice was steadily rising. "Lionel Stanton is old. Who knows when a relapse may occur? I've heard some strange things about this marriage and I don't intend to let the matter rest."

Laura forced herself to remain calm but her skin burned, feeling the curious stares of all turning upon them. Guy stuck his head forward like a bull preparing to charge. His small eyes glittered with vengeance as he glared at Matt. "You're a man with little history I can trace. You're not what you seem, Thorne."

"Gentlemen!" Lord Clifton placed himself between the two antagonistic men. "This is most unseemly. I must ask you to desist in this abuse. You are upsetting my guests." He turned to Guy. "You came as a guest of my nephew and I would ask you and your companions to leave without further trouble."

Blood suffused Guy's face. "I'm the one who's been wronged. This man's a scoundrel and not fit to grace decent society. He's a fortune-hunter."

Laura heard Matt suck in his breath, and as she held his arm to restrain him she felt the muscles harden with the force of his anger.

"You're cupshot, Guy," she said contemptuously. "Fairfield is not yours; it is mine. And my husband is not the fortune-hunter in this room. You are."

Lord Clifton eyed Guy sourly. "Will you leave quietly, or must I have you thrown out?"

Guy swallowed, his glare vitriolic. "I'm leaving." He turned on Laura a look of such hatred that she involuntarily flinched and leaned closer to the protection of Matt's figure. "You had better pray you've borne a son before Lionel is in his grave. That's the only way you'll keep Fairfield for certain. My father still has powerful friends. I want Fairfield." His eyes glazed with a fervour which filled Laura with dread and his voice lowered to a whisper. "Fairfield will be mine! By whatever means it takes."

Chapter Eight

A child.

A son for Fairfield.

It was the only way to ensure that Guy Stanton did not inherit her home.

The statements revolved through Laura's mind on the carriage ride home from Clifton House. But to save Fairfield by such drastic measures—what would be the price? Surrender to her husband. That would be far from a penance. Her cheeks flushed and her limbs tingled at the thought and she was glad of the darkness within the carriage. Since leaving the ball Matt had withdrawn into his own thoughts. He had been deeply affected by meeting Sir James Breten and the confrontation with her cousin. Even though they sat in silence, both absorbed with their own problems, Laura was acutely aware of her husband's presence.

When the carriage swung round a corner she was thrown against his figure, her breast and thigh prickling with sensation. She closed her eyes to combat the frantic racing of her blood. It would be no hardship to honour all her marriage rites and conceive Matt's child. Yet Matt did not love her, and she certainly did

not love him. The enforced companionship and intimacy of their arranged marriage was affecting her,
making her aware of a man as she had never been
before. He had roused her passion, shown her that she
was capable of desire, but most harrowing of all was
the knowledge that it was him she wanted to initiate
her into its little secrets.

Once consummated, her marriage could never be
annulled, a dark voice reasoned. Her fingers locked
together until her knuckles cracked. Why was forbidden fruit always the greatest temptation?

Nothing in her upbringing had prepared her for
this. Gentlewomen were expected to be virtuous mod-
els of decorum and respectable pillars of the community. But when had she ever been able to endure
the constraints placed on gentlewomen? Minor acts of
rebellion and misdeeds had followed her through her
youth. As a young woman she had ridden the countryside unchaperoned, which had scandalised the local
matrons in Essex. She never hesitated to speak her
mind and was not afraid to tell a man when he was
acting in a high-handed manner, or with little regard
to the welfare of servants or the poorer classes.
Women were expected to bow in silence to the judgement of their menfolk. Submissiveness was not
Laura's way.

She could not deny the wild pounding of her heart.
Was not Matt her husband? Why should she not
yield? A sigh escaped her and she pressed her fingers
to her temple. Such reasoning was madness; her future was not with Matt. But the frantic racing of her
pulses would not be stilled. Excitement and temptation lured her; a deep subconscious knowledge glo-
ried in what destiny decided would be inevitable.

A warm hand took her icy fingers. "It's been quite a night, Laura."

"We both have enemies," she said brokenly, desperate to shake off the sense of foreboding which had settled over her. "I'm not going to be intimidated by Guy's threats."

"That's my woman."

The warmth in his voice destroyed her fragile hold on her composure. As they alighted and entered her grandfather's house the future loomed as dark and menacing as a bottomless chasm. Despair crushed her spirit. The strain of the evening and the charged emotions—one moment euphoria in Matt's arms, the next stark fear at all she could lose—overwhelmed her. Matt had paused to speak with Jedediah and Laura hurried to her room. She was pacing in agitation, her oyster silk gown rustling as it swirled cloud-like around her at each furious turn. Hearing Matt enter, she continued her pacing, and pulled the pins from her hair to ease the tension of its high-piled tresses, shaking the auburn locks free so that they unfurled over her shoulders to her waist. Her eyes were dark as sapphires, the pupils widely dilated, and her lips were moist and parted as she drew each fractured breath.

"I'm going to lose Fairfield." She clenched her fist in impotent fury. "Guy will not rest until he has it in his clutches."

"You won't lose Fairfield. You've come too far for that to happen." Matt stood by the fireplace, watching her. When her agitated movements took her past him he reached out and, taking her arm, drew her towards him. "This isn't like you, Laura. You're a fighter. Guy won't win. Haven't you right on your side?''

"Have I?" Her voice was tortured. "What of the web of deceit and lies I've woven thus far to keep Fairfield? Perhaps I'm as bad as he is.''

The firelight flickered over his face, deepening the hollows of its contours, and his eyes glittered like jet. "At least your motives were for the good of the people of Fairfield, not just for its wealth.'' He took her chin between his fingers, forcing her to hold his penetrating stare.

Matt heard the snatch in her breath, his gaze drawn to her parted lips which seemed to be begging him to kiss them. Did she know the effect she had upon him? He wanted her. God, how he wanted her! Was she using her wiles to ensure that she kept his protection?

"I'm not going to desert you while you need me, Laura. Guy Stanton can do nothing while we remain together.''

"You have honoured our bargain," she replied, fighting the tears that glistened in her eyes. "You have your own life to lead, Matt.''

That she did not plead with him to stay rankled. Why was she so stubborn? And so independent!

"Do you want me to stay, Laura?''

"Of course." Her voice broke and her defiance crumpled. "I'm out of my depth, Matt. The lies and deceit are stifling me. I don't want to live a lie.''

Her honesty shattered Matt's reserve. His willpower was stretched to its limit to control his senses, which were in tumult at her nearness. Her eyes were soft and beguiling, their colour deepened by fear and also the inner struggle she was exerting against her aroused sensuality. He wanted to kiss her until she was trembling and her eyes heavy-lidded with passion. The sudden surging of desire was so powerful that it shredded his will. He craved to hold her naked in his arms while he discovered all the wonderful mysteries of her body which he had only envisaged in his dreams.

"We are bound by more than a piece of paper." His hand slid along her jaw to rest each side of her face and he stared deep into her eyes.

She swallowed, appearing to capitulate for a moment, then a change came over her expression, guarding her thoughts from him. "Sir James Breten has a vendetta against you. You don't need Guy as your enemy as well."

"I can handle Breten and your cousin. Fairfield will be yours."

"It is no longer enough. I want a child to ensure that Fairfield stays in my family." As she spoke she spread her hands across his broad chest.

Golden sparks of anger flashed in his bronze eyes. Good God, did the woman know no shame? He desired her, but a child was not part of their bargain. His future was not at Fairfield. He'd lost one child and he still grieved for his bonny, merry daughter. To father another and never be able to watch it grow to adulthood was beyond enduring.

His lips curled back in disdain. "For a time I began to believe you were different from the class which always seek to manipulate others. You'll stop at nothing to achieve your ends, will you? What manner of creature are you? You'd condemn a child to a fatherless existence with no thought of its needs, but only to satisfy your own selfish aims."

His voice was like needles pricking into her heart.

"My son would inherit Fairfield," she retaliated, hiding her hurt by defiance.

"And a life without love."

At the contempt which darkened his swarthy face Laura reeled with shock. "I'd love my own child!"

"Are you sure it would not be just another piece of property to you?" he raged. "The means to secure Fairfield?"

She struck his face without thinking, her palm stinging from the force of her anger. He caught her wrist, his eyes sparking with fury.

"Now I see the true Laura Stanton." That lethally quiet voice flayed her. "The soft seductress offering herself with such innocent enticement is an image as false as your lying tongue."

Matt released her hand and stepped back. She was staring at him with a shocked expression, her beauty enhanced by the pallor of her face, her blue eyes signalling anger—or could it be pain? He would not believe it was pain. The need to possess her flared like a forest fire and he was perilously close to losing control. He turned away. He dared not look at her. A single touch would fan the inferno he was battling to keep in check.

"You wrong me, Matt." The whisper reached him. Then the seductive rustle of silk told him that she had entered her dressing-room.

The thought of sharing the room with Laura for another night was intolerable. Tearing off his velvet jacket and long embroidered waistcoat, he took a plain green broadcloth jacket from his clothes press. His periwig was thrown around its stand and he paused only to push his fingers through his shoulder-length hair before the door banged behind his departing figure. The taverns on the dockside beckoned. There at least the doxies were without deceit in offering their favours, and he could shrug off the irksome graces he had adopted and enjoy a drink with a humble sailor. Even the company of cut-throats and sneak-thiefs would seem refreshingly honest after the sly intrigue and petty vendettas of the gentry.

Horror. Dark, cloaking horror gripped the silent spectator. Destiny mocked. The wheel of fortune had turned, revealing the bottomless pit of terror. It coated skin in a freezing sweat. It clogged the senses so that breathing was fractured in tortured gasps. Through a widening tunnel of darkness rose a scarlet sunrise. Black shapes became visible, setting a mind screaming in hysterical denial. The hangman's noose was silhouetted black and menacing against the blood-red sky.

A figure in black breeches and white shirt materialised to mount the scaffold. The man's features were shaded as he stood beneath the triangular wooden structure on the platform of Tyburn's gallows. The jeers of the crowd deafened like thunder.

Quaking shivers invaded limbs already manacled by terror. Another figure, a woman dressed in virginal white, was led to the man's side. The menacing shadow of the noose fell across her bowed features. The spectator became the woman on the scaffold and her body was doused by icy terror which turned her knees to pulp and she staggered.

"Courage," a voice taunted. "Our destiny awaits us."

The chanting of the crowd became a death-knell. The burly, hooded hangman stepped forward, and as he placed the noose around the man's neck he tore off the hood and looked at the woman. A soundless scream scratched at frozen vocal cords. Guy Stanton was laughing evilly into Laura's face...

With a sob Laura came awake. Her heart was pumping wildly and her body was wet with sweat. She lifted a shaking hand to sweep her auburn hair from her face and drew in several long, steadying breaths. It was the third time she had had that dream during the night. Did it portend the future? Her stomach churned with nausea. Was it a warning that Guy wanted her and Matt dead? He was cruel and vindictive, but was he capable of murder to gain his own ends? Guy was certainly capable of arranging a convenient accident to kill Matt and herself and thereby become the heir to Fairfield.

The sound of splashing water and muffled male voices coming from the ante-room told Laura that the servants were filling her bath, though she could not remember ordering one. A hot, relaxing bath would dispel her fears. Above the sound of water being poured into the tub she discerned the steady drum of torrential rain on the window-panes. Another miserable wet day ahead.

In the dim morning light she could see that the pillows and cover she had placed on the day-bed had not been slept on. Her heart sank. Matt had not returned last night.

What a fool she'd been to antagonise him. So much depended on his goodwill. She lay for a moment, her head buzzing with the events of last evening. She had better rise and put away the covers and pillows before Sarah entered her room. Things could not continue as they were. It was her own fault that she was in this mess. Matt had only honoured their bargain. Her problems were not his problems.

The outer ante-room door clicked shut and then she heard the footmen who had finished filling her bath chatting as they walked along the corridor to the servants' stairs at the back of the house. She sat up, suddenly resolved. The deception must end. She would release Matt from his bargain. It was too late now to visit the priest at the Fleet and have all records of her marriage struck from the register. Her marriage was legal. She would accept the role of deserted wife, retire to Fairfield and live in seclusion. There would be no child, but at least Matt would be free of the danger from Guy.

Rising from the bed, she quickly threw the covers on the day-bed back on to the four-poster and, in her flimsy-nightgown, hurried to take her bath. In her haste she pulled the silk over her head as she entered the ante-room. As her head emerged from the folds she gasped with shock, and clutched the garment against her naked body.

"Such solicitation," Matt chuckled as he lay back in the water, watching her. "I had not expected my wife to join me, but the tub is large and my back is in need of a good scrub."

She backed away, conscious of her own nakedness and of the vast expanse of his bare chest with its manly spread of hair across the hard muscles. Once through the door she pulled the nightgown back over her head.

"Laura, would you pass me the soap?" Matt called.

"Get it yourself. It's on the side-coffer."

"I can't see it. Would you ring for a servant?" His

voice was smooth, too smooth for Laura's peace of mind. "Perhaps your maid would be more accommodating."

Exasperated at realising she could hardly summon a servant to hand her husband a bar of soap, she returned to the ante-room and picked a bar of sandalwood soap from the dish on the table. Keeping her eyes fixed on a small painting of an Italian landscape, she held it out to him. Her hand was grabbed and she was impelled to stare into his teasing bronze eyes.

"I could do with my back being washed," he suggested. "Or perhaps you would prefer that I call a servant? A pity, though; they're bound to question the scars which have not yet faded."

"What does it matter now?" she replied wearily. "Soon the scandal of my marriage will be common gossip. You can leave whenever you wish, Matt. No more lies—no more deceit. Our marriage was a mistake, but I won't tie you to a woman you despise. I shall consult my grandfather's lawyer to see how it can be annulled. At least our marriage got an innocent man out of prison, so some good came of it."

"Pigheaded to the end," Matt taunted, showing none of his previous anger. "I did not have to agree to our marriage. All is not yet lost." He smiled. "Are you going to wash my back, or must I summon a servant?"

"Give me the soap," Laura said, retrieving it.

She moved behind him and kept her gaze on the crown of his head as she lathered the soap on to the natural sponge and massaged the suds into his shoulders. She worked with a clamped jaw, her senses steeled against the warmth of his firm flesh and the heady scent of sandalwood which now permeated the water. She worked furiously, needing several rinses and massages before his skin glowed golden beneath her ministrations.

Matt clenched his teeth against the seductive play of her hands and the sponge over his flesh. He had taunted her to wash his back because he had spent a wretched night on her account. He had not stayed more than a half-hour in the tavern. The three doxies who had tried to win his attention had nauseated him. They had smelled rancid with their body odour, their hair had been lank and greasy, and their coarse voices had disgusted him. He had downed two tankards of ale before he'd realised that no amount of beer was going to ease the agony of his mind.

At first Laura's strokes had been terse and far from gentle, but after each rinsing her touch had gentled, and now each sweep of the sponge or touch of her fingers over his flesh became a sensual caress.

"Lean forward." Laura was startled by the huskiness in her voice.

Matt drew up his knees and bent his shoulders over them as she worked lower over his back, her movements becoming ever more tender as her fingers skimmed the weals of criss-cross scars. They had healed, but the deeper ones had raised swollen ridges which would take months to disappear.

Guilt assailed her. "You suffered so badly on my account. And now this business with Guy will place you in greater danger," she said hollowly. "Guy will only inherit Fairfield if we are both dead. I fear..."

"Laura, don't think that way." He gripped her hand. "Guy is a bully; his threats were meant to scare you."

"You don't know him as I do. You've kept your

side of the bargain. The marriage can be annulled. I'm going to tell Grandfather everything. He's become very fond of you. I'm sure he'd understand how desperate I was. He'll ensure you have a replacement ship for the *Sea Maiden*.'

''I want nothing from your grandfather,'' he answered harshly.

''Then take my jewels and buy a ship to enable you to sail from England. Guy meant what he said. He's capable of arranging an accident so we die.''

''Our marriage is legal, Laura. I don't run away from my enemies.'' He turned to take her wrist, drawing her round so that she stood in front of him. Bronze eyes bored into her soul and there was a faint flush of colour on his cheeks. ''But I am touched that you care, Laura.''

His dark hair snaked into curls around his neck where it was wet. He was regarding her gravely. Her gaze slid from his to linger upon the contoured muscles of his chest and arms, and the powerful strength in his thighs as he sat with his knees bent. Her free hand held the soapy sponge and she absently began to wash his arms and chest.

Her cheeks flushed as her awareness of him set her pulses racing. Matt leaned back against the rim of the tub, his eyes partially hooded as he studied her expression, and then let his gaze wander down the column of her throat and lower still to her bosom. She saw him swallow. Glancing down, she was appalled to discover that her nightgown had become splashed with water. It was now transparent, and moulded to her breasts and narrow waist.

Without warning her free hand was gripped. With

a twist of his arms and a chuckle, he pulled her off balance and she joined him in the tub.

"Oaf! Baboon! Let me go!" she fumed.

Matt's laughter echoed in the chamber as she struggled against him. His leg was clamped across her hips and the length of his body pressed intimately to hers. Matt had intended only to teach his wife a lesson by making her soap his body. He should have realised that the restraint he had put on his desire was dangerously close to breaking-point. He had wanted her for so many nights, the memories of her response to his kisses bedevilling his dreams. Now the touch of her body against his destroyed his resolve. His laughter was muffled as his mouth found the hollow of her throat and then moved to her lips, halting her stream of abuse with a kiss so profound that it robbed her of breath.

Her mouth moved beneath his, mastered by the same delicious rapture which had overtaken her at the ball last evening. Memory had not played her false; his tongue teased the velvet softness of her mouth, shattering her reservations. She was powerless to resist. Her senses were devastated once more by the expertise of his caresses as his hands moved slowly along the length of her figure. They returned with tantalising slowness to tangle in the cascading tresses of her hair. Easing her head back, he stared deep into her eyes. Her lips parted, and with a soft groan of surrender she brought her mouth down to meet his.

An unfurling tongue of heat spread through her veins and expanded to a raging inferno, making her move sinuously against him. She clung to him. Earlier fears were decimated as his skill cast everything from her mind but the euphoric pleasure and the inevitable discovery of pleasure still to unfold. Her blood coursed through her veins to the rising crescendo of her pounding heartbeat.

The water was a warm cocoon around them, lapping sensuously against their forms. Kisses were pressed against her throat and Laura closed her eyes, sighing softly as he slid the clinging nightgown from her body and tossed it on to the floor. Instinctively she tried to shield her breasts from his gaze, but he pushed her hand aside.

"I'm tired of you hiding yourself away from me," he murmured throatily. His gaze moved languorously over her full breasts, narrow waist and curved hips, like a connoisseur consigning to memory Venus's perfect form. "Your body is glorious. It was made to be kissed and caressed."

His mouth took hers once more. His caresses aroused sensations which brought sighs of pleasure from deep in her throat. Passion dispelled her embarrassment and she yielded to the magical world of sensuality that he was weaving upon her senses. She writhed against him, consumed by a hunger which seem insatiable. She could not get enough of the taste, smell and touch of him. A slow, pulsating ache rose from the core of her, intoxicating in its demands as her body revelled in the pleasure created by the play of his lips and hands. Slow caresses traversed her thighs and up to her ribcage, then skimmed across her taut belly in tantalising strokes. Her body tingled with heavenly promise as he licked droplets of water from her skin. His mouth was a subtle inducement, playing havoc with her senses, moving from her lips to the peak of her breast, which set her blood on fire.

Emboldened, she wanted to feel his body as he had

explored hers. Her fingers slid over the firm muscles of his torso, skimming lightly at first, then returning with greater pressure, wanting to know every part of him as he was likewise discovering her. When his fingers sought the moistness between her thighs she bit her lip to stop a cry of pure pleasure. Was it possible for a woman to give a man equal joy? she wondered, drugged by the power of awakened passion. Her hand moved into the water over the fine hairs on his thigh to close around the virile tumescence. He gasped and shifted higher in the water, his hand over hers stilling the movement of her fingers.

Her eyes opened and she stared into his taut face. "Does that displease you?"

He swallowed with apparent difficulty and his voice was strained. "My sweet love, it's a pleasure beyond endurance, but I would initiate you in the joys a man can bring a woman before I seek my own release." He favoured her with a crooked grin. "Besides which, I have yet to finish my bath."

In answer she searched for the soap, which had fallen from her grasp. With it firmly in her hands she reared up out of the water, her knees astride him in the large tub, and began to complete the soaping of his body. She could feel the tension building within him and her own excitement was at fever pitch by the time she had completed her task. She was about to rise from the water when he put a hand on her shoulder to stop her.

"Now it is my turn."

She thought she would swoon from the sheer pleasure of his touch as he tenderly soaped her body, lingering with tantalising provocation over her breasts, stomach and thighs. She was breathing heavily and her legs were so weak that when he rose from the water and drew her up against him she was incapable of standing.

Laughing wickedly, Matt picked up two towels and wrapped one around her before scooping her into his arms. He walked into the bedchamber and laid her reverently on the bed before drying her with such adoration that her body became a living fire of longing from her neck to her toes. In turn she performed the same task for him, devouring him with her gaze as the towel moved over his sleek body.

Again her hand was stilled, and for a long moment their gazes burned into each other's, then he slowly drew her down over him. The touch of his flesh against hers was like a lighted fuse reaching the powder-keg.

Matt clasped Laura in his arms and rolled her on to her back. He had wanted to bring her to the joy of fulfillment slowly, but the months of his abstinence were against him. The pliant softness of her body was almost his undoing. She was writhing beneath him, her body arched in response to the skilled inducement of his hands. He drew her hips up higher and gently entered her, restraining himself until his will-power was in shreds.

Her velvet heat enclosed him and she quivered. He felt her tense as he met against the resistant membrane, then it parted and he entered deep within her. He moved slowly, rhythmically, wanting her to experience the same pleasure that his own release would bring.

Laura gasped as he drove deeper, filling her. She moved to accommodate him and her legs were lifted and guided to wrap around his waist. A myriad sensations expanded, bursting like shooting stars through her entire body. She locked her arms around him, unaware that in her rapture her nails pressed into his back as she arched higher, wanting to feel him deeper inside her as they moved in perfect unison. She was driven by a force as old as time, moving towards an unknown plateau, each explosion of sensation carrying her higher within a maelstrom of iridescent waves.

She cried out in abandonment at the height of her ecstasy. They lay satiated in each other's arms, locked in a passionate embrace as their heartbeats stilled to a semblance of normality. With the slowing of her clamouring heart Laura became aware that at the moment of his climax Matt had rapidly withdrawn from her, his seed spilling against her thigh. He had deliberately ensured that there would be no child. The knowledge numbed her. He had used her not as a wife, but as a whore.

Tears burned behind her eyes, and, unable to control the pain she turned away from Matt, unwilling for him to see her shame.

Matt felt the scald of a tear upon his shoulder and looked askance as Laura turned her back on him. She lay rigid, freezing him out. Did she resent being taken by a man of his kind? A man she did not regard as her equal? The years of resentment and anger against her class scoured him. Did she think, now that the marriage was consummated, that she was trapped with him to the end of her days? Did she think he had no plans? His future had been mapped out before he met her. His duty remained to avenge Susannah's and Rachel's deaths. Yet a part of him regretted those tears. He was unprepared for the degree of compassion he felt for her.

"Did I hurt you?" he asked, putting a hand on her shoulder.

"Would you care?" Her bitterness flooded out.

"I wanted to give you pleasure, not pain."

She glared at him over her shoulder, her eyes brilliant with silent tears. "You wanted a woman to serve your needs. You made damned sure I wouldn't carry your child. I was a whore to you, nothing more."

"I told you, Laura, I will not father a child just so you can keep Fairfield." His temper began to rise as he felt he was the one who had been used. Her responses had been as false as her lying tongue. And like a green youth he had been beguiled to her. Never again. He knew her now for what she was. She had set out deliberately to seduce him. She hadn't wanted him. All she had wanted was a son for Fairfield.

He rolled from the bed and opened a coffer which contained his breeches. By the time he had pulled them on his iron control had mastered his fury. He spun round and glared down at her. "Your ploy has failed. A child should be conceived in love and cherished. It's not a weapon, the means to your own selfish ends. Having lost one child, do you think I'd allow another to be born and taken from me? Or was I just a convenient means to an end, too lowly in station to have my feelings considered?"

The words were like knives slashing into her heart. Hadn't he made it clear how much he despised her class? Until she had felt his seed on her thigh she had not realised how much she wanted a child. And it was not for Fairfield. It was for her. For her it would have been conceived in love. God help her, she had fallen in love with Matthew Thorne. And he had made his hatred for her clear.

She sat up and pulled the sheet to her chin. Her years of training as the daughter of a gentleman had taught her to hide her emotions well. Though her hurt was buried deep within her, she would not let Matt see her pain. "I return to Fairfield at the end of the week. You are free to lead your own life." She came up on her knees, clasping the sheet to her figure. "I shall tell my grandfather of our arrangement and face his censure. I just hope he can forgive me. I'll explain everything. I'll take the blame. You were paid for a service."

His lips curled back in self-derision at the way he had been duped into believing that she could one day see him as her equal. A painful ache gripped his chest. He had glimpsed something wonderful within his reach and it had been snatched from him before it could be nurtured. Regret harshened his voice. "Don't be so naïve. Now the marriage is consummated there can be no ending it."

His stare was scathing but he was plagued by the vision of her loveliness as she sat with her auburn hair loose about her shoulders, her eyes wide with shock and shattered innocence. The sheet was moulded to her high, firm breasts and revealed the line of her lithe hips and thighs. He was tempted to strip the sheet from her and prove once and for all that he could make her his in a way which proved he was her master. But that would show his own vulnerability and weakness, and he would not give her that ammunition to turn against him.

"We both made a mistake and we're stuck with it," he snapped. "However onerous that may now prove."

He pulled a shirt from a second coffer and continued to dress. "At Fairfield I trust we shall have separate rooms," he added. "I've business of my own to attend first. It will keep me from your home for some days."

The door slammed behind him and Laura stared at it for a long time, her heart searing in her breast. He could not have made it plainer that he hated her. Or did he? Her body still glowed from the tenderness of his lovemaking. But did he truly not care? Surely a man who had made love to her with the tenderness Matt had shown was not as immune as he appeared?

It was a beginning. Laura crushed down her own ruffled pride. To give in to it would be to destroy her chance of happiness. She loved Matt. She wanted her marriage to work. While they were together there was always a chance that she could turn his hatred into love.

Her eyes glistened with determination. Matt was obsessed with his need to avenge what had happened to his first wife and daughter. She respected that. But what of the future? Could she heal his hatred and distrust? Could she make him acknowledge that his desire was not for her body alone, but for the possession of her love?

Chapter Nine

The day before Matt was due to join Laura at Fairfield it snowed. She awoke to the pristine brightness of a white landscape, and the ache which had settled over her heart in her husband's absence deepened. She stared disconsolately out of the window as the flock of geese flew across the sky to the marshes bordering the river estuary. From the moment she had returned to her home there had been constant callers as news of her marriage spread. All had been eager to meet Matt and had looked askance when she'd explained that he had been called away on business.

"So soon after your marriage," one startled matron had cried. "And I thought it was a love-match."

Three other neighbours present had looked archly at each other and Laura had felt her cheeks begin to burn.

"As you will have heard, my marriage took place hastily. Grandfather insisted I wed when he was close to death. I returned to Fairfield with my grandfather to ensure that he rests during his convalescence. My husband still had business to attend in London. He will be here in a few days."

Had she imagined it, or had there been knowing looks of disapproval? One woman had stared pointedly at Laura's stomach. "Marry in haste—repent at leisure, they say. But then there's some as have no choice."

"I am not with child, Mrs Chadwell," Laura had responded sharply.

The pinch-faced woman was the wife of a wealthy yeoman farmer and a gossip. She was the terror of the local vicar, always demanding that women of uncertain morals be pilloried for their wantonness. She resented Laura's return to Fairfield which meant her own status in the community was diminished. Several times Laura had condemned Mrs Chadwell's malicious persecution of lone women and vagabonds.

Under the impact of Laura's angry glare Mrs Chadwell had sniffed and sucked in her lips. She turned her stare on her companion, a nervous woman of middle years. "Time always tells in such matters, does it not, Mrs Rushmer?"

"Oh, well—I..." Mrs Rushmer, who was the curate's wife, had fidgeted with the lace edging on her sleeve. Few women stood up to Mrs Chadwell's bullying tactics. "We are, of course, delighted to see Laura wed."

"So when shall we see this husband of yours?" Mrs Chadwell had persisted.

"I expect his return in two days, if the weather holds."

But the snow had put paid to Matthew's return. It was several inches thick, and in many places along the roads it would have drifted into the hedgerows to the height of a man.

Another week passed. The road from the village

had been cleared, but the rutted, icy track was still treacherous. The temperature remained freezing and the shepherds on the estate were predicting more snow. And they were rarely wrong. Still there was no sign of Matt. What if he did not come? Had he changed his mind about continuing the ruse of their marriage? He had been so adamant in London that the arrangement stood. But that was before they had made love and then quarrelled so bitterly. She had not realised it could hurt so dreadfully to be absent from him. And what if Sir James Breten had pursued his vendetta against Matt? Her husband could be in prison and she would be none the wiser.

Matt eased himself forward in the saddle. He was concealed by a coppice of trees on the hilly ridge in the growing twilight. His legs ached after the two-day ride, but he was grateful to Laura for having insisted that he learn. His narrowed stare was riveted upon the coach in the valley below. It was speeding along a driveway towards a sprawling stone manor house built a century and a half earlier in the shape of an E to commemorate the reign of Queen Elizabeth. Everywhere was evidence of the owner's wealth. The stone-built stables and carriage-house were topped with a clocktower and formed a quadrangle behind the house. Formal knot-gardens and rose-arbours with fountains could be seen from his vantage point high above the manor. Behind them was a long orchard and a vegetable garden which looked huge enough to feed an army. Before the coach drew to a halt in front of the house six liveried footmen and a dozen maids and menservants formed a line to greet their master. His gaze lifted to scan the estate and a resurgence of grief clutched at his chest. This was where Susannah and Rachel had died. What could have brought them here to Kent, so far from their home in London? Susannah had no relatives that he knew of. There was a prickling at the back of his neck which always occurred when he tried to fathom how his wife and child had died. So far he had learned nothing. He had not been able to get close to Sir James five and a half years ago and had only seen him from a distance. During his last visit here, the locals had been close-mouthed about anything concerning Sir James. He was a man feared as much as he was respected, and it seemed that everyone within a five-mile radius of the estate either worked for him or was in need of his goodwill too much to risk alienating him.

This time he would learn the truth.

But there was something unmistakably secretive about the locals' manner when he mentioned anything to do with a woman and child's death in the area six years ago. He was more than ever certain that it had been no accident. Yet that made no sense.

He puzzled over it for hours. Had their deaths something to do with the vendetta Sir James had initiated against himself? It seemed absurd, but once the suspicion was there it began to grow. What did a man of Sir James Breten's wealth and position fear from him? Even if he had been responsible for their deaths, he was too powerful to be brought to account for it. He had too many friends in high places who would save his neck and career should any scandal break.

Yet Matt could not rid himself of the notion that Sir James was hiding something...that he had arranged Matt's imprisonment because he feared that he knew too much. Matt rubbed his stubbled chin. A week spent on the trail of Sir James had told him a great deal about the man. Sir James owned several estates in various counties but the Hall was his major residence. He had a son, Robert, who was the same age as Matt and who was reputedly touring the Continent at the present time. Sir James had been a widower for many years and had never remarried. His mother, Lady Henrietta, the daughter of an earl, doted on him. He was a Member of Parliament, a respected adviser to King William, and was immensely wealthy. It just did not make sense that he should go to such pains to ensure that Matt spent years in prison on trumped-up charges of debt. Surely even the gentry needed a reason to act so vindictively towards another man?

Matt stayed in the area for four days, often riding about the countryside in disguise to learn more of Breten and his family. He learned little from the close-lipped community.

"We don't like nosy strangers," one innkeeper said sourly. "It's not our way to gossip about our betters."

Two other barmen came to stand behind the innkeeper as he spoke, and Matt knew he was being warned off.

When he left the inn a short time later, the stableboy sidled up to him as he collected his horse from the stable. Twice that week Matt had tipped him handsomely for looking after his horse. The boy looked over his shoulder to ensure that they were alone before speaking. "Bain't good ter ask questions, mister. Not here."

"Why's that, lad?"

The boy shuffled his bare feet, which were blue with cold, but seemed reluctant to say more.

"Why are you warning me?" Matt asked, taking some coins to press them into the stable-boy's grimy hand.

The lad pocketed the coins and lifted his long, greasy hair back from his face. Both his ears had been cut off. He nodded to the far end of the stable where a dozen pack ponies were tethered. "Those ponies won't be here come morning—they'll be heading for the coast, if you get my meaning."

"You mean they're smugglers' ponies?"

The boy nodded.

"Is Sir James involved?"

"No. But he's got his secrets jus' as the smugglers have theirs. Wouldn't like to see yer body face-down in a ditch one morning, mister. That's wot happen to them as pry in these parts."

Matt knew that smuggling was rife, even though England was no longer at war with France. There was always a profit to be made by avoiding the high taxes on various imports.

"Is it what happened to a woman and child some six years ago?"

The boy looked at him blankly. "Don't know nothing about that, mister."

Matt handed over some more coins. "Get yourself a pair of shoes, lad."

Warned about the smugglers, Matt was more careful in his investigations. He had no reason to suspect that Sir James was involved with the "Owlers", as the smuggling gangs were called.

On the fifth day a new incident occurred which alerted him to another danger. He was concealed in a coppice, his spy-glass trained on Breten's house, when two riders passed below him on the road. One rode behind the other and was obviously a servant. Matt turned his spy-glass on the bulky figure of the leading horseman. The rider was muffled against the cold. The collar of his cloak was pulled high and a kerchief hid the lower part of his face, but there was no mistaking those heavy-hooded cruel eyes or the strawberry roan the man rode.

Matt felt a shaft of unease pierce him. What was Guy Stanton doing here? It was no chance visit. He must have learned of Breten's vendetta against himself and meant to find out more about Laura's new husband.

A new fear gripped him. If Guy was here, there was also danger to Laura. He had already been away from Fairfield longer than he had promised. Talk was bound to have started about his absence. His fingers were stiff with cold as he replaced the spy-glass in his saddle-roll. The temperature had dropped drastically in the last hour and as Matt turned his horse towards the nearest inn he looked up at the sky. He sighed at seeing the dun-coloured clouds laden with snow. Before he reached the inn it had begun to fall. By morning the entire valley was cut off.

Laura's fears grew with each day that there was no news of Matt's arrival. For the third Sunday she must now attend church without her husband at her side. And the gossip would be growing.

Her grandfather was waiting in the entrance hall of Fairfield as she descended the stairs. Over her gown she wore a midnight-blue velvet cloak, its hood and hem trimmed with a wide band of white fur. In her hand she carried a matching fur muff.

"You look beautiful, my dear," he said, leaning heavily on his gold-topped cane as he smiled at her. He looked at her with concern as they walked to the carriage, Laura slowing her stride to keep pace with him. "Stop worrying about that husband of yours. He'll be here when he can. The roads are treacherous this time of year."

In the last week her fears for Matt had grown so out of proportion that she was tempted to confide in her grandfather. He was looking at her with such devotion; she could not bear to see the pain and disappointment in his eyes when she revealed the truth to him about her marriage. She must bear the burden of her fears alone. If Matt had not returned by Wednesday she would send Jedediah to London to discover what had happened.

They were among the last to take their places in the small Saxon church. The Stanton family pew was next to the choir and opposite that of Mr and Mrs Chadwell. As they walked slowly up the aisle to their places Laura kept her head high and a smile fixed on her face as she acknowledged the curious stares of her neighbours and villagers.

"He's still not turned up, then," a woman's voice carried to her. "Odd love-match if the husband'd abandoned her after a month."

Laura knew that the words referred to Matt and that they echoed the thoughts of most of the people gathered in the church that morning. As she settled in her pew Mrs Chadwell commented in a harsh whisper to her husband, "I'm beginning to suspect that Mrs Thorne's marriage is a figment of her imagination.

She always was a wild one. I've said all along that she'll come to a bad end. She's been very reserved since her return. Not like her old self at all. You mark my words, she's hiding something..."

Laura ignored the spiteful tirade, aware that Mr Chadwell was shuffling uncomfortably in his seat and trying ineffectually to silence his wife. A glance at her grandfather showed him nodding amiably to old acquaintances. His hearing was not as strong as it had been once and he had obviously missed Mrs Chadwell's comments. For that Laura was grateful.

Throughout the service her head remained high. She would not let anyone see how Matt's absence had upset her. Neither would she allow herself to answer the spiteful gossip. When Matt arrived it would silence their tongues. If Matt arrived.

At the end of the service the Stantons were always the first to leave the church, followed by the Chadwells, then the rest of the congregation. Laura hid her unease as she faced the double row of inquisitive faces each side of the aisle.

Oh, Matt, where are you? Laura silently asked.

The church door opened at the far end of the aisle. Light blazed into the dark church as though from a long and distant tunnel. To Laura's overstretched nerves escape from the curious gazes looked to be at the furthest end of the earth, and her grandfather's slow pace drew out her torture. The whispers were louder now as she passed.

"There's rumours in Colchester that the marriage is one of convenience. It were all over the market last week," a milkmaid giggled to her companion. Laura recognised her as a woman she had once seen in Guy's company on one of his rare visits to Fairfield.

"Whoever heard of the gentry making a love-match?" The milkmaid pitched her voice higher. "It were for the property. Thought she'd cheat that cousin of hers out of what's rightly his."

Murmurs followed the remark, and Lionel covered Laura's hand on his arm with his own. "Don't let such gossip upset you," he whispered. "Anyone has but to see you with Thorne and it's obvious you love each other."

If only that were true. Had they really deceived her grandfather so thoroughly? Laura's heart ached, knowing how well Matt had played his role of adoring spouse. Too well. And like a fool she had fallen in love with the charming rogue, knowing that he still loved his first wife.

When they stopped to speak a few words with the vicar, Laura saw that the kindly man's eyes were solemn with concern.

"Good sermon, Reverend," her grandfather said. "But I thought you would have included a reference to psalm…"

Laura moved away from her grandfather's side, knowing that he always liked to challenge the vicar over a point in the sermon. She needed a moment or two alone to compose herself before the rest of the congregation emerged from the church.

She wandered several paces to the family burial plot and looked at the row of gravestones all bearing the Stanton name. The last four grouped together were of her mother, father and his two brothers. Had any one of the three men lived, all of whom had died before their fortieth birthdays, she would not have married Matt and be feeling this wretchedness. She grimaced, despising the self-pity which had overtaken

her. If she was unhappy it was her own fault. She had
insisted upon the deception of their marriage. So
many suitors had paid court to her that she had never
expected that when she fell in love it would be un-
requited.

If Matt were here she would do all in her power to
make him fall in love with her.

Behind her footsteps scrunched on the churchyard's
gravel path. She ignored them, resenting any intrusion
and loath to face the curious questions of the villagers.

"Have I been so long away that you have forgotten
you have a husband?" a deep, familiar voice mocked
softly.

With her heart clamouring, Laura swung round.
Matt was grinning at her. He was swathed in a black
cloak which reached the ground. He swept his cocked
hat trimmed with ostrich feathers from his head and,
placing it over his heart, bowed reverently to her.
When he straightened he was grinning at her look of
delight.

"Matt! Thank God you are well and safe." She ran
into his arms.

"My dear, I had not dared to hope for such a welcome." His amused chuckle deepened as he embraced her and, uncaring that they were observed by
fifty staring villagers, he lifted her off her feet to kiss
her cheek. His voice was husky as he whispered,
"Then, for you to show such joy in our reunion will
stop the gossips. You never miss a chance, do you,
Laura?"

His words ruined the pleasure of his arrival. He set
her back on her feet and she pulled up the hood of
her cloak which had fallen back from her auburn ring-

lets. "Must you always believe me so callous? I was worried about you. Both Breten and my cousin Guy are powerful enemies."

He raised a dark brow, but if he had intended to mock her statement the genuine anxiety in her eyes stopped him. He laughed and linked her arm through his. "Still, there is too much at stake for us ever to forget our roles."

At seeing Lionel Stanton advancing towards them with several of the most important landowners in the parish, his gaze became tender. Even though she knew that look was false, Laura found her heart racing harder.

"I had forgotten how beautiful you are," he said as her grandfather came into earshot. He lifted one hand from her muff and pressed a kiss upon her wrist, exposed above the embroidered leather of her glove.

"Thorne, I thought the weather would keep you indefinitely in London. I should have known you'd risk the treacherous roads to be reunited with your bride."

Matt smiled at Laura. "How could I stay away? Even a new husband is foolish to neglect a woman as beautiful as Laura. She has transformed my life. Because of her there is light where once there was only darkness."

"A poetic speech, Thorne." Lionel chuckled. "Let me introduce you to my friends."

As her grandfather made the introductions Laura kept her arm linked through her husband's. All the women hurried forward to be included in the introductions and Laura was satisfied that Mrs Chadwell had been ostracised by her companions.

Throughout the day visitors called at Fairfield. The

news of Matt's arrival had spread and it seemed that everyone wanted to meet Laura's husband. It was some hours later when they were alone for the first time. The last of the guests had left and her grandfather rose from his chair.

"I will bid you both goodnight." He paused and smiled at Matt, who had also risen to his feet. "I hope you will be happy at Fairfield, Thorne. You've made quite an impression on the neighbours. Fairfield needs a man of foresight to continue to make it prosper."

"I am a sea-captain, Mr Stanton, not a farmer," Matt said smoothly. "I had planned to set sail again this summer."

"You will not give up the sea for Fairfield?" Lionel Stanton stared at him sternly.

"I will not be supported by my wife. I want nothing to do with her money. Fairfield belongs to Laura and she has plans for its future. Naturally I will do all in my power to assist her."

"You became part of Fairfield when you married Laura," Lionel flared. "You cannot escape that. This is nonsense. The land does not manage itself. You cannot evade your responsibilities, Thorne."

"I evade nothing. But I will not be supported by my wife's income."

Lionel eyed him stonily. "You are allowing your pride to blind you. Fairfield needs a strong and farsighted man at the helm. You haven't a ship as far as I am aware," he challenged. "Or had you expected Laura to provide you with one?"

Matt paled, and his eyes glittered dangerously. "Nothing will induce me to live upon my wife's bounty."

"Fairfield needs a man to run it," Lionel raged.

"Why else do you think my grandfather imposed the entail on the property? Your place is at your wife's side. Fairfield—"

"I will be no paid servant to the glory of Fairfield."

The atmosphere in the room sparked with tension. Laura intervened, alarmed that her grandfather would push Matt too far. "Grandfather, I did not marry Matt to make a farmer of him. He loves the sea. I would never force him to give up the life. Matt did not marry me for my wealth. He despises it. I respect his wishes to lead his life as he sees fit."

"If he loved you, he would not abandon you," her grandfather accused.

"Rather that as I love him I will not force him to give up so important a part of his life, or his self-respect. I am capable of managing Fairfield."

Laura braced himself against her grandfather's anger. To her surprise he bowed his head and seemed to be hiding a smile. "It's not the time to speak of such matters. I am tired." He looked at Matt, who was standing with his feet planted firmly apart, his stance uncompromising. For a long moment the two men held each other's stare. Finally Lionel said, "You have been at Fairfield less than a day. In time you will feel differently. It has that effect on those who call it home."

Matt did not answer, but from the tension in his face it was clear that he was mastering his anger. Unexpectedly Lionel laughed.

"Aye, Laura chose well for her husband," he said with returning humour. "They say true love never runs smoothly—pride had been many a lover's downfall. Remember, Matt, that no one truly owns the land;

the land owns them. We are its custodians during our lifetime, nothing more. And we have a duty to those who toil upon it.'' With that parting shot he left the room.

Laura sighed wearily. All day she had been stingingly aware of her husband's presence and the knowledge that soon he would leave her life forever. ''I fear Grandfather will persist in his argument. He wants what is best for Fairfield. I'm sorry if it makes things difficult for you.''

Matt had been watching Lionel's departure with a frown. ''He's quite a man, your grandfather,'' he said simply. ''I don't like deceiving him.''

''You haven't. You've always been honest. I'm the one who has lied and cheated. I'm not very proud of myself, Matt. But I would do it all again to save Fairfield from my cousin. Grandfather meant what he said about believing us to be the custodians of the land.''

Matt laughed in sharp derision.

''Don't mock,'' she responded.

Aware that it was time for them to retire also, Laura strove to ease the tension between them. Earlier Matt had been shown to his own rooms which adjoined her chambers by an interior door. Here at Fairfield they at least had more privacy from one another, while being forced to continue in their roles of devoted husband and wife. She moved to the spinet and touched one of the keys. ''Would you like me to play for you, Matt?''

He lifted a dark brow and smiled. ''Another evening. Won't the servants be expecting that we retire early? There will be gossip and speculation aplenty now that I have arrived.'' He took her hand. ''What's wrong, Laura? You've been tense and ill at ease all evening.''

His touch almost destroyed her self-control. She lowered her lashes and gave him a sidelong glance. How could she tell him that she loved him, that she wanted nothing more than for him to be truly her husband? She forced a teasing smile. ''At moments like this we are strangers. I have glimpsed a far-away look in your eyes this evening, Matt. I sense all did not go well for you in your investigations.''

''No.''

He had withdrawn behind a barrier which she could not breach. Even so, she had to try. ''Would it help to talk about it? My grandfather is not without influence.''

''I settle my own scores in my own way,'' he said tautly.

''Why do you reject my help? Do you hate me so much?''

He expelled his breath harshly. ''I don't hate you, Laura.'' His voice was strained and husky. ''I find it difficult to speak of my wife and daughter, but I believe Sir James Breten was involved in their deaths. He is also the man behind my imprisonment.''

Laura swallowed a rush of jealousy. He had not said first wife but simply ''wife''. Susannah would be the only woman Matt regarded as his true wife. ''Then why did you return,'' she managed to force out, ''if to discover the truth is so important?''

His expression darkened. ''I gave you my word that I would be at Fairfield last week. The snow delayed me.''

For an instant she thought she had seen something deeper in his eyes, revealing that there was much he was withholding from her, but as she held his gaze his eyes were carefully guarded. He did not remove his hand from her shoulder. The clean, manly scent of him stirred memories of his kisses and his love-making, causing a bittersweet pang of pain and pleasure. What she would not give to be loved by Matt as he loved Susannah—as he still loved Susannah. How could she compete with a ghost?

She broke away from the web of emotions he was spinning around her and led the way to their rooms. Outside her bedchamber door she paused and, seeing a maid bob a curtsey as she passed them on the landing Laura inclined her head for Matt to enter her room. Once inside, she indicated the adjoining door. "At least now you can sleep in a proper bed."

"I was becoming used to sharing yours, even if it was just for a few minutes." He grinned wickedly. "Will you miss my company also, Laura?"

"I am legally bound to you, Matt. But you do not regard me as your wife. Your marriage rites are just a mockery of that ceremony."

"You are my wife, Laura." He moved closer and she felt her breath stifle in her throat. She yearned to be taken in his arms, to feel the magic of his kisses on her heated flesh. As she stared into his eyes she saw tenderness and also devilry, but there was not the love she craved.

"By deed, but not in your heart," she answered raggedly.

"And what am I to you, Laura?" His manner became cold as he captured her arms and held them behind her body. She was pressed against him, not with desire but with contempt, as he sought to prove his mastery over her. "Am I not the stud to provide Fairfield with a child?"

"Do you think I could give myself to you if I thought you merely that?"

She felt a shudder go through him and found herself abruptly released. "Are these more lies to achieve your own ends, Laura?"

"When have I ever lied to you, Matt?"

"You lie readily enough to your grandfather, whom you profess to love. You'd do anything to save Fairfield from your cousin; you've told me that enough times."

He flared back with such vehemence that she flinched. She could not humble herself further. "Then remember that well, for it will be the maxim I live by." She pulled away from him.

"I told you, I will not give you a child which I will never see raised to adulthood."

"I would never stop you seeing it. We may live separate lives in the future but you will always be the child's father." She swallowed against her pain. "I do not want to be childless all my life."

"Then you gravely erred when you took me for your husband."

"We both erred," she said huskily. "But our vows were made."

As if of its own volition his hand came up to stroke the soft flesh of her shoulder. "You gave me my freedom from prison. You have many qualities I admire, but I don't trust you, Laura." Startled by the glitter of unshed tears sparkling behind her lashes, he added ruefully, "I certainly don't trust myself when in your company. You are a temptation I find hard to resist.

Having made love to you, I want you all the more in my bed.''

"You delude yourself, Matt." Laura's pride rose; she wanted to wound him as he had wounded her. "You did not make love to me. We fornicated. You cannot even say we performed the act of procreation expected within a marriage. You ensured no child would be conceived. If I am condemned to barrenness then I will not be your concubine."

Without another word she walked into her dressing-room. Matt watched her with confused emotions. Her head was high and her shoulders squared in defiance, but there was a sensuous sway to her hips which brought an ache of longing to him. Was he a fool to deny her a child when his own body throbbed to possess her? Could there be a future for them? The devil whispered in his mind. A beautiful, passionate wife, wealth and social standing would all be his.

Pride crushed temptation. There was one barrier he could never breach. His bastardy was a stigma he could never overcome. How could Laura ever accept him as her equal while he remained a penniless sea-captain without even a ship to call his own? To continue the marriage upon her terms would eventually destroy him, and he would truly come to hate her.

Chapter Ten

A week later, when the snow had thawed, Laura ordered the horses saddled and asked Matt to accompany her on a ride.

"Perhaps when you see Fairfield you will not be so hostile towards your responsibilities here," she said as she urged her mare to canter.

Matt narrowed his eyes, unprepared to be swayed. Fairfield was Laura and Lionel Stanton's obsession. It had nothing to do with him and had no place in his future.

Yet when he saw how the ploughmen, working behind the horses as they prepared the ground for the first crops, would halt in their work to wave to Laura, and she would call out to all of them, asking after their families by name, his mood began to change. It was the same with the ditchers who were clearing the draining ditches of winter debris, and also the herdsmen and shepherds. Sometimes as they rode past a tenant farm the children would run out to greet Laura. She would halt to press a small bag of freshly baked cakes into their grimy hands, and occasionally a small flask of medicine for an ailing member of the family, to ease his or her suffering.

Matt watched Laura closely. In the last week he had been aware that she took special care that there was no physical contact between them. Dressed in a military-style velvet riding habit, she would ride out early and inspect the estate, then return to spend an hour or two working on the accounts. She spared nothing of herself in the management of Fairfield. When she emerged from the study and sought his company her manner was teasing and witty, making him laugh and briefly forget the problems which plagued him. She would get him to talk of his voyages and to his surprise he found himself confiding in her more than he had with any other person. In the evenings she would play the perfect hostess—one moment listening to a discussion of politics, the next playing the coquette, provocative and alluring in a way that made Matt burn to possess her again. Yet always she was elusive. She would smile enticingly as she played the spinet, singing a tender love-song with the voice of a nightingale. Then she would grow serious, and sit frowning over a game of chess or backgammon with either himself or her grandfather. There were many facets of her character which were at variance with the spoilt heiress he believed her to be.

When dealing with the people of the estate there was no sign of the haughtiness she often showed to those neighbours of her own class. There was never any sign of patronage as she enquired after the health of tenants and servants. When they bobbed their curtsies or tugged their forelocks, respect and affection was clear on their faces. He was surprised at the good repair of the farm cottages. Clearly the Stantons cared for their tenants and workers. The estate itself was larger than he expected, but neither its size nor the large herds of cattle and sheep impressed him. Neither did its landscape. It bordered the marshes, and the land was flat almost to the point of bleakness. In the distance a mist rose from the reed-beds and the honking of geese could be heard as they flew overhead.

As they returned to the house itself he studied the rambling building. It was built of grey stone, with mullioned windows, and most of the stark walls were covered with ivy. One ancient wing even had a turreted tower and a filled-in moat, which was all that remained of the original fortified manor. The house was built around a quadrangle with a shingle roof and was unremarkable. Behind the house were the stables and outbuildings with their wattle and daub walls freshly whitewashed and their new thatch still golden. It was a jumble of buildings. Yet as Matt rode up the winding drive, lined with oak trees to protect the house from the wind which came straight off the marshes, he felt a strange stirring in his breast.

It was Fairfield's lack of perfection which appealed to him. Through the wintery mist, the leafless trees spread tentacle-like branches to embrace the charcoal sky, and smoke curled upwards from half a dozen tall red-brick chimneys. From several windows candles burned like welcoming beacons and from the walled vegetable plot could be heard a jaunty whistle and occasional laughter as the gardeners worked.

It dawned on him that the sound of laughter had been frequently heard during his ride. The people of Fairfield were content in their lives, and that was a rarity. Despite the harsh winter none of them appeared to be hungry, but then during his talks with Jedediah Hames and Barker both servants had been quick to praise the Stantons for their generosity to their tenants. Both had told Matt that in hard winters Lionel would dispense grain from his own store to ensure that no one went hungry.

Fairfield was not an impressive estate with a grand house, but it had an atmosphere of contentment and well-being which even the marsh mist could not dispel. He could understand why Laura was so obsessive about her home, but he could not afford such weakness. He must arm himself against the spell that Fairfield was capable of weaving and, more importantly, he must be on his guard against the seductive enticement which Laura constantly presented.

Late that night he prowled his room, unable to sleep. Knowing that only a door separated him from Laura's bed and the sweet ecstasy of her passion made sleep impossible. Twice he had gone to the adjoining door, but his hand had halted before it reached the latch. The boundaries of their marriage had been clearly written and agreed.

He sat in front of the fire, staring into the flames. To banish thoughts of Laura from his mind he tried to summon the image of Susannah. It remained elusive and undefined. Yet through the shrouds of time he could hear Rachel calling him, her shadowy figure running with arms outstretched. "Pa! Pa! Catch me, Pa!"

He sank his head into his hands and groaned. There would never be another daughter like Rachel. But until now he had not realised how empty his life would be if he never held another child of his own in his arms. He stood up abruptly and at a noise from the corridor outside swung round. Soft voices came from Laura's room and when he heard her door open he moved quickly to his.

Laura looked startled to find him on the landing before her. "Did I disturb you, Matt? I'm sorry."

She was fully dressed and wrapped in a thick coat.

"What's wrong?" he asked.

"Widow Croke has taken the fever. I've herbs which can help her."

"You cannot mean to ride out in the middle of the night?"

Laura glared at him scornfully. "By morning she could be dead of neglect. She's a young woman with four children to rear."

"Then I will come with you," he said, impatient at her stubbornness. "You cannot ride alone."

"Jedediah has been summoned. He usually accompanies me."

"Not while I am here. He's getting on in years."

"I cannot delay. Be in the stables in five minutes."

She hurried away without a backward glance, her mind on her patient.

Something changed in Matt that night. He stood helplessly by while Laura risked taking a fever by tending the young widow. The children, the oldest of whom was ten, sat crying by the meagre fire. To stop them crying, which would upset their mother, he kept them amused by using the sleight-of-hand tricks he had learned as a youth. He would suddenly produce a penny from behind a child's ear or a kerchief from an empty pocket. He kept them entertained for an hour, and before each of the four children was a small pile of copper coins that they would keep. He took the youngest girl on to his knee and began to tell them stories of the wonder of the strange lands he had visited. He looked up to find Laura watching him, her expression fixed and staring as though she was in pain.

"What's wrong?" He glanced significantly towards the corner of the room where the mother lay behind a partitioning blanket.

Laura shook her head. "Widow Croke is sleeping comfortably. Her fever has broken. I'll get the children back to their beds and stay until a servant can be sent from the house to tend to the family in the morning."

"You look exhausted," Matt said.

Laura dragged her gaze away from the child sitting in his lap, and with a shrug turned away, sat down on a stool by the fire and laid her head against the wall. "The children cannot be left. I'll sleep in the chair. In an hour it will be dawn. If you wish to return to the hou..."

Her words slurred as she fell asleep. Matt hushed the children and got them into bed. Taking his cloak from the peg on the wall, he laid it over Laura, and stooped to build up the fire.

Unable to sleep, he busied himself with preparing a meal of oatmeal for the children. Hearing a noise from behind the curtain, he went to the widow's side. The rushlight had burnt out, but dawn was already lightening the sky and he could just make out the woman's form. He put a hand on her brow and was relieved to find it cool. The figure stirred beneath his hand.

"Mr Thorne, what are you doing here?" Widow Croke asked hoarsely.

He crouched by the bed and was surprised to see how young the woman was. She was in her middle twenties and beneath her linen nightcap her blonde hair was braided into two thick plaits.

"I could not allow my wife to stay here on her own."

The widow smiled. "It wouldn't be the first time. She's nursed many a family through different fevers. Took it herself last winter, and we all feared she might die. Thank God she recovered. What would our lives have been like if Cecil Stanton had returned? They were bad days, according to the old folks who were alive then. Every winter people died of starvation—Cecil Stanton never cared for the people. He took all the land could give." She sighed.

"You should rest, Mistress Croke," Matt urged gently. "A maid will be sent to help with the children until you are strong enough to rise from your bed."

His hand was grabbed. "You chose an angel when you took Mistress Laura to wife," the widow said. "That Cecil Stanton would never have let a widow stay on in a tithe cottage. I got a lame leg and can't do much work, but Mistress Laura took not a penny in rent this last year since my husband died. We are all proud to serve you as master of Fairfield," the widow added. "Bill Waters has been waiting to speak with you. About us marrying."

"Then he should speak to Mr Stanton, not myself."

"No. You are master here now. It's your blessing Bill and I'd be wanting."

Matt felt a lump rise to his throat. "You have it with pleasure."

He rose abruptly, ill at ease with the pleasure that

the woman's request had brought to him. He was getting too involved with the estate and its people. He did not want them to feel beholden to him.

Laura awoke with a start when a cat jumped on to her lap and began to knead her thighs with its paws. Her eyes widened in astonishment as she saw Matt ladling out the oatmeal into five wooden bowls. He held one out to Laura.

"Take this into Widow Croke. She's awake and hungry and fretting to get up. I ordered her to stay abed."

He smiled at the growing surprise on Laura's face as she saw that the children were all dressed. Then she bowed her head, and he thought he detected the glitter of a tear on her cheek, but she had picked up the bowl and disappeared behind the curtain to tend the widow before he could question her.

Laura felt as if her heart had been clamped in a vice. To see Matt dealing so competently and with evident pleasure with the children had hurt her more than she thought she could bear. Clearly he loved children. Yet he had condemned her to barrenness, even after she had promised him that she would never stop him seeing the child. She had not realised until now just how much he must despise her.

Laura stayed in the cottage while Matt fetched a maid from the house to tend the widow until she recovered. She was surprised that he also returned, but their ride back to Fairfield was strained. It was her fault. Matt was at his most charming, but she was hurting too much to respond.

When they dismounted in the stable-yard she turned to him and said heavily, "I must thank you for all you have done for the Croke family."

He smiled his most disarming smile, which only served to make Laura's heartache more painful. "It is what the people would expect of your husband, is it not?"

"For a man who professes to despise Fairfield and all it stands for, you make a natural and considerate benefactor. Few landowners would trouble themselves as you did. The children especially..." Her voice shook. "The children adored you."

She broke away from him, and since Matt was standing between her and the house she ran into the stable, leaving him staring after her in puzzlement. She stumbled blindly to the horse-boxes and, seeing the groom leading in her mare, she climbed the ladder into the loft. She wanted to be away from the prying eyes of the servants. She needed to be alone with her pain. Sinking down into the hay, she allowed her tears to flow, biting her lip to stop the sound of her sobs. Eventually her lack of sleep overcame her and she drifted into a doze.

Matt had steeled himself against following Laura into the stables. Clearly she was upset, but with each day it was becoming harder for him to control his desire. When he eventually settled the score with James Breten he intended that the baronet would repay all the money taken from him on the false charges of debt, together with the price of his ship and cargo. Then he could set sail and put this bizarre marriage behind him. His frustration welled up and, waving aside the groom, he remounted and set off towards the distant riverbank. He needed to see the river and taste the salt in the air. He'd been land-bound for too long, and that was making him restless.

Away from the estate the undrained land became marshy, and he picked his way with care across the squelching grass. A man carrying a bundle of drift-wood on his back tipped his slouch hat respectfully to him.

"Good day, Master Thorne."

"Good day, sir."

"It's not for you to call me sir, Mr Thorne. I'm Hal Weddell."

"Of West Farm?" Matt queried. "You've a brother Ben who is gardener at the house."

"Aye." Hal looked pleased that he knew who his brother was.

"I'm afraid I've been remiss in visiting the farm-steads," Matt apologised.

Hal grinned. "You're recently wed, Mr Thorne. You can't be expected to know everyone. With re-spect, sir, I'd like to bid you welcome to Fairfield. It's good to see Mistress Laura so happy."

Matt urged his horse forward until the ground be-came too treacherous underfoot to approach the river any closer. The mist shrouded the skyline and the only vessels visible in the estuary were a small cutter and two fishing crafts returning to land. He breathed deeply of the salty air. It did not give him the satis-faction he craved. From along the lane the game-keeper and his son ambled towards him. They carried a dozen ducks between them and each had a gun slung over his shoulder.

"Good day, Mr Thorne. Mrs Thorne mentioned that you were partial to duck. Gil and I thought we'd make sure Cook got these for your dinner."

"That's very kind of you. It's Jacob, isn't it?" Matt

answered. "You should not have gone to so much trouble."

"Ain't no trouble at all. Right glad we are to have you here. There were times we thought Mistress Laura would never wed. Should have known she'd pick a real man and not one of those milksops who came calling."

Matt frowned as he rode on. It was impossible not to respond to the warmth of the estate workers and tenants and it was beginning to annoy him. Fairfield could never be his home. There was no point in his becoming attached to it, or the people here. A hunger welled within him to be with Laura. He had ridden out to put her from his mind; instead she was more firmly lodged in it than ever. The memory of her anguished face as she ran into the stables tortured him. It was no good; he must return and seek her out.

The stables were deserted and he could hear the grooms working in the tack-room in the opposite outbuilding. He waved aside the groom who stuck his head round the door.

"I'll tend Neptune," he said, leading his gelding into his stall.

Tethering his mount, Matt ran a hand over its muscled flank and patted the horse. He had been surprised at how fond he had become of the gelding, and that he enjoyed riding and the isolation of the countryside. The horse rubbed down and picking contentedly at its hayrick, Matt glanced around the stable, his gaze moving up to the hayloft. Something told him that Laura was up there. He moved stealthily up the ladder and paused at seeing her asleep in the hay. She lay on her back with one hand thrown over her shoulder. A single tear sparkled on her lashes. The response of his blood was immediate. Lying in the straw, she no longer appeared the grand lady out of his reach. She was as lovely as a wood nymph, free of constraint. She was his wife, and if he was ever to get her out of his system he must possess her one more time. Maybe then he could banish her from his thoughts...

He sank on to the hay beside her, his mouth gentle and slowly rousing upon hers. From deep in her throat she murmured, and her eyes opened. Her instant awareness of him froze his movements. Even wanting her to the point of madness, he could never force her. He looked down at her. Time was held in a breathless moment. All sound was stilled. Even the horses ceased to fidget in their stalls.

Laura stared up at her husband, transfixed as he slowly lowered his head and his mouth skimmed her parted lips.

"Matt," she groaned, her hand flexing to push against his chest in protest. But her fingers had no strength to resist him, any more than her body could deny the frantic pounding of her heart. Her body was tingling, weightless in a sea of anticipation. Her dreams had all been of him making love to her, and to awake to discover herself in his arms ignited her desire, too long held at bay.

When Matt drew back to search her face for her response, his bronze eyes were dark with the hunger of his passion. It mirrored the craving building in Laura. His mouth was poised so enticingly above her own, and her hand reached behind his head, gently easing him down to meet her lips. Wounded pride and anger melted into passion, resentment blazing into unequivocal desire. All misunderstandings, conflicts of will and misconceived agreements were drowned by the engulfing waves of desire. After nights of longing for his touch, Laura could not fight the wayward demands of her body. Nothing mattered but the powerful sensations which transported her. It was like being tossed in the tumbling waters of a millrace. The kiss was passionate but infinitely tender, demanding with a thoroughness which threatened the destruction of her sanity.

Pinned against the powerful length of his body, Laura was lost to the fevered clamouring of her blood. She was impatient with the feel of rough clothes instead of warm flesh, her fingers shaking as she tore at his buttons and felt her laces loosened. Her breasts were freed from the confines of her stiffened corset, and when her skirt and petticoats were hoisted to her waist a wild, explosive heat expanded within her.

Matt was beyond coherent thought. When Laura was in his arms, her mouth parting under his, her body arching to press closer to him, he forgot everything but the need to possess her, to make her irrevocably his. His mouth was against her throat, his lips feeling the moans of pleasure vibrating from deep within her. She was trembling, her body moving, abandoned, unashamed, joyful at every caress and kiss. She filled his senses, her figure a living flame engulfing him, and his passion became volcanic.

There were no barriers between them in their passion. He was not only her equal but her master...her teacher...the focal point of her pleasure...her destiny. He didn't seek mindless release. He wanted to carry her beyond the stars to a sensual world of mystical pleasure, where they could be as one in body, spirit and mind—equal and invincible.

Laura gasped, ''Matt, please, please.'' Her head

rolled from side to side, unable to contain the exquisite sensations which roused her body to ecstatic torment, prolonging each moment of pleasure. When he entered her the last scrap of her restraint snapped. With building rhythm they reached the edge of oblivion, encompassed by a rapture that was soul-searing.

Her cheek resting against Matt's bare shoulder, Laura sighed in contentment and rolled on to her stomach to press a kiss against his throat. When he did not respond she raised herself on to her elbows and smiled into his eyes. Their expression was sombre and she frowned as she pushed back the mass of her auburn hair which had come loose from its pins.

"Did I not please you?" she said fearfully.

His throat worked. "You pleased me mightily."

"Then why the frown?"

Matt stared up into her lovely face, still flushed from the aftermath of her passion. Again he had possessed her body and experienced a fulfilment he was not prepared to acknowledge. The pain of wanting her hurt more than he had bargained for. He gathered her into his arms so that he would not have to look into the bewitching beguilement of her eyes. When he found the strength to let her go he knew he would never hold her close like this again. He could not risk it. She had conquered him with her passionate response and he knew he would never meet her equal again.

Laura sensed the tension in Matt. She wriggled to sit up and stare down at him. She guessed why he looked so bleak. This time he had not withdrawn from her, and she could have conceived his child. She hid her pain that the thought so displeased him. She would not let him see how deeply she was wounded.

But as she stared into his handsome face, and saw the stiffness of pride in every line, she knew she had to be the one to make the first conciliatory move.

"Matt, I've never regretted our marriage. I know we can make it work."

"You know that is not possible."

"Why not? We enjoy each other's company. We give each other pleasure. That is more than many marriages have."

Matt sat up and began to straighten his clothes. "Here in the hayloft we are equal, Laura. Step outside and the vastness of Fairfield and all its wealth swamps us. And what am I...?"

"You are my husband."

"Bought and paid for."

"No, Matt. It's no longer like that between us."

"It will always be like that between us until I own a ship and can restore my fortunes and repay to you the money which cleared my debts. *Nothing* has changed, Laura." He paused in tucking his shirt into his breeches and touched her cheek with his hand. "I don't want your charity, or your pity. You are proud, and will never respect any man who is not your equal in all things."

Laura came up on to her knees. "That's foolish, Matt. I love you."

He smiled tenderly. "It's not love you feel for me. Don't confuse the way your body responds to mine with love. I'm the only man you've lain with, and women feel as you do for their first lover."

She shook her head to deny his words, and he put a finger over her lips.

"Don't say any more, Laura. Our worlds are separate. Don't tempt me to believe that there is a chance. I only have so much control.''

She could not believe that he was so callously rejecting her. Her pride flared and with it her temper. ''Damn you, Matt! You're a stubborn, ox-headed churl!''

He grinned ruefully. ''That's more like it, Laura.''

She slapped his face and instantly regretted her action. He did not flinch, but stood up and raised a brow as he smiled down at her.

''I'm sorry. We made an unholy pact. Let it end before it destroys us both.''

She stood up, shaking down her skirt and fastening the bodice of her riding-habit. Matt was at the head of the ladder, about to descend.

''Mr Thorne!'' A groom called from below. ''Is Mistress Laura there?''

''I'm here, Simon.'' Laura finished fastening her jacket and was appalled to find her skirt and hair covered in hay-stalks.

''There's visitors, Mistress Laura. Barker says for you to hurry. It's Mr Cecil Stanton and he's quarrelling with your grandfather.''

Laura hurried to the loft ladder.

''Just a moment, Laura.'' Matt put a hand on her arm to stop her. ''You can't go into the house like that.'' He picked some hay off her shoulders, but she was too anxious to learn what was happening to stand still.

''If Uncle Cecil knows anything about our marriage and tells Grandfather, it could kill him,'' she said, banging her knee on a rung of the ladder as she missed her footing. She hurried across to the house, picking bits of straw out of her hair, uncaring that it was loose about her shoulders and that she must look a fright.

As she entered the house she became aware of raised voices.

"Prison bait, that's what he is," Cecil Stanton bellowed.

Laura's blood ran cold.

As she ran towards the parlour she heard her uncle continue his accusation. "A debtor. A common debtor. Married in the Fleet."

She heard Matt following her as she entered the room unannounced. Cecil Stanton was striding back and forth, waving his walking-cane angrily at her grandfather. Laura's worried gaze flew to Lionel. To her surprise he was standing by the fireplace, one hand holding the open edge of his jacket, the other resting negligently upon the marble mantel. It was a pose he frequently adopted when he was enjoying a debate and his expression did not change as he saw Laura approach.

"Prison bait, I say," Cecil Stanton continued to rage. "One thousand pounds in debts. It was never a love-match. Laura bought herself a husband. She did it because you were dying and she wanted to cheat the entail. When did our family ever wed gallows' meat?"

"Matt was wrongly accused." Laura defended not herself but her husband. "He never owed that money. His business partner trumped up charges against Matt and stole his ship."

"By your defence of the prisoner you condemn yourself." Cecil rounded on her. He was a large man and, like his son, used to bullying to get his own way.

Laura stiffened her spine and glared back at him. "I am legally married."

"To a man totally unsuitable."

"There you are wrong. I am proud to be the wife of Matthew Thorne. He is a man of honour."

"So proud you planned to have all evidence of the marriage struck from the records once Lionel was dead and Fairfield was in your hands." Cecil's lips curled back into a snarl. "Never trust someone who can be bribed as you bribed the prison warden. For a higher price they will always betray you."

Laura glanced across at her grandfather, fearing to see the condemnation in his eyes.

"You do not dispute what Cecil has said?" He spoke quietly.

"I am ashamed only of the lies I had to tell you." She moved closer to her grandfather, her eyes pleading with him to understand. His continued calmness puzzled her and she said, "You don't seem surprised."

"Even on my sick-bed I was not taken in by your tale of a love-match—though the act you and Thorne put on was a good one."

"Why did you not say anything?" Laura could not control her curiosity. She had believed she had duped everyone. "You must have been so ashamed of what I had done."

"I was disappointed that you did not confide in me." He looked at Matt, who was standing protectively at Laura's side. "From the first Thorne proved himself to be a man of principle. Many of his answers to my questions were as carefully worded as any courtier's, but he never lied to save his own hide. I questioned Jedediah. He was reluctant to betray your confidence, but his first loyalty was to me. And since then I have made other enquiries about your husband. I learned nothing which would make me wish to see the marriage dissolved.''

''I still don't understand why you allowed us to continue,'' Laura said hollowly.

Her grandfather smiled. ''The more I discovered about Thorne the more I was convinced you had made a good choice for a husband.'' He again looked pointedly at Matt. ''Principles can be more important than wealth for the new master of Fairfield.''

A bellow of rage from Cecil Stanton interrupted them. ''You can't cover this up, Lionel. Thorne was bought. The man's a debtor.'' He bore down upon his brother. ''By tomorrow the news will be all over London and Essex. Your family will be a laughing stock, shunned by society. And don't think I shall let it end at that. I told you on the day you reclaimed Fairfield after your exile that the estate would again be mine.''

''I've already ensured against your taking any such action. I've petitioned King William to revoke the entail.'' Lionel faced his brother with open scorn. ''You ruined Fairfield once with your greed. I could not let that happen again.''

Despite his defiance, Laura was alarmed to see that her grandfather was beginning to grow pale. The strain was showing on him so soon after his illness.

''Grandfather, please sit down and rest.''

She whirled on her uncle. ''Stop this bullying. It won't do you any good. My grandfather is ill. Do you want to be the death of him?''

''You think yourself so clever.'' Cecil turned on Laura. When Matt stepped protectively forward he took one look at her husband's angry face and backed away, growling out, "Laura has disgraced her family. Matthew Thorne is a nobody. His mother was a whore and he's a bastard."

Laura felt Matt tense at her side, but before he could speak her grandfather pronounced in a voice intended to end the matter, "Thorne's mother was married, and was deserted by her husband. She wanted no links with the blackguard and reverted to her maiden name, which is an old and revered one. Her father may have been an impoverished preacher, but he was the fifth and youngest son of Henry Thorne, one of England's finest lawyers. Although a Puritan, Henry Thorne was often consulted by Charles I during his reign, and I met him on several occasions and respected his views and judgement. The family lost all its money supporting the King's cause against Parliament."

"A story no doubt put about by yourself to cover up your granddaughter's shame."

"You can check the details easily enough, as I did," Lionel said haughtily. "I suggest you do. Otherwise it will be you who will become the laughing stock and an outcast from society, for besmirching the good name of my family."

Cecil Stanton was breathing heavily as he outfaced his brother and thrust a menacing fist in front of Lionel's face. "Fairfield will be mine!"

"That will never be," Lionel raged. "Now get out of my house and don't ever return."

Rage turned Cecil's face puce, and without warning his fist slammed into his brother's face. Laura screamed as her grandfather was knocked to the ground, blood streaming from his cut eye.

Matt leapt forward and dragged Cecil from his

brother before he could bring his walking-cane down on to Lionel's head. As her husband and uncle struggled, Laura ran to her grandfather's side. Matt hauled both of Cecil's arms behind his back, forcing the man on to his toes, and frogmarched him from the house.

"You'll pay for this, Thorne." Cecil Stanton continued to shout his threats. "You'll all pay for this."

Laura was helping her grandfather to a chair when Matt returned and assisted her.

"I regret you had to find out about our marriage in so unpleasant a manner, sir," Matt said. He could see that the old man was badly shaken from his brother's attack. "Shall I call Barker?"

Lionel Stanton gave him a long and subjective stare. "Now it is all out in the open I want some questions answered." He reached out and took a stalk of hay from Matt's hair, and another from Laura's, she having come to kneel by his chair. His expression was enigmatic and, pointing to a carved wooden box on a table, he said, "Would you fetch me that box?"

Matt did so and watched as the old man opened it and drew out a familiar document.

"This is the agreement you and my granddaughter signed?" he said unnecessarily. "I obtained it from the lawyer. First I want to know if the marriage has been consummated."

Laura drew in a sharp breath and was betrayed by her blush.

"It has been, sir," Matt answered guardedly.

Lionel took the document he was holding and ripped it in half, and tossed it on to the fire. "Then this is worthless. The marriage will stand. Now, what are your intentions, Thorne?"

Matt swallowed down a rush of anger and resentment at the cavalier way Lionel Stanton was arranging his life. Why did the gentry always think they could dictate the terms? But even as the resentment formed it began to wither. Throughout the exchange with his brother Lionel Stanton had stood by Matt and his mother's family. He had known nothing of his family's background. His mother had spoken only of her father.

He was aware that Laura was looking at him with uncertainty. She had defended him valiantly and the memory brought a tightness to his chest.

"I am a sea-captain," he replied, his own pride making him stubborn. "I want my ship back. That is how I earn my living."

"That is no life for the future master of Fairfield," Lionel declared.

"I will not be supported by my wife's income," Matt rejoined.

"That's your pride talking. Your responsibilities are to Laura and to Fairfield."

Matt controlled the anger welling within him. "Obviously I will stand by Laura. But my life is upon the sea and not here in Essex."

"Your pride is misplaced, Thorne. You say you are proud to bear your mother's name. There is nothing to be ashamed of in your Thorne heritage."

"It isn't as simple as that," Matt said heavily. "My life at this moment is not my own. I know that it was no accident which killed my first wife and daughter. Their deaths must be avenged. I have no future until I can lay to rest the ghosts of my past. To do that I have business in London. I leave in an hour."

"This business," Lionel asked, "is it to do with Sir James Breten?"

Matt held himself stiffly, his voice taut with suppressed emotion. "It was upon Breten's estate in Kent that Susannah and Rachel died. Breten was the one who laid the false charges of debt against me and had me imprisoned. I want to know why. He believes himself above the law, but he will answer to my pistol. I intend to challenge him to a duel."

With a curt bow to them both he left the room. In truth he no longer knew what he wanted. He was still reeling from the information Lionel had given him about his family. He needed to think, and he had delayed too long his confrontation with Sir James Breten.

As the sound of Matt's footsteps faded Lionel turned to Laura. "Talk to this husband of yours and make him see sense."

"No, Grandfather," Laura said firmly. "Matt must decide his own future. It doesn't matter that you have burned the agreement we signed. I will not tie Matt to a marriage he does not want. He is free to decide."

"But I thought you loved him."

"I do."

"Then why risk losing him?"

"Because Matt can never be bought or ordered. Yes, I love him. But he is a proud man. If our marriage is to survive it must be upon his terms or not at all."

Chapter Eleven

Laura was torn between love and duty. She was worried about Matt and had received no word from him since he'd left Fairfield. She could not rid her mind of the feeling that he was in danger. Yet it was impossible for her to follow him to London. Matt had left Fairfield an hour after Cecil Stanton had confronted her grandfather, and that evening Lionel had collapsed. The physician had warned her that her grandfather had suffered another seizure of the heart. Another attack could kill him. For a week she had not left his side, but in the last few days be had begun to recover his strength, though he was still forbidden to leave his bed.

She had just retired, but could not face sleeping alone. She knelt by the fire and sighed. She missed Matt and it had taken all her will-power not to write and entreat him to return to Fairfield. She feared the consequences of his confronting Sir James Breten. If Grandfather were not so ill she would have gone to London to be at her husband's side and support him. Matt had denounced her words of love as nothing more than infatuation. He was so wrong. This crippling ache she felt when he was absent was not infatuation. Neither was the dizzying heights her senses soared to at his slightest touch. She had rejected enough ardent suitors to know that she loved Matt with all her heart. And she was determined that he would acknowledge it.

If he did not believe her avowals of love then only by deeds could she ever convince him. And for that she must be in London. Yet how could she leave her grandfather when he was so ill? She had written a short letter to Matt, telling him that her grandfather had collapsed and had been ordered to rest. Matt had his own affairs to set in order and she would not add to his burdens by causing him to worry over matters at Fairfield.

Matt had returned to Stanton House in Lincoln's Inn and in the following week saw Breten twice. Each time he was in the company of his mother, Lady Henrietta, and to spare the woman's sensibilities he refrained from challenging Breten to a duel in front of her. By day he visited all the fashionable coffeehouses and meeting places, hoping to discover Breten alone, and in the evenings he accepted the invitations which poured in for him to dine or attend a reception.

There were many curious questions about his presence in London without his wife, the most persistent of which came from Mary Montgomery. Her reputation preceded her, and once Matt would have found the attention of such a beautiful and notoriously passionate woman difficult to resist, but though he flirted with her he was unmoved by her beauty, and her obvious intention to win him to her bed. After the freshness and honest passion of Laura he had no wish to become another trophy for the jaded palate of London's most notorious wanton. In short, he was fast losing patience with Mary Montgomery's pursuit, and when, one evening, he attended a gaming-house he was relieved that she was not present. Breten often frequented the place and Matt hoped that tonight he would not be disappointed. An hour later Sir James sauntered into the main salon with several companions. Matt delayed no longer. His frustration at waiting had fanned his temper. He wanted justice, and he wanted it now.

With single-minded purpose he crossed the room and was several feet from Breten before the latter recognised him. A look of hostility flickered over the older man's haughty features.

"You are a liar and a blackguard, sir." Matt slapped Breten's cheek with his glove. "I demand satisfaction."

There were several shocked gasps from the players watching from the gaming-tables, but also many expressions in the room showed pleasure in Sir James's discomfiture. Breten was unpopular; his overbearing arrogance had won him many enemies.

Sir James's dark eyes narrowed with hatred as he glared at Matt. "I don't fight with those beneath me."

"Then you are a coward as well as a blackguard, sir," Matt announced.

One of Breten's companions, a pompous figure in white satin, declared arrogantly, "Why, it's the upstart who married the Stanton heiress. The man deserves to be horsewhipped for his insolence."

Matt ignored the outburst, his concentration focused on Sir James. "You wanted me silenced for some reason of your own, Breten," he taunted. "Are you man enough to answer my challenge?"

"You need a lesson taught you in manners," Breten sneered. "You're an upstart who needs to know his place. As the challenged party, the choice of weapons is mine. Pistols." He gave a malevolent smile. "Name your seconds, and mine will attend them to arrange the details."

Matt looked at Adam Melchet and Sidney Harris, two gentlemen he had befriended since his marriage. "Will you be my seconds?"

"Yes, if you are determined on this course," the tall, blond-wigged Adam Melchet replied, looking concerned. "But I beg you to reconsider."

"Breten has escaped justice for too long," Matt said sharply. "He will answer to me."

Another of Matt's companions cautioned, "Duelling is illegal. We could all be thrown in prison."

"Then you need be no part of it, my friend." Matt turned to Sidney Harris, who nodded his agreement.

An hour later Matt was in the study of Stanton House, staring at the letter he was trying to write to Laura. It was meant to be a simple missive, but as he began to write the image of her was so clear and temptingly lovely in his mind that he found it impossible to form the words. He owed her more than a terse explanation, and there was, of course, the possibility that he would be killed on the morrow. Who would then protect her from her cousin when Lionel Stanton died? He shook his head to clear his thoughts. Once a widow, Laura would be free to marry again, and to a man who was her equal in status and wealth. Why should that thought cause him such regret? For years he had awaited the day he could bring Susannah's murderer to account.

Adam Melchet was announced and Matt rose from his chair, offering his friend a brandy. Melchet took it and drained it in one gulp, his thin face drawn beneath his blond periwig.

"Breten won't reconsider," he said at last. "It's to remain pistols at dawn, tomorrow on the heath. The arrogant cur says he has an important engagement at ten in the morning and wants you, and this unpleasant incident, out of the way. He spoke as though this was no mere matter of satisfying honour. He wants you dead, Matt. Why?"

"Does a man like Breten need a reason?"

"Then for God's sake, Matt, send him an apology! This is madness. Breten is a crack shot. In his youth there were several scandals linked to his name and he spent a month in the Tower when he shattered the arm of an earl's son in a duel. His mother petitioned King Charles II for his release. Some say she even slept with him to gain it. There's nothing Lady Henrietta would not do for her precious son."

"There can be no apology unless he explains the circumstances of the deaths of my wife and child. And why I was imprisoned. He's guilty as hell. This time he will pay the penalty for it."

"If you kill him, Matt, you'll hang." Adam swung his lithe figure out of the chair and paced the room. "Dammit, Matt, you've just wed one of the most beautiful women in England. Why throw all that away?"

"Because Breten cannot be allowed to escape justice."

"Then I hope you've made your will," Adam groaned in frustration.

For another hour he continued—in vain—to try and persuade Matt to send an apology to Sir James while drinking heavily from Matt's brandy decanter. Eventually he fell asleep in a chair. Matt put a hand on his shoulder and gently shook him awake.

"Go upstairs and sleep in comfort. I'll call you when it's time to leave in the morning."

"Can't leave you alone," Adam insisted.

"I've some letters to write and would prefer my own company."

Adam nodded, and as his friend climbed the stairs and the great clock in the hall struck midnight Matt sank on to a chair in the study and bowed his head in his hands. Avenging Susannah and Rachel's deaths had been an obsession for so long, but now that he was close to achieving his ends he felt no elation. He felt only a great weight of sadness. As he thought of his young daughter his eyes filled with tears and his heartache increased. He should never have gone to Fairfield. There he had begun to lose sight of his goal—his craving for revenge. He still loved Susannah, but it was Laura's image which was always in his mind. He could not help feeling that he had betrayed Susannah. He could not allow her death to go unavenged, and beyond that he was not prepared to consider his future.

There was a tap on the door and a footman entered. "There's a woman to see you. She would not give her name."

"It's gone midnight," Matt said wearily. "Send her away. I've no wish to see anyone."

The door was pushed open and a strong, musky

perfume filled the study as a cloaked woman glided into the room. "I heard of the duel tomorrow and came at once."

She threw back the hood of her cloak, revealing her blonde hair, and pulled the mask from her face. Mary Montgomery removed her cloak and moved towards him, her hips swaying provocatively and her large breasts exposed almost in their entirety in the plunging neckline of her scarlet gown.

"You cannot spend the night before a duel alone, and your wife is still at Fairfield," she said, pouting as she put her hands on his shoulders and pressed her body against his.

Matt captured her hands and drew back. "You should not be here, Mary."

"Indeed I should not. It's scandalous the way you have ignored me, Matt. You should have come to me." She pulled his hands so that they were pressed against her breasts, her voice a soft, seductive purr. "No man should be alone on the night before a duel. I will give you a night you will never forget."

"Your offer is generous, but I must decline."

She laughed and rubbed her hips provocatively against him. "No man has ever refused me."

Matt's patience was stretched to its limit. "You are a beautiful and desirable woman, but you forget I am but recently wed. I love my wife."

Beneath the layer of rice powder on her face, her cheeks mottled with angry colour. Her eyes, which moments earlier had been filled with invitation, were now slitted with venom. "That's absolute rot," she spat. "You married the Stanton heiress for her money. You don't love her. It's all over town that you challenged Breten to this duel because your first wife was found dead on one of his estates.''

"Who is spreading those rumours?" Matt demanded.

"It's no secret that you and Breten hate each other. Since your meeting at Lord Clifton's ball Society has been laughing at Laura Stanton behind her back. You did not marry her for love, did you?"

"I think you had better leave." Matt snatched up Mary Montgomery's cloak and flung it around the woman's shoulders as he propelled her towards the door.

"No one rejects me," she seethed as he escorted her to the front door. "Especially an upstart of a fortune-hunter. I hope Breten does kill you. By all accounts you and Laura Stanton deserve each other. She only married you to ensure that her cousin never inherited Fairfield. She's as much of a rogue as you are."

Matt was grim-lipped as he closed the waiting carriage door on the courtesan, and as he turned to enter the house he caught a movement in the shadows of the house opposite. A figure detached itself from the darkness and ran off down the street. He considered chasing Guy Stanton's spy, but knew the man would disappear in the maze of alleyways.

As he closed the study door behind him he felt a sick wave of despair engulf him. Tomorrow he honoured his vow to bring Breten to justice. He had not expected to feel this emptiness at having failed Laura. Their ruse to convince society that she and he had married for love had failed. The duel tomorrow would only fuel the gossip about their marriage. A marriage, he realised too late, that he did not want to turn his back on. Laura was in his blood and he did not want to lose her.

His mind raced, forming plans for his future. The marriage would have to be on his terms. It could succeed if he was again in possession of the *Sea Maiden.* Two years at sea, dealing only in precious spices and materials from the Orient, and he could make enough to buy a second and third ship and begin to build up a small fleet. In five or seven years his fortune would be made.

He checked the rapid pace of his thoughts with a bitter laugh. He was confident of his marksmanship with a pistol. At sea there had been hours aplenty when the ship was becalmed, and he had used those hours perfecting both his fencing and shooting skills. If a ship was boarded by pirates a man's life could depend upon such expertise. But the outcome of a duel with pistols was never certain. Breten was also a skilled marksman. It was not unlikely that, even if he killed his adversary, Matt would himself receive a mortal wound.

Laura started violently as the bedchamber door was flung open and Sarah entered in her nightclothes. The candle-flame flared dangerously in the maid's shaking hands and her face was ashen.

"Mistress, come at once. It's your grandfather..."

The sight of the maid's white face filled Laura with dread. Snatching up her robe, she ran to her grandfather's bedside. Barker barred her way as she entered the bedchamber.

"He's passed away, mistress," he said hoarsely. "I've sent for the physician."

"No, Grandfather can't be dead!" Laura pushed

Barker aside and stumbled to the four-poster bed. She pulled the bed-hangings apart and sank to the floor at his side, her throat aching with the depth of her loss. Two coins had been put over his eyelids, but apart from that he looked so peaceful, as though he merely slept.

"Oh, Grandfather, you were recovering so well. Why did you have to die? Uncle Cecil and Guy are responsible for your relapse. Their greed for Fairfield brought your death about."

Sarah was sobbing quietly behind her and Laura's own tears were threatening to overwhelm her. She put her hands together and prayed that his soul would be at peace, then rose stiffly to her feet.

"See to what must be done," she said to Barker.

The need to be alone with her grief made her flee the room. Grief tore through her with such ferocity that she slumped on the bed, unable to stifle her tears, and in the midst of her misery she began to feel the familiar stomach cramps. Her wretchedness increased at realising that she had not conceived Matt's child.

Matt was still struggling to write to Laura—a letter to be delivered only if he did not survive the duel. For his own peace of mind he did not attempt to analyse his feelings for her. But this was not a letter he could write without being honest, and it was that honesty which was making it so hard for him to face death with equanimity on the duelling field. He knew now that he had so much to live for.

Outside in the street he heard a carriage draw up. He glanced at his pocket-watch and discovered it was an hour before dawn. Suspecting that Sidney Harris had brought a carriage to drive them to the heath, he finished the letter in a rush and stared for a moment at the manner in which he had signed it. "Your devoted and loving husband, Matthew Thorne."

He only wished he could have spoken the words to Laura when last they had made love in the hayloft. He'd been a fool to allow his pride to build so many barriers between them. He would always love Susannah, but Susannah was the idealistic love of his youth. Laura was different. She was the abiding love of his future...

He stood up to answer the knock on the outside door, knowing that the servants would still be abed. His flippant greeting to Sidney Harris dried in his throat as he saw the tall figure of a veiled woman in black standing on the step.

"I have not come all this way to conduct my speech with you on the doorstep like a common tradesman, Mr Thorne," a strident, cultured voice announced. "Stand aside and invite me in."

Taken aback, Matt moved aside. It was only as he found himself following the imposing figure towards the lighted study that his anger rose at the way the woman had spoken to him as though he were a lackey.

"Madam, what is the purpose of your visit?" he said, drawing level with her and preventing her from entering the room.

She nodded in the direction of the study. "I will discuss it behind closed doors. Servants gossip."

"The servants are abed at this hour."

She ignored him and entered the study to take up a commanding stance by the fire. "I want you to call off this duel you intend to fight with Sir James Breten."

"That is none of your affair, madam." Matt struggled to control his anger at the woman's interference.

"It is very much my affair, and you can curb your insolence, young man." The woman lifted her black veil back over her high lace head-dress *à la Fontage* and he recognised Lady Henrietta Breten.

"I have nothing to say to you, Lady Breten," Matt said stiffly.

"But I have much to say to you, young man. When I have finished you will understand why it is impossible for you to fight this duel." She seated herself on a chair by the fire and glared up at him. "Please sit down. You wanted to learn the truth about the deaths of Susannah Thorne and her child. They were nothing to do with my son James."

"They died on Breten land."

She bowed her head and a look of pain crossed her still refined features. But there was no softness in her face; her mouth and eyes were scored with hard lines of bitterness. This was a woman who did not know the meaning of compromise. There was no spare flesh on her high cheekbones and in her prime she must have been a beautiful woman. Her dark eyes were as sharp and bright as a viper's as she studied him.

"I can see you will not be satisfied until you have the whole story," she announced reluctantly. "James was my only child and his duty was clear—to marry well and provide strong sons to inherit the Breten lands. He failed me, but I stood by him. He has a son, Robert—a wild, undisciplined man, several months younger than yourself. Robert was responsible for your wife and child's deaths, not James."

"Then he must be brought to justice," Matt demanded.

"That is not possible!"

Matt's fiery outburst was halted as he saw that Lady Henrietta was struggling to keep her face devoid of emotion. She was failing. Her eyes were haggard and her mouth a grim slash from some long-suppressed torment. She drew a deep breath, her stare bleak as she faced him.

"My grandson is shut away in an asylum for the insane. The woman and child's deaths proved he was unbalanced. There had been other incidents on the estate. First of unnecessary beatings of people who defied him. When a milkmaid was found strangled in a wood I still did not believe that Robert could be involved. Even when the body of a young cowherd was found, beaten and floating in a stream, Robert convinced me that he knew nothing of the incident. But when your wife's body was found I knew that Robert was responsible and that he was capable of killing again."

Matt stifled the rage burning through him. Lady Henrietta spoke so dispassionately about Susannah's death, when it had wrecked his life. "I was at sea when Susannah died. When I docked I travelled to Kent and made extensive enquiries about her death. I met with silence. No one in the area would speak of the incident."

"The people who owe their livelihoods to Sir James had been given warnings. Everyone in the district has some relative who is beholden to my family for their homes and jobs," Lady Henrietta said primly.

"I never understood why Susannah should have been in Kent?" Matt voiced the question which had baffled him for so many years.

"She was fortune-hunting, what else?"

Matt shot out of his seat and paced for several moments to control the scalding heat of his temper. Finally he managed to say in a reasonable voice, "That is preposterous."

"Come, now, don't play the innocent with me." Lady Henrietta's dark eyes flayed him contemptuously. "Your mother sent her. I thought I had dealt with that scheming whore, Penelope Thorne, but the woman must have learned something of the truth. She thought I'd pay for her to keep silent."

"I will not have my mother spoken of in that manner," Matt flared. "Out of respect to your venerable years, your ladyship, I have tried to be patient. I have no intention of stepping down from the duel with your son. I must ask you to leave. I have matters still to attend to before I meet Sir James."

"Sit down and listen to what I have to say," Lady Henrietta rapped out.

"I will not, your ladyship," Matt responded with chill civility. "You tell me blithely, and without any apparent remorse, that your grandson was responsible for the deaths of my wife and daughter. Then you malign my mother and expect me to sit and listen to you. You may have Sir James firmly tied to your apron-strings, but you have no hold over me. I've no wish to use force, but I will if you do not immediately leave this house."

Matt strode to the study door and opened it. When the woman remained firmly in her chair he lost his patience. "There is absolutely nothing you can say which will stop the duel. Sir James has done everything in his power to destroy me. Why only he knows. Because of him I was arrested for a debt I did not owe and would have spent the rest of my life in prison.''

"I acted in my son's name. He knew nothing of your imprisonment.''

Matt glowered at her pathetic attempt to lie for her son. "Your story does not hold water, your ladyship. Breten bought out my partner in the *Sea Maiden* some months before.''

Lady Henrietta Breten smiled tautly. "I had those papers forged with my son's signature. Your foolish wife told me much about you. The rest I learned from Caleb Van Steenis. I was prepared to do anything to save my son's reputation. It was the only way I could stop you from snooping and finding out the truth.''

Matt retraced his steps into the room. The woman did not flinch as he glared at her. What she said made no sense. Yet a feeling of foreboding tightened his stomach. He dismissed it as caused by tiredness and his concern for Laura. The contempt he felt for Lady Henrietta's family blazed out. "What did I ever do to harm you? If your grandson is safely locked away in an asylum, how could I discover anything to harm your family?''

"By existing!'' she said harshly. "When your wife came to me with her absurd notion that I would help Penelope Thorne, Robert overheard our conversation. It was what finally tipped his unstable mind into madness.'' She paused and dropped her gaze from his furious glare. Clenching her hands together, she swallowed several times, clearly having difficulty in continuing. Her eyes, when they returned to hold his stare, were like chips of black ice. "You cannot duel with Sir James Breten because he is your father.''

Matt recoiled as though a battering-ram had thudded into his stomach. "That's not true. My mother was married to my father. The knave deserted her. Breten was wed to the Lady Cynthia at that time."

Lady Henrietta snorted in disgust. "He married Cynthia later. He married Penelope Thorne first. I would not accept that he had wed a nobody—the daughter of an impoverished preacher. Your mother knew her place; I grant her that. More than you do. You jumped at the chance to wed the Stanton heiress."

Matt rubbed the back of his neck and stared in disbelief at Lady Henrietta's haughty figure. Every instinct, all sense and reasoning made him reject her declaration. His hatred for Sir James Breten was so deep that he stubbornly refused to listen. It was the wild story of a desperate woman trying to save her son from being killed in a duel. "I heard you would stop at nothing to protect your son. But this…this is…"

"It is the truth. And don't think I'm proud to admit that you are my grandson. After all I worked for—it has come to naught. I have already seen the first signs of instability in my two-year-old great-grandson. Through Robert, the Breten line is now cursed with madness."

Matt sank down into a chair opposite his visitor, his voice accusing. "I think you had better tell me everything. I'm still not convinced this is not some ruse to stop the duel. And why should you be telling me this? Sir James is a notable marksman and has fought several duels. I have not."

"You are no novice with a pistol. Sidney Harris came to my house earlier to try and persuade my son not to fight you. Sir James was out. Harris is an honest man. I believed him when he said you were capable of hitting a sixpence which has been tossed in the air.''

Matt stood up, rubbing his chin as he paced the study. ''If I am to believe your absurd claim, hadn't you better tell me the full story?'' he said tautly. He still believed that Lady Henrietta was lying, but he hoped to learn why Susannah had been on Breten land.

''James married Penelope Thorne after falling in love with the wench.'' Lady Henrietta spoke in a clipped voice without looking at him. ''He kept it secret from me, knowing that I planned he should wed Lady Cynthia Minton. I did not intend that my plans would be thwarted. James was sent to our Scottish estate to oversee a matter there. While he was away I visited Penelope Thorne and told her that since James was already contracted to wed Lady Cynthia her marriage to him was illegal. She was distraught, of course, but she understood how unsuitable the match was. She had enough breeding to know that one should always marry within one's station...that like must marry like... She refused my offer of money, saying she would move to London.''

Her piercing stare studied Matt's closed expression. He gave no sign of the turmoil of his emotions. Lady Henrietta had certainly checked on his past.

Her lips thinned to a sneer as she continued. ''It was only later that I learned she was expecting a child. A bastard child in my eyes. One I vowed would never set foot on Breten property. But I digress... The wench was too ashamed to return to her family, which I suppose showed she had some scruples. When James returned from Scotland he was told that Penelope Thorne had run off with a soldier. When he could find no trace of her he finally believed the story and agreed to marry Lady Cynthia. I had all records of his marriage to your mother struck from the parish registers. The priest was a drunkard and easily corruptible."

Matt stood rigid, only a muscle pumping along his jaw betraying the effort it was costing him to control his anger and not have the woman thrown out. It was she who had no scruples. The entire absurd tale was a lie from beginning to end. It would not save her son from his retribution.

"If what you say is true," Matt said with lethal quietness, "which I believe it is not, then you condemned an honourable woman to shame and penury."

A more rational part of his mind reasoned that Lady Henrietta Breten could have bullied his gentle mother into believing everything she said. Marriage contracts were considered as legally binding as the wedding ceremony, but in many cases they had been overturned, provided the couple had never consummated the union. But Sir James Breten was not his father. He would not accept that.

He went on coldly, "I was imprisoned because of the papers signed by Sir James Breten, and my wife and daughter died mysteriously on his land. Avenging their deaths is all that concerns me. That is why I will face Sir James on the heath tomorrow."

"I have told you the truth," Lady Henrietta said hollowly. "We reap what we sow. My son's marriage to the Lady Cynthia was supposed to strengthen our ancient lineage. Instead the creature came from mad stock—carefully hidden, of course, over the generations." She paused, and it seemed to take a great effort for her to continue. "James knew nothing of your birth."

Lady Henrietta eyed Matt, defiant and unrepentant. "Your mother had been grievously ill. Your wife tended her, and heard during the delirious ramblings of Penelope Thorne's marriage. My son's name was also spoken. Misguided romantic that your wife was, she thought Sir James would help Mistress Thorne."

Again she halted, her expression uncompromising and haughty.

"Go on," Matt ground out. "I'm interested to learn just how many lies you'll weave to save your worthless son's hide."

"I wish they were lies," Lady Henrietta said heavily. "James was away when your wife arrived. I saw her in his stead. There was no disputing that Rachel Thorne had Breten blood; she was very like my sister as a child. I gave your wife a hundred pounds and of course denied everything. I was not aware that Robert had overheard her story."

For the first time since her arrival her glance failed to hold Matt's. She fidgeted for a moment with the gold knob on her walking-cane. "Robert must have followed her when she left the house." Her voice had lost its strident edge. "He ran them down with his carriage. When questioned he said the woman was a thief who had stolen the money in her possession, and that, terrified of arrest, she had thrown herself under the carriage wheels."

Matt slammed his fist against the wall, unheeding of the pain which shot up his arm. Lady Henrietta's head was bowed, but he felt no sympathy for her. She had felt none for his mother, if there was any grain of truth in this preposterous tale. The years of pent-up fury burst from him. "So at last the truth. Robert Breten was responsible for the deaths of my wife and child. He was a true son of his class. He murdered them cold-bloodedly. For what reason—sport?"

Matt paced the room. So Sir James had not been responsible for Susannah's death, but clearly the man had been scared witless lest Matt should learn the truth.

"Your story has a flaw." Only his iron control kept his anger in check. "If Sir James knew nothing of my imprisonment or Susannah's death, why is it that since my marriage he has been so openly hostile towards me?"

"I told him that you were an impostor; that you had heard the story of his marriage to Penelope Thorne and were passing yourself off as his son. Such a scandal could destroy his career at Court."

"Again you betray yourself, Lady Henrietta. If you truly believe that Sir James is my father, you have but to tell him the story you have told me. That, if he was married to Penelope Thorne, she did not run off with a soldier. You drove her away."

"And risk losing his love? He's all I've got in the world."

"As Susannah and Rachel were once all I had." Matt controlled his slipping temper with difficulty. How like the gentry to stoop so low to get their own way. Lady Henrietta must think him a fool to swallow this absurd story.

Lady Henrietta stood up and drew a leather pouch from beneath her cloak. "There is one hundred pounds in gold here. In my coach I have another nine hundred, awaiting your agreement to flee London and forget this duel."

"I cannot be bought, Lady Henrietta." Matt blazed all his contempt for the gentry. Her attempt to bribe him confirmed to him that everything the woman had said about her son was a lie. The woman had no morals or scruples. It was likely that her grandson was in an asylum for the insane and had caused Susannah's death. He was out of Matt's reach. Not so Sir James.

"Laura Stanton bought you for the same sum," Lady Henrietta sneered.

Matt's lips thinned into a bleak line. "I suggest you leave, Lady Henrietta."

He opened the door of the study, and this time Lady Henrietta replaced the veil over her face and rose. He escorted her to her carriage where three coachmen and a linkboy awaited her. As one of the coachmen opened the door she nodded to a small chest on the floor. "One thousand pounds, Mr Thorne. Take it and leave London tonight."

A muscle throbbed along his jaw and his voice was harsh. "Have your coachmen take it into the house."

He watched in silence as two of the men struggled up the steps with the heavy weight. Lady Henrietta gave a satisfied sigh. "I admit I did not think I could buy you so easily, Mr Thorne."

"But you haven't, your ladyship," he answered, backing up the steps. "You stole my ship from me, and a valuable cargo. I'm taking this money in partial repayment of that theft. It will repay Laura Stanton for settling the debts on the papers you forged to have me imprisoned."

Matt stood at the top of the steps, his back protected by the open door and his hand on the hilt of his sword lest the coachmen should try to rush him.

"I believe you are capable of weaving the absurd

web of lies you told me because I am the younger man and you fear my skill with a pistol.''

"Every word is true." Her voice had lost its strident edge.

"Then your family has a great deal to answer for."

"You mean still to fight my son?"

"I do."

"Then you and your father will both be damned."

As soon as it was light Laura left her room and took up vigil by her grandfather's corpse. His body had been bathed and laid out; his hands, folded over his shroud, held a large gold cross, and four large candles were placed at each corner of the bed. The Reverend Mr Harvey stood at the head of the bed, his prayer-book open. Laura knelt at his side and one by one, as word of her grandfather's death spread, servants, tenants, neighbours and acquaintances came to pay their respects. The funeral was to be at noon tomorrow. Laura's head remained bowed in prayer until gradually an ominous silence fell over the mourners gathered in the room.

Turning her head, she saw Cecil and Guy Stanton standing at the foot of the bed. She was astonished that they were here. Her uncle and cousin lived a two-day ride away. Their expressions were malevolent and without grief and they had not even troubled to remove their hats in respect of the dead.

"If you cannot show the proper respect to your kin," Laura said coldly, "then leave."

"We have a right to be here for the reading of my brother's will," Cecil Stanton declared. "When we heard that Lionel had suffered another seizure we stayed close by. I want to see the document purportedly signed by King William which robbed me of my inheritance.''

Laura was too weighted by her grief to argue with them. ''The lawyer will not arrive from Colchester until tomorrow. You are not welcome in this house. There are rooms aplenty at the inn.''

''Do you hear how the haughty bitch commands us?'' Cecil Stanton spoke to the Reverend Mr Harvey. ''Fairfield is rightly mine.''

The vicar stepped forward. ''If you cannot show respect for the dead I will ask the servants to remove you, sir. There is no question who is the rightful heir to Fairfield. It is Mistress Laura, as decreed by King William himself.''

''Come, Guy,'' Cecil snarled. ''We will return tomorrow. I would not miss the pleasure of seeing my brother lowered into his grave.''

Laura shivered at the hatred in her uncle's voice. He would never accept that Fairfield was lost to him.

The heath was covered in thick mist and Matt paced back and forth in front of the carriage as he fretted on the arrival of Sir James Breten. The man was late. Matt had deliberately cast Lady Henrietta's story to the back of his mind. He conceded that it was a clever ruse. Just one second of hesitancy on his part was all it would take for him to lose the edge in the duel and be mortally wounded by Sir James. He stared bleakly towards the London road; his nerves were taut and all he wanted was for the affair to be finished with. He did not think for a moment that Sir James would not come. The visibility on the roads was so bad that their own journey had taken longer than they expected.

"Get back into the carriage, Matt," Adam said. "You'll be frozen to the bone and miss your aim."

"Matt never misses," Sidney spoke, his voice muffled by his cloak, which was wrapped about his lower face as he hugged his arms about his shivering figure. "How much longer do you intend to wait?"

"I've already waited six years," Matt said, leaning on the side of the carriage. His rapid pacing had warmed his body and he was glad of the cold air which chased the cobwebs from his brain. He had not slept. All night Lady Henrietta's words had given him no peace. He still refused to believe her story. For too many years he had despised the gentry, and Sir James Breten most of all. On his encounter with him at Lady Clifford's ball he had felt such overwhelming hatred that it was inconceivable that the man was his father. Surely if Lady Henrietta had spoken the truth he would have felt some bond, some link of affection, no matter how small?

He was composed as he watched the carriage appear out of the mist. The first lesson he had learned in combat was to clear his mind of all thoughts, to concentrate on the matter in hand. It had served him well in his street-fights as a lad and had been invaluable in the occasional battles he had waged at sea against pirates. However, he had never fought a duel before and he felt the same triggering of nerves in his stomach that he experienced before every sea battle. He was not afraid to die for what he believed was right. At last he was to honour the vow he had made on Susannah's and Rachel's graves. His expression was grim. Guiltily, he was surprised to find how much he wanted to live. On the point of avenging his wife's and daughter's deaths he regretted that he might never now share a future with Laura.

Resolutely, he pushed that remorse aside. If there was regret for a future which might have been, the time for that was past. To survive he must concentrate only upon the next few minutes. If God was on his side Sir James's shot would not be a mortal wound to him.

He spared only a cursory glance at his adversary as he stripped off his cloak and jacket and approached the seconds in his long vest and shirt-sleeves. Sir James had also removed his outer garments. Sir James's second produced a walnut inlaid box and opened the lid to display two of the finest duelling pistols that Matt had ever seen.

"If you approve of the weapons, both are primed and ready," Sir James's second stated.

With a steady hand Matt chose one, tested its weight and balance, and nodded his approval.

There was no tremor in Sir James's hand as he took up his own weapon.

Sidney Harris cleared his throat. "I must ask you both to reconsider."

"I do not retract my challenge," Matt said firmly. He turned to hold Sir James's stare, unconsciously searching for some look or familiarity of feature which would confirm Lady Henrietta's words. There was none, and the hatred he felt for the man was almost choking him in its vehemence. Sir James's expression was set and uncompromising.

"Then, gentlemen, take your places, and on the count of three you may fire," Adam Melchet said in a tight voice. "May God guide your hand, your conscience and your judgement."

Matt took up his position, his legs braced and his body turned sideways to present the smallest target to Sir James, who was some twenty paces distant. Against the greyness of the mist Sir James's figure was clearly outlined and Matt could even see the glitter in the older man's dark eyes.

On the count of one Matt and Breten raised their pistols simultaneously. On the count of two both men released the safety catch with their thumbs, their eyes squinting over the metal barrel as they aligned it with their opponent's heart.

"Three!"

Breten twisted his mouth into a lopsided smile and a dimple appeared briefly in his cheek as his pistol fired. Matt's finger on the trigger hesitated. Pain flared through his side and he staggered back a step. He could feel the warm gushing of blood, chilling as it spread across his shirt in the cold air. There was an expectant silence as the seconds ticked by and Matt kept his pistol levelled at Sir James's heart. The man was at his mercy.

Yet as he stared into the older man's proud and unflinching face still he hesitated. The seconds coughed and fidgeted.

"Why doesn't he fire?" one of Sir James's companions whispered hoarsely.

Matt drew a steadying breath and the pain in his side drained the colour from his face. Sir James stood rock-still, awaiting the shot which could kill him. He showed no fear, and again his lips twisted and the dimple appeared. Matt's expression did not alter in its hostility as he fired contemptuously into the ground. Without a word he turned on his heel and walked towards the carriage. At each step pain slashed through his side and he could feel the wet stickiness of his blood spreading down across his hips. He had received other wounds in battle and he did not have to look to know that his wound was not a fatal one. Sir James's bullet had scored a deep channel just below his rib, but the shot had not entered his body.

"Let me see your wound," Adam demanded.

"It's not as bad as it looks, just a deep graze. Sir James's sight must be failing him for him to miss at such close range."

"Why did you fire into the ground?" Sidney asked. "I thought you wanted him dead."

"There have been too many deaths." Matt shrugged aside an explanation. He winced as Adam eased his shirt from his waistband and examined his wound.

"You've been lucky. That's if you don't bleed to death," he said. He removed his linen cravat, made it into a wad and pressed it against Matt's side to stem the flow of blood.

Sir James's second had come to his side. "How badly are you hurt?" he enquired stiffly.

"You can tell Sir James I shall live. But there are still accounts to be settled between us after he has spoken to the Lady Henrietta about my ship, the *Sea Maiden*. I shall call on him tomorrow with my lawyer."

"What is this about a ship?" interrupted Sir James, who had been listening as he pulled on his jacket and cloak. "And what has the Lady Henrietta to do with anything which concerns an impostor like yourself? For you are an impostor, sir. That is what all this is about, is it not? And I want the matter ended here."

"I claim to be no one other than who I have always been. I am the son of Penelope Thorne." Sir James stood stiffly, his dark eyes snapping with an arrogance that Matt found difficult to stomach, so that he added, "I was born ten months after a wedding took place in a small village church outside Bath." His voice was becoming hoarse as the effort to control his temper and speak civilly began to take its toll. "My father was supposedly a gentleman, though his conduct was that of a reprobate who seduced an innocent woman then abandoned her. She died shamed and in poverty, too proud to reveal the name of the man who had betrayed her."

Aware that the seconds were listening with growing curiosity, Matt put his foot on the step of the carriage, preparing to step inside. Loss of blood was beginning to make him light-headed. He had no wish to be humiliated and give Sir James the satisfaction of seeing him faint. As he sank down on to the carriage seat he leaned forward to hold Breten's grim stare.

"I will call at your house tomorrow with my lawyer. I want my ship back, which your mother contrived to have confiscated for imaginary debts. She wanted me in prison and unable to ask awkward questions about the deaths of Susannah and Rachel Thorne on your land six years ago."

"You say their name was Thorne." An edge of disquiet was apparent in Sir James's voice, but his eyes remained cold and guarded. "The woman and child were beggars who stole money from the house. The woman panicked when my son pursued them and in her terror ran across the path of his carriage. It was a terrible accident, but the woman would have been hanged for theft if she had been caught."

"And you believed that story?" Matt's lip curled back. "I know where your son is now, and that their deaths were the cause of his confinement. It was no accident."

Sir James's face paled and he waved away the hovering seconds. "I would like a word in private with Mr Thorne." As his companions stepped back he climbed into the carriage and sat down opposite Matt.

Adam Melchet remained by the door. "Matt, you should see a physician."

"I will speak with Sir James. It is time everything came out in the open. I have no wish for this vendetta to continue if it can be resolved. All I want is my ship and the money for its cargo returned so that I may get on with my life."

Sir James waited until Melchet had joined the other men before speaking in a low voice. "I will not pay you if you want a bribe to stop this preposterous story you are spreading that you are my son."

"Don't flatter yourself, Breten. I have never claimed to be your son, only the son of Penelope Thorne. I want nothing from any man who could desert my mother after his lust had abated and leave her to live in penury in the poorest quarter of London. Poverty never broke her; she remained a gentlewoman to the end of her days. All I wanted on my return to England was to learn the truth of my wife's and daughter's deaths on your estate."

Matt found himself subjected to Breten's dark and inscrutable stare. The haughtiness had gone from his face and he looked suspiciously on his guard.

"Why did you fire into the ground?" Sir James asked.

"Perhaps for the same reason your shot went wide."

"I misjudged my aim in the dim light."

Matt stared at him fiercely until the older man looked away. He was certain now that Sir James was hiding something. The evasion was momentary. When Breten's dark glare returned to hold his it was pitiless and condemning.

"You say you've waited six years to avenge the deaths of your wife and child, so why back down when I was at your mercy?"

Matt laid his head back against the leather upholstery and sighed wearily. "Your mother called on me last night, demanding that I cry off from the duel. She had concocted an absurd story which I disbelieved because it was easier to discount it than question an unpleasant truth. But as I looked down my pistol barrel her words could not be ignored. I have mourned my daughter for six years. You have a dimple, Sir James. It was that which stopped me killing you. Rachel had a similar dimple, that is all. When it came to it perhaps I was not man enough to shoot a man down so cold-bloodedly."

Sir James had grown very pale. "You have Penelope's stubbornness and her colouring. So the soldier deserted her in London, did he?" The sneer had returned to his voice.

Matt felt the years of resentment and hatred begin to boil within his gut. "There never was a soldier. And you were the man who abandoned her to take a wealthier wife. Lady Henrietta did not lie when she said you were my father."

"So you continue that ruse," Sir James said, recovering his composure. "You've ferreted deep to get your information. Penelope Thorne ran off with a soldier."

Matt started forward, his fist clenched, but he was brought up short by the agonising pain from his wound. Gasping, he fell back on the seat and bit out, "That's what Lady Henrietta wanted you to believe. When you were in Scotland she visited my mother. She explained to her how you had married beneath your station. That like should always marry like... That in fact you were not legally married at all since you were precontracted to the Lady Cynthia."

From the fixed bleakness of Sir James's stare, Matt knew he had hit upon the truth. He would show no mercy now. "Lady Henrietta struck me as a very persuasive woman. And if you knew my mother you will know how fiercely proud and stubborn she could be. She went to London so that you would be free to marry the woman she then believed that you were legally bound to. In her heart she hoped that you would find her. She never married, and rejected any suitors."

There was a choking sound from Sir James and his knuckles were white as he gripped his hands together and bowed his head.

Matt went on. "I never knew why Susannah went to your estate. Lady Henrietta said that it was because Penelope was grievously ill with a fever. In her delirium she spoke your name and of her marriage. My ship had been battered by a storm and needed substantial repairs. I was two months late returning to England and they had no money for a physician to attend my mother. Susannah travelled to Kent in des-

peration to ask for your mercy. You were away and
Lady Henrietta dealt with the matter. Apparently your
son overheard their conversation. Robert Breten murdered your granddaughter, Sir James. I think that
knowledge is punishment enough for your crimes. I
only learned all this last night. Even now Lady Henrietta fights your battles for you. The dimple saved
you, but I still was not certain that you were my father
until you confessed to knowing my mother."

There was no arrogance now in Sir James's
haughty features, only pain. "I did not know you ex-
isted. I swear I did not know. I followed Penelope to
London, but could not find her. It never occurred to
me that she would be forced to live in the poorest
quarter. When I still balked at marrying the Lady
Cynthia I was told that Penelope had died while mis-
carrying the soldier's child. I loved your mother as I
never loved another woman." A ray of hope dawned
in his eyes. "Did she survive the fever? Is she alive
now?"

"She recovered from the fever, but it left her lungs
weak. She died the following year."

Sir James closed his eyes, and his throat worked as
he struggled to combat his emotions. When he opened
his eyes again he stared at the blood spreading
through the wadding and over Matt's fingers which
were placed over his wound. "I nearly killed my own
son—Penelope's child."

"Yes, Penelope's child and proudly so—but not
yours, sir."

"But you are my son! And I was married to your
mother before I wed Cynthia. We never divorced.
You are my heir—not Robert. My marriage to Cynthia was bigamous."

All his life Matt had wanted to know the identity of his father. He had wondered how he would feel. Hatred? Affection? He had not expected to feel pity. No amount of remorse on Sir James's part could wipe out the suffering of his mother and he could never forgive him for abandoning her.

"I want nothing from you except what was stolen from me—my ship and the money for its cargo," Matt answered coldly. "I will never permit my mother's name to be linked in a scandal which will rock England. I have married again and would also protect my wife from the repercussions of such a scandal. It would also destroy your career, Sir James."

He no longer felt hatred for Sir James. He saw his father for the still handsome but dissolute and weak creature that he was.

"But I am offering you wealth," Sir James stared at him in puzzlement. "And land beyond your wildest dreams."

"I am refusing it. If you had really wanted to find Penelope you would have done so. You chose the easy way out. I am as I have always been...the son of Penelope Thorne and no one else."

Sir James Breten bowed his head for a long moment, and when he lifted it Matt saw that his dark eyes were clouded with pain. "You are right to be proud of being Penelope's son. Would that I had proved worthy of her. My mother is not an easy woman to overrule, or to live with, when she is set upon governing your life. I always gave in to her, preferring a quiet life. But not over the matter of your ship. I will see to it that you are fully compensated for your loss."

"Then there will be no need for us to meet again, sir." Matt felt the last of his hostility for the man ebb. He glimpsed a moment's sadness in Sir James's eyes. Both men knew they could never be close as father and son should be. Penelope's, Susannah's and Rachel's ghosts stood too firmly between them.

Chapter Twelve

The silence of a tomb followed Mr Tooley's reading of Lionel Stanton's will. As Laura had expected, she had inherited everything.

"And if Mrs Thorne dies without issue?" Cecil queried in a bombastic tone. "Then surely the property passes to my family, as the only other Stanton kin?"

The thin, pale lips of Mr Tooley pinched tighter, but there was a satisfied glint in his eye as he continued. "No. Before his death Lionel Stanton again petitioned King William to end the entail of the estate. This time the King, in light of Miss Stanton's recent marriage to Mr Thorne, granted the request. And I think we can safely say, don't you, Mr Stanton, that neither you nor your son will be appearing as beneficiaries in the wills of Mr and Mrs Thorne?"

With a thunderous expression mottling his fleshy face Cecil stood up and left the room without speaking. Guy followed, but turned to pause by the door. Laura, still struggling with the shock and relief of what she had just learned, turned to look at him. Guy's expression was malevolent.

"Enjoy Fairfield while you can, Laura." Every word was laced with threat.

Laura suppressed a shudder. Would she have to spend the rest of her life guarding against her cousin's spite?

Remembering her duties as mistress of Fairfield, she turned to Mr Tooley. "Would you like to stay to dine? You have a long journey back to Colchester."

The lawyer collected his papers and stood up. "Thank you for the invitation, but I must decline."

Laura escorted him to the door, but it was obvious that the lawyer was troubled.

"Is anything amiss, Mr Tooley? Are my grandfather's affairs not in order?"

"Your grandfather was very specific in his instructions. My concern is for yourself, Mistress Thorne. I am surprised that your husband is not at Fairfield at such a time. Your cousin is a dangerous man to cross. Perhaps it would be wise to engage more staff. Men who know how to use a weapon to protect—"

"Mr Tooley." Laura cut across his warning. "Surely, should any harm befall me, Guy Stanton will be the first person they suspect? He is a bully, but I don't think he is foolish enough to risk being hanged to get Fairfield."

"Don't underestimate him, Mrs Thorne."

"I won't. Thank you for your advice, Mr Tooley."

After the lawyer left Laura felt crushed by her grief. She gazed disconsolately out of the window. The interminable winter's mist obscured the line of oaks in the drive and the ground was crisp with a coating of thick frost. The weather was as depressing as her mood. Where was Matt? She missed him so desperately. There was such a void in her life. The ache in her heart at the enormity of her loss was almost unbearable. She had sent word to Matt of her grandfather's death, but to arrive at Fairfield in time for the funeral he would have needed to ride hard, sparing neither himself nor his horse. The frost had ensured that the roads would be passable, for often in winter they became quagmires and carriages were bogged down in the deeply rutted mud. Since the messenger had not returned she did not even know if Matt had received her letter. With Cecil and Guy so close at hand, she had felt the need for the funeral to be over quickly. The funeral arrangements had kept her mind from dwelling on the problems of her marriage but now, mingled with her grief, her pain at loving Matt intensified. She had never felt so lonely.

"Matt, I love you so much," she breathed in an agony of longing, and hugged her arms around herself. "What must I do to convince you that you are a worthy master for Fairfield?"

Jedediah came into the room and coughed discreetly into his hand. "Has there been any word from Mr Thorne?"

Laura shook her head. Jedediah's own mourning for the man he had served for nearly forty years had bowed his stocky frame and made his features haggard. "How will it all end, Jedediah?" She gave in to her need to confide in someone. Jedediah alone of all the servants knew the circumstances of her marriage. "I must have disappointed my grandfather when he learned the truth about my marriage, but he never condemned me."

"He knew you had made the right choice." Jedediah absently massaged a hip joint. He had been limping when he'd entered the room and Laura suspected that this winter his joints ached more cruelly from the cold and the damp weather.

"Please sit down, Jedediah. I need to talk to you."

A grimace of pain crossed the old servant's face as he lowered himself stiffly into a chair. Laura's grief, the uncertainty of Matt's feelings and now Guy's continued threats were making her feel vulnerable. She poured the servant a glass of brandy before voicing her fears. "Matt will never settle here. His life is on the sea. He is too proud to be supported by my money. It's not as if he loved me. He kept our bargain and, though I have come to love him, I cannot bind him to it for the rest of his life."

"Master Lionel was a very wise man," Jedediah was quick to reassure her. "And, yes, Mr Thorne is proud, believing that the man should provide for and support his wife. That is a credit to him. You would despise him if you thought he was a fortune-hunter. But you are his wife. He will never abandon you. He said so to Master Lionel when he first came to Fairfield."

"He spoke from a sense of duty and honour. If he does not love me, he will come to despise me as he despises all the gentry. I do not think I could bear that."

"How can you think that he does not love you?" Jedediah said solemnly. "Mr Thorne adores you. It is plain to see in the way his gaze follows your every movement when you're in a room. If you're absent he can't keep from glancing at the door, awaiting your appearance."

"It was agreed that we would pretend ours was a love-match. You know the circumstances, Jedediah. It is but a role he plays."

"And I know when a man is looking at a woman he loves," he said with a grin. "Mr Thorne may not have admitted it to himself yet, but he loves you. Why else do you think your grandfather did not challenge the motives for your marriage after he had learned the truth? He had several long talks with Mr Thorne and he trusted your husband. He died content, assured that your future and happiness were secured."

Did Matt love her? Had her grandfather and Jedediah really seen what she had been too blind to see? Was Matt no longer play-acting when they were alone? Had his desire turned to love? Her heart pounded so hard that she felt it would suffocate her. All her fears for Matt's safety returned. What if he was in prison, or Sir James had challenged him to a duel? What if he did not admit that he loved her until he had set sail again? He would not return for months. Suddenly she could not bear the agony of waiting. She would go to him.

"Order the carriage ready in an hour," she said to Jedediah. "I'm going to London. Will you accompany me?"

He rose slowly and with obvious pain to his legs. "I will be happy to, mistress."

"Oh, Jedediah, I should not have asked you. The pain in your joints must be severe in this atrocious weather. I shall go alone. In my absence I would know that Fairfield is in good hands. I will travel with just my maid and return in a week."

Upon entering her bedchamber she found Sarah sneezing violently and her face was flushed with un-natural colour.

"Sarah, help me pack just a few things for a week's

stay in London, then go to your bed. You look to have a cold and fever starting.''

''You can't go to London without a maid.'' Sarah's protest ended with a coughing fit.

''I can manage well enough. Jane, the chambermaid at Stanton House, can serve my needs for a day or two.'' She looked worriedly at her maid. ''Now off to your bed. I can pack what I need. I've spare dresses and such in London. I want you well when I return.''

Her departure was delayed when one of the coachmen could not be found. It was not the first time that the man had been neglectful of his duties in recent weeks and Laura ordered Barker to give him a warning.

''It's late in the day to be starting for London.'' Barker voiced his anxiety. ''Would you not be better served by waiting until morning?''

''Whenever I start my journey I shall need to stay overnight at a coaching-inn. At least this way I'll reach London by noon tomorrow.'' Laura would not be dissuaded. She wanted to see Matt to assure him that in her eyes he was the most worthy of men to be her husband. She did not care that his fortune was lost, or that his past was not as respectable as society would wish. She loved him. And she was desperate to convince him that their marriage could work.

Fifteen minutes later the village was far behind them and they were travelling across flat, marshy country. The landscape was bleak and unwelcoming, with few cottages or workmen's huts. The mist enclosed the marshland in an eerie silence and Laura shuddered. She would feel more comfortable when they reached the next town and the road to Colchester was less deserted.

When the horses began to slow, she felt an inexplicable unease. The silence was unnatural. No birds announced their territory in the trees and in the empty fields no rabbits scurried to safety at the sound of the horses and carriage. Someone had passed this way shortly before. Or was lying in ambush. Fear clutched at her throat. It was not unheard of for highwaymen to work this area.

There were shouts from the road ahead. The carriage swayed to an abrupt halt and Laura heard an alarming thud, like a body falling to the ground. Her instincts warning her of danger, she reached for the pistol under the seat, but as her fingers closed over it the carriage door was thrown open.

A pistol-barrel was pointed at her face and a gruff voice commanded, "Easy now. I wouldn't do anything foolish, ma'am."

The man wore a kerchief across the lower part of his face and the wide brim of his hat shaded his eyes. The sour, musky smell of a body which had never seen soap made her gag.

"Is it jewels yer trying to hide under the seat?" he said, roughly grabbing Laura's hand. When he felt the pistol in her fingers he laughed cruelly. "Give me the weapon slowly, and no tricks. Try and use it and I'll kill yer."

When the barrel of his pistol was placed against Laura's temple, she froze in terror. She had no choice but to loosen her hold on her own weapon. The cloaked robber snatched it from her and stuck it into a leather belt at his waist.

"Now yer purse and jewels."

276 *Marriage Rites*

"I will give you nothing," Laura fumed, her defiance covering the fear she was feeling.

"Spirited, ain't yer?"

The pistol was cold against her temple and Laura struggled to stop her body trembling as the man's free hand tore open her cloak. A diamond brooch in the shape of a lover's knot was ripped from her velvet bodice. Then her diamond earrings were pulled from her ears and stuffed into the thief's pocket. He began to tug the rings from her fingers and she cried out in protest, "Not my wedding-band, it belonged to my mother."

"Me 'eart bleeds, it does really. My ma never 'ad no wedding-band—never 'ad no wedding either," he growled. "Where's the money and the rest of the sparklers? Gentry never travel without a jewel-box."

"There are no more jewels."

His free hand grabbed her chin and she could see the evil glitter in his eyes, making her heart pump harder in terror. "Jewels ain't no use to the dead. Tell me where they are."

There was a grunt from the roadway and Laura's blood ran cold as she heard Seth the coachman cry out in pain.

"There are no more jewels," she declared, refusing to give in to her fear. Her eyes blazed their contempt as she defied him. "What's happening to the coachmen? They have nothing of value."

"Yer speak too much." He swiped a hand across her mouth and Laura tasted blood. "Where's yer purse? I've only to shout out to have yer servants shot."

Laura could feel the money-pouch pressing against her hip where it was hidden under her petticoats. As the robber leaned closer she could see his small, cruel eyes and their expression was merciless.

"Where's the money?" The robber's tone was menacing. "I ain't got all day. Got it hidden on yer person, 'ave yer?" He cackled with delight. "Then I'll just 'ave ter look fer it."

"I will give it to you," Laura said, nausea rising to her throat at the thought of the man's dirty hands on her body.

He withdrew the pressure of the pistol from her head, but when her hand slid to the hem of her gown to raise it as decorously as possible he slapped it away. A second blow to her cheek sent her sprawling across the seat. She screamed as he hoisted her skirts to her thighs, his fingers probing the soft flesh of her legs as he groped for the purse. It was fastened securely to her waist by a strong cord and he would have to put down his pistol to cut it with a dagger.

"Sam," he shouted as he hoisted himself inside the coach. "Deal with the coachmen. Then come and hold this one down. There's more than a money-purse she's got between her legs worth the taking."

There was the sound of heavy blows and a grunt of pain before the second masked man appeared. "Jus' take the money," Sam snapped, drawing out a dagger and slicing the cord. "And let's get on with it."

"Get your filthy hands off me!" Laura shouted. She kicked out as the first man ran a hand along her inner thigh and he drew back with a mocking laugh.

The pistol again pointing at her face froze her struggles. Her own eyes were wide with terror as she stared into the highwayman's eyes. They gleamed

with satisfaction and there was no mercy in his ruth-
less glare.

"Come on, Zach," Sam shouted. "Get on with it.
We've got to be well away from here before a hue
and cry is raised."

"You won't get away with this," Laura declared.
If they were going to kill her anyway, she would die
fighting. Her hand snaked out to rake the man's face
and the robber's pistol was raised. Then pain seared
her skull and scarlet stars exploded in her head before
darkness swamped her.

Matt swung wearily out of the saddle. Still unused
to long hours on horseback, his back and legs were
stiff and aching. The wound in his side was not serious, but it had bled copiously and the hard ride had
again opened it up. However, the discomfort was
slight compared to the worry he felt for Laura. He
had been appalled to receive her letter saying that
Lionel Stanton was dead. Without Lionel's protection
he could not rid his mind of the notion that Laura was
in danger. Guy and Cecil Stanton would not miss any
opportunity to use her vulnerability and strike against
her.

A startled groom came out to lead Neptune into his
stall and as Matt entered the house Barker appeared,
his lined face creased and anxious, confirming the
worst of Matt's fears.

"Mr Thorne. Is the mistress not with you?"

Matt felt his stomach knot in alarm. "I've come
from London, Barker. Is your mistress not at home?"

"She left three hours ago for London to be with
you." The major-domo glared at him accusingly.
"You should have been here when she needed you,

not chasing your own interests in London. She's been beside herself with grief over Master Lionel's death. You were her husband and sworn to protect her from that scheming uncle and cousin.''

The servant's fear for Laura's safety was so obvious that Matt did not rebuke him for his insolence.

''I had no idea Lionel was so ill. He looked well enough when I left. Tell me quickly what has passed. Are Cecil and Guy Stanton still in the district?''

''They left an hour before Mistress Laura took it into her head to go to London. I was anxious when I learned that one of the coachmen could not be found. He's not worked here long and I think he could have been one of Guy Stanton's spies.''

Matt felt as if he had been rammed by a runaway horse. ''I passed neither Cecil Stanton's carriage nor Laura's on the way from Colchester.'' His voice was shaky with unspoken fear. ''Though I stopped to speak with Mr Tooley. He seemed very relieved that I was returning to Fairfield tonight. Had the Stantons threatened Laura in any way?''

Jedediah Hames hobbled into the hall, his voice hard. ''Mistress Laura stood up to them, but the ordeal, on top of her grandfather's death, clearly upset her.'' His stiff manner and cold appraisal condemned Matt for his neglect. ''Your place was at her side, Mr Thorne.''

''I truly wish I had been here.'' Anguish was stark in Matt's grim face. ''Have another horse saddled for me and I want as many men as can be raised armed and ready to ride out in ten minutes.''

Barker paled and his hand shook as he raised it to sweep through his thinning hair. ''You could be riding into a trap.''

"I must risk that. I would risk anything to save my wife." He turned too quickly and staggered as an agonising pain shot through the wound in his side. A maid carrying a taper to light the candles in the fading light screamed as she stared at his figure.

"Mr Thorne, there's blood on your jacket!"

"It's a graze, nothing more," he said irritably, impatient now to ride after Laura. He was convinced that she was in danger. He had been selfish in pursuing his own plans when he owed Laura so much. She had saved him from being treated like an animal in prison and given him back his self-esteem.

"With respect, Mr Thorne," Jedediah cut in, "if you continue to lose blood you will be too weak to help Mistress Laura if she has need of you."

Matt nodded. "A bullet nicked my side. It looks worse than it is."

"Let me tend you," Jedediah offered. "I served Charles Stanton all through his days in the army. I have some skill with wounds. And a glass of brandy will help restore your strength."

Matt was about to refuse, but the elderly eyes which regarded him were no longer antagonistic. Jedediah had never approved of Laura's marriage plan and neither had he approved of Matt. He had always been disdainful, considering the sea-captain no better than any other criminal. Now his gaze was respectful and also admiring.

"Thank you, Jedediah," he said, putting a hand on the servant's arm. "I will never forgive myself if anything has happened to Laura."

Within half an hour Matt had covered two miles of road. Twenty men from the estate had joined the search and the anguish in Matt's heart was mirrored in all their faces. The frosty ground made it difficult to look for fresh tracks and now the light was fading fast.

"Light the torches," he said tersely. "I want every foot of ground searched. Are there any turn-offs near here?"

"A few to desolate farms," the estate bailiff remarked. His stout figure and heavy-set face were stern. He also clearly blamed Matt for abandoning Laura.

"I want them all searched, even if it takes all night," Matt ordered. "Split up into twos. We'll cover more ground that way."

"But why should Mistress Laura visit those?" The blacksmith's son scratched his head. "There ain't no one in these parts would harm our mistress."

"Perhaps she had no choice," Matt returned bleakly.

"If anyone's harmed Mistress Laura," the bailiff snarled, "I'll kill the swine with my bare hands."

"That will be my privilege," Matt said savagely, and held the bailiff's beligerent glare. The antagonism left the older man's eyes and he nodded.

A shout from one of the grooms ahead drew his attention. "There's blood on the side of the road here, and from the way the grass has been flattened it looks like there's been some sort of a scuffle."

Matt rode over to investigate. "The ground is so hard it's difficult to see any tracks clearly. But over there on the side of the road looks like a pool of horse urine." He felt his panic rising for Laura's safety. "Four of you search the hedgerow to see if there are any hidden bodies. The others keep your eyes peeled for any other sign of disturbance, or of tracks leading off the road."

Twenty minutes later, as darkness was rapidly falling, wheel-tracks were found leading through a gate to a field.

"Two of you follow those tracks," Matt ordered.

"They be a farm wagon, sir," the bailiff answered.

"I still want the tracks followed," Matt insisted.

One of the riders rode back through the gate, his voice rising with excitement. "Mr Thorne! There's a carriage hidden in the wood. The horses have been taken. It's the Stanton carriage, I'm sure of it. But there's no sign of Mistress Laura, or our men."

Matt galloped to where the carriage was hidden and wrenched open the door. As the light from the torches fell on the interior his heart clutched with fear. There was blood on the upholstery and the floor.

"Mount up, men!" Matt ground out. "Every building in the area must be searched no matter how ramshackle. Your mistress's life may depend upon it."

As he swung into the saddle he felt a black despair. Let Laura be safe, he prayed. Had his need for vengeance against Breten robbed him of this second chance of happiness? His life would be nothing without Laura.

Pain throbbed through Laura's head as consciousness slowly returned and she was aware of voices. Her body was swaying uncomfortably and something dug painfully into her ribs. Her returning senses warned her of danger. She cautiously opened her eyes and in the twilight found herself staring at the ground, and with each sway of her body a spurred boot came into view. Memory flooded back. She was being carried like a sheaf of hay over a man's back. Without making any betraying movement which would warn her captors that she was conscious, Laura carefully checked to discover if any of her limbs were bound. Thank God they were not.

She had no idea where she was, but assumed her abductors were the highwaymen. Did they intend to hold her to ransom? Whatever their intention she was determined to escape. The best chance of that lay with the element of surprise.

Her nose wrinkled at the sour, musty smell of the man carrying her. He was the one who had stolen her jewels. The throbbing in her head made it difficult to think clearly, but she was certain that the pain in her side was caused by the pistol the man had taken from her and stuck into his belt.

The indignity of being carried in such a manner fuelled her anger. When her sharp ears heard the snufflings of horses, she turned her head very slowly and saw that they were walking away from a dilapidated barn. Within half a dozen strides Zach was crossing a poorly kept garden and then he braced himself as he kicked open a door. Light flooded out from the interior of a cottage. It smelled of dust, damp and rats' droppings, and must have been deserted for months. Laura had been unable to see anything of the countryside to guess where she was being taken.

Across the room she saw the figures of the two coachmen, bound and gagged. Both were shaking their heads as they fought to regain full consciousness.

''Good work.'' Guy Stanton's voice rasped from

across the room and Laura felt her rage intensify. "My threats must have frightened her and she wanted to run to her husband's side. How convenient for us. Put her down on the bed and bind and gag her. It could be some days before Thorne is drawn into our trap. Then they will die together."

Laura bit her lip to contain her fury. She was too angry to feel fear. Guy had not been bluffing. She had been a fool not to heed Mr Tooley's warning. Guy was more evil than she had believed.

She closed her mind to her mounting anger. To outwit her cousin she needed a clear head. Through lowered lids she saw a dirty, rush-covered floor and glimpsed a mildewed mattress on a truckle-bed. She held her breath, hardly daring to breathe. She had to get the pistol from her captor's belt. If she failed all would be lost.

"Once she's tied up," Guy continued, "you can go. The jewels and money on her were reward enough."

As Zach half turned and stooped to deposit her on the bed, Laura moved swiftly. Her hand shot out to close around the handle of the pistol in his belt and she dragged it out as she was tossed on to the mattress. The three men froze as they saw the pistol clutched in her hand.

"Stay back!" she warned, her thumb cocking the pistol ready to fire.

Zach had removed the kerchief and his face was pale beneath several days' stubble of red beard. "That's the pistol I took from her," he said stupidly.

"And I'll use it. Don't any of you come any

closer." Keeping her eyes on all of them, she rose slowly to her knees.

"Fool!" Guy shouted. "Get the pistol from her. She won't shoot."

"Yes, I will," Laura said as she stepped on to the floor, the wall protecting her back. The two robbers were closest to her and she waved the pistol at them, adding, "Get over there by my cousin."

They backed away, their faces white with terror.

"Get the pistol!" Guy screamed, his face puce with anger. "She's only a woman, damn it! And tie her up."

"The first one to come near me dies," Laura said. Her heart was thudding wildly. She only had one shot. She didn't know for how much longer she could hold them at bay before they rushed and overpowered her. Her mind was racing, searching for a way to trick them and escape.

"You didn't pay us to get shot," Sam said sullenly as he edged towards the door. "I ain't staying here."

"Stop bleating, man," Guy sneered. His eyes never left the pistol in Laura's hand and she saw him grin as he noticed that her hand was beginning to shake. "She can only wound one of us," he urged. "She's seen your face. Do you want to hang for kidnapping her if she goes free?"

"If I only have one shot, it's for you, Guy." Laura levelled the pistol at his heart, her face set with resolve. "I won't allow you to kill Matt."

The two robbers were poised indecisively by the door. Clearly they were men used to taking orders and not thinking for themselves. But Laura remembered the lust in Zach's eyes in the carriage. Even if she shot her cousin she would still be at the mercy of two violent and unprincipled men.

"You took what was mine, Laura. Now you must pay," Guy stated.

"Fairfield was never yours, Guy. Your father stole it from my grandfather in the first place."

An evil grin twisted his fleshy features. "Is Fairfield worth dying for, Laura?" he taunted. "For you will die. You and that prison-bait of a husband you profess to love. Where is your devoted spouse? He did not even care enough to attend the old man's funeral."

"Your quarrel is with me, not Matt." Laura refused to rise to his baiting. "I won't allow Matt to die. It was my idea that we marry and I save Fairfield from your clutches."

"How ardently you defend him," Guy sneered. "What happened to your fierce Stanton pride? Not fallen in love with that fortune-hunter, have you?" He gave a crack of malicious laughter. "Oh, but I believe you have. Will you still want to save the lecher you married when you learn that all the time he's been in London he's been whoring with Mary Montgomery? My spy saw her leaving Stanton House early yesterday morning."

Laura swayed as jealousy stabbed cruelly through her. Zach made a lurch for the gun, but she swung round on him, the deadly light in her eye stopping him in his tracks. He put up his hands and backed away.

"Don't shoot. I ain't going to take that bullet so Guy Stanton can go free."

"That's very wise, Zach," Laura said coldly,

though her heart was aching at the news that Matt had been with Mary Montgomery. The woman had been making a play for Matt for weeks. Matt might not love her, but he was still her husband, and because of her his life was now in danger.

Her brittle stare was again on her cousin. "Whom my husband was with in London changes nothing. I will not allow you to kill him. This is between us, Guy."

Guy had begun to edge closer and her finger tightened on the trigger. He showed no fear and laughed mockingly. "How long do you think you can stand like that? What will happen when you grow tired? You're outnumbered three to one." Guy's grin was evil. "If you kill me these two men will fall on you like the vermin they are. They'll kill you to save their own hides from the gallows, but first they'll make you suffer and enjoy a bit of sport."

Laura's gaze darted from Guy to the two robbers. They had recovered their composure and were regarding her with malevolent glares.

"You can't win, Laura. You'll never get away." Guy continued his taunts.

"But you will be dead too, Guy." Fear was closing her throat. She could not see how she could escape all three men. All she knew was that she must save Matt's life. Their marriage had been doomed from the beginning. She could not be responsible for his being killed because of her cousin's greed for Fairfield.

"You haven't got what it takes to pull that trigger, Laura," Guy jeered, and suddenly rushed her. Her death was written on his face. She fired and saw the shock in his expression as the shot entered his chest.

He stumbled two steps and fell to the floor by her frozen figure. One hand clawed out to her and gripped her skirt; the other clutched at his wound where blood pumped through his fingers.

"Bitch!" he croaked, almost toppling her as he tugged at her skirts to keep his body upright. "She's done for me. Have your sport with her, men. I want to hear her beg for mercy before I die."

Laura turned the pistol on the man advancing towards her. In a corner of the room she saw the bound driver and coachman, their eyes wide with fear. There was no one to save her. And she had fired her only shot. Backing away, she tried to pull her skirts from Guy's fingers, but he held fast.

"Make her beg for mercy," Guy croaked.

Laura screamed. There was no escape. Turning the pistol in her hand, she held it aloft to use it as a club, but she was trapped between the bed and Guy's prone figure on the floor.

"The bitch must die, and the coachmen," Zach said as he lunged for her. "Or they'll see us swing."

Laura screamed again and struck out, the pistol glancing off the side of Zach's head. His hat protected him, and the stench of his rotting teeth hit her full in the face as he grabbed her wrists and forced her down on to the mattress.

Terror made Laura writhe and kick, the flesh shrinking on her bones as Zach lay across her. Her hair had come loose in her struggle and it fell across her face, but her eyes were screwed shut to blot out the lust-crazed face of her attacker.

"For God's sake, Sam, get the pistol," Zach yelled as the butt of it contacted with the side of his head.

It was wrenched from Laura's fingers with bruising ferocity. Zach captured both her wrists in one large, grimy hand and pinned them above her head. His free hand began to grope between their bodies, seeking the fastening of his breeches. Her struggles increased in desperation as she felt his aroused member against her thigh.

"Make her beg," Guy said faintly. "Hold her down, Sam."

"No!" Laura screamed. The blood was pounding in her temples as terror turned her body to ice.

She fought on bravely, scratching, kicking, biting, but each movement was slower and less effective than the last as his weight overpowered her. Her lungs were labouring for air and her muscles trembled from straining to hold her attacker at bay. Her mind froze with the loathsome horror of his assault and she screamed again, knowing that it was only a matter of minutes before her strength gave out.

"Touch her and you die!" a voice rang out from the doorway.

Laura felt Zach's body wrenched from her and she pushed her hair back as she sat up, her eyes blinking in disbelief and relief as she saw the dozen men crowding into the cottage. Matt had thrown Zach across the room when he had pulled him from Laura and now two servants held him. Two pistols were trained on Guy's slumped figure on the floor. After a cursory glance at his bloodied jacket Matt stepped over him and, taking Laura's hand raised her to her feet and drew her away from her cousin's groaning figure. His arms went around her and his lips were against her hair.

"My darling, thank God we arrived in time," he said hoarsely.

For a moment she clung to him, his arms a welcome harbour after her fear. "Guy wanted to kill us both." She strained back from him, her eyes misty with tears. "I could not let you die because of my obsession with the estate." She began to shake with reaction and Matt's arms tightened around her, drawing her towards the door.

Laura shuddered and looked over Matt's shoulder to where her cousin lay on the floor. "I shot Guy. If he dies, they'll hang me."

"You were defending yourself," Matt consoled her as he led her outside to the horses. "Guy won't die from that wound. He'll live long enough to face trial."

He turned to the bailiff and ordered him to take Guy and the two robbers to Colchester gaol.

"It's over, Laura," he said with infinite tenderness. "You are safe." He tipped her chin up with his finger, and as she gazed into his handsome face he smiled. It was the most heart-rending smile she had ever seen.

"Oh, Matt, I love you so much. All I wanted was for our marriage to have a chance."

As she stared raptly into his bronze eyes she saw that they were bright with unshed tears. "I thought I'd lost you," he said gruffly.

He pulled her close, their gazes so intense that several of the men who had ridden with Matt discreetly turned away to give them a moment's privacy. The wild pounding of Laura's heart was matched by the frantic rhythm of his own as they embraced. She spread her hands across his broad chest, her heart too full to put her love into words. When their mouths fused, they tasted the salt of each other's unashamed tears. Their breath mingled in a brief, searing kiss, foretelling the pleasures still to discover, the ecstasies still to unfold.

With a muffled groan Matt broke them apart, and a loud cheer went up from the men.

"God bless you, Mistress Laura. And you too, Mr Thorne," the bailiff said with a pleased grin.

"Aye," the other men chorused. "God bless Mr and Mrs Thorne."

"You'll not be leaving us now, Mr Thorne, will you?" someone ventured. "You'll not be going back to the sea? Fairfield needs you."

Matt's expression stiffened, but Laura could see that he was pleased with the men's concern. He did not answer, and lifted Laura on to the saddle of his horse. When he swung up behind her she felt him draw a sharp breath and hold his side.

"Matt, you are hurt. What happened?"

"It's a long story. I'll tell you back at Fairfield." He stopped her further questions with a kiss and then turned his mount towards the estate. "Let's go home, Laura. You are so brave and I am so proud of you, my darling."

As they rode Matt told her of the duel and his discovery that Sir James Breten was his father. He had expected her to be outraged that he had rejected his Breten inheritance. However, "It would be an insult to your mother to accept it," she said softly.

"Well, at least I have the money for my ship, and the money from Lady Henrietta will repay you for settling my debts. You may not have married a wealthy man, but I am not a pauper. Nor need you feel shamed by the inequality of my birth.''

"I never cared about your lack of money, Matt. Or your background. You had higher principles than most men of our station. That was what impressed me most.''

"But I cared, Laura," he said in a tone which made her heart ache with anguish. "I still do.''

Laura's heart clenched. Would she ever be able to chisel through his obstinate pride?

They were approaching the village, the blazing torches which lit their passage bringing the villagers out of their houses. Some of the men had already ridden ahead and as Matt and Laura were recognised the people cheered.

"God bless you, Mr Thorne, for saving our dear mistress," Widow Croke shouted.

"A long and fruitful marriage to you both," another woman cried out.

"Long may Matthew Thorne be our master," several men chorused together.

Laura leaned back against her husband's chest and laid her hand over his, which rested on her waist. "The people love you, Matt. How can you desert them? Does Fairfield truly mean nothing to you?''

Matt was having difficulty controlling the welling emotion that the villagers' cheers had brought to his chest. The lines of faces, grinning and smiling in the torches' yellow light, destroyed his composure. Fairfield had captured him in its spell.

An hour later Matt emerged from his dressing-room, bathed and with a fresh bandage over his wound. His breath caught in his throat as he saw Laura reclining on a day-bed by the fire in her bedchamber. She wore a white satin robe which clung to her figure like a second skin and her thick, curling auburn hair hung loose to her hips. The room was lit with only a few intimate candles and covered silver servers kept a meal hot on a table beside Laura. She swung her legs to the floor and stood up to hand him a glass of wine.

"I thought we would dine privately tonight," she said softly. She stood very close as he reached for the wine glass and the perfume of her skin and hair tantalised his senses. He took a glass from her and smiled deep into her eyes. Since the villagers had challenged him on his plans for the future he had become very quiet.

"What shall we toast, Mrs Thorne?" he queried, raising a dark brow, his expression enigmatic. "Fairfield is at last safely in your hands."

"Fairfield is no longer so important to me. I feared I had lost something infinitely more precious."

Matt put aside his goblet and, gazing in to her beautiful upturned face took it reverently between his hands. "Laura, it's time we put the circumstances of our marriage behind us and thought only of our future—together."

"I want that more than anything, Matt, but I don't want a loveless marriage, or a husband who will betray me with the likes of Mary Montgomery. You can have your freedom if you wish it."

He did not doubt that Laura loved him. It was evident in the strain of her voice and shone brightly in her eyes as she gazed adoringly up at him. Now that he knew the truth of his parentage, he also knew that he was her equal in birth, but not in wealth. That would come in time, and with the villagers' cheers still echoing in his mind that was no longer as important as it had once seemed.

"So Guy told you that the Montgomery woman came to Stanton House? It was not at my invitation. I sent her away." When he saw her eyes misting with tears of joy, he held her tighter. "I almost allowed my obsession with the past to ruin my only chance of happiness for the future. I had to honour my vow to Susannah and Rachel, but it had blinded me to so much else."

"I would not love you so much if you were not a man of such impeccable honour." Laura slid her hands over his shoulders to entwine them in his long hair, her love shining like a beacon in her eyes. "I was jealous of the power your first wife still seemed to have over you, but I accept that as right and proper now. Their deaths could not go unavenged. I accept that you still love Susannah and that any child I give you will never replace Rachel. But I want our child, Matt. Not for Fairfield but for us."

The demand of his kiss silenced her. When finally they broke apart he continued to press kisses against her throat. "My darling, it's you I love. In my foolish pride I nearly lost you. I hated everything that you stood for, but one by one you broke down my reserves and conquered my aversion," he said huskily. "You were not like the gentry I despised. I began to realise how much it hurt you to lie to and deceive your grandfather, even though your motives were to save the people of Fairfield, not the fortune most would have craved. You showed me a generosity of spirit I thought had faded into the legends of outdated chivalry. I did not know how precious was your love until I nearly lost you." He kissed her brow and then her lids until, with a soft sigh, he captured her mouth with a fierce, possessive passion.

She moaned with delight as his hands caressed her breasts, her body pressing provocatively against the sleek muscles of his powerful figure. Desire was throbbing through her blood, but she struggled to keep control over her senses until she had finished what needed to be said between them. "I don't want you to give up the sea if it means so much to you," she said, her voice rich with seductive promise.

"Do you think I could bear to spend months at a time away from you?" he smiled. "But the sea will be part of my life. For I will never live off your money. With the price of my ship and cargo returned to me I can afford to buy a new vessel and hire a captain to sail it for me. In five years I intend to have a fleet of ships. I will prove myself worthy of you and worthy of Fairfield."

Laura traced the line of his jaw with her finger, her heart swelling with the fullness of her love. "Always so proud," she teased, with a provocative smile. "My love, I wonder if I and Fairfield are worthy of you? I can think of no more honourable or fitting man to be its master, or the master of my heart." She rose on to her toes, her lips tremulous as they parted in a seductive whisper. "I intend to spend the rest of my life proving how much I love you."

A wicked, enticing smile tilted his lips and made

her whole body tremble with longing. His hands tightened possessively around her, gathering her in a passionate embrace; his lips were warm and demanding upon hers, but with a tenderness which seared her soul.

"My dearest love," he breathed, between pressing kisses against the throbbing pulse in her throat. He lifted her effortlessly into his arms and strode into their bedchamber. "I love you so much. And you have brought me something even more precious than love. Something I never thought to have again. Peace... I love and adore you, my darling."

Kisses replaced his words, their masterly sweetness and hunger weaving a magic which would encompass them for the rest of their lives.

* * * * *

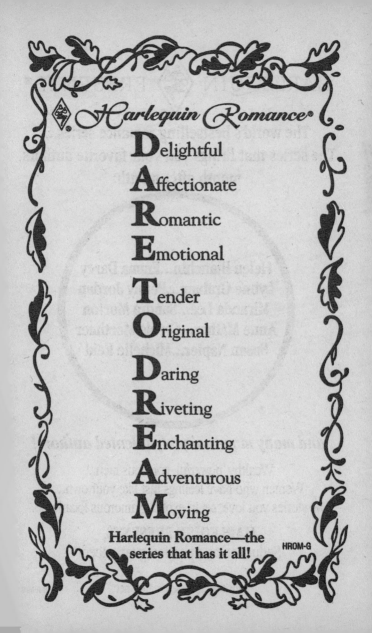

Harlequin Romance®

Delightful

Affectionate

Romantic

Emotional

Tender

Original

Daring

Riveting

Enchanting

Adventurous

Moving

**Harlequin Romance—the
series that has it all!**

HROM-G

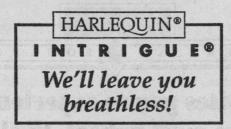

HARLEQUIN®
INTRIGUE®

We'll leave you breathless!

If you've been looking for thrilling tales of
contemporary passion and sensuous love stories
with taut, edge-of-the-seat suspense—
then you'll *love* Harlequin Intrigue!

Every month, you'll meet four new heroes
who are guaranteed to make your spine tingle
and your pulse pound. With them you'll enter
into the exciting world of Harlequin Intrigue—
where your life is on the line
and so is your heart!

THAT'S INTRIGUE—DYNAMIC
ROMANCE AT ITS BEST!

HARLEQUIN®
INTRIGUE®

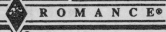

HARLEQUIN SUPERROMANCE®

...there's more to the story!

Superromance. A *big* satisfying read about unforget-
table characters. Each month we offer
four very different stories that range from family
drama to adventure and mystery, from highly emotional stories to romantic comedies—and
much more! Stories about people you'll
believe in and care about. Stories too
compelling to put down....

Our authors are among today's *best* romance writ-
ers. You'll find familiar names and
talented newcomers. Many of them are
award winners—and you'll see why!

If you want the biggest and best
in romance fiction, you'll get it
from Superromance!

Available wherever Harlequin books are sold.

Romance is just one click away!

online book serials

➤ *Exclusive* to our web site, get caught up in both
  the daily and weekly online installments of new
  romance stories.

➤ Try the Writing Round Robin. Contribute a chapter
  to a story created by our members. Plus, winners
  will get prizes.

romantic travel

➤ Want to know where the best place to kiss in
  New York City is, or which restaurant in
  Los Angeles is the most romantic? Check out
  our Romantic Hot Spots for the scoop.

➤ Share your travel tips and stories with us on the
  romantic travel message boards.

romantic reading library

➤ Relax as you read our collection of Romantic
  Poetry.

➤ Take a peek at the Top 10 Most Romantic Lines!

Visit us online at

www.eHarlequin.com
on Women.com Networks